TAIL-WAGGING PRAISE FOR THE BARKING DETECTIVE MYSTERIES

THE BIG CHIHUAHUA

"This series is hilarious! The antics of Geri and her talking dog make the reader laugh out loud. An interesting cast of characters, an enjoyable read."

—*RT Book Reviews*

"Pepe and Geri make a great crime-solving team. Guaranteed: lots of smiles."

—*Hudson Valley News*

CHIHUAHUA CONFIDENTIAL

"Hollywood is the stage for this enjoyable caper starring amateur PI Geri Sullivan and her talking Chihuahua/partner, Pepe. The characters are comical, especially Pepe, who will have you laughing out loud. A great read."

—*RT Book Reviews*

"Light as a feather and a whole lot of fun."

—*Seattle Times*

"Hop on board the TV-studio tour bus for this light cozy."

—*Library Journal*

"An adult mystery with young adult appeal . . . The second in Curtis's fun new series featuring Geri and Pepe is tailor-made for anyone who can't get enough dog mysteries and those readers who never miss an episode of *Dancing with the Stars*."

—*VOYA (Voice of Youth Advocates)*

DIAL C FOR CHIHUAHUA

"Three woofs and a big bow-wow for *Dial C for Chihuahua*. Pepe is one cool sleuth—just don't call him a dog! I really loved the book."

> **—Leslie Meier**, author of the Lucy Stone mysteries

"Readers will sit up and beg for more."

> **—Sushi the Shih Tzu**, canine star of the *Trash 'n' Treasures* mysteries by Barbara Allan

"Writing duo Curtis has created a humorous but deadly serious mystery. Pepe is a delight and more intelligent than most humans in the book. An ex-husband and current love interest keep Geri's life hopping. Crafty plotting will keep you engrossed until the end and have you eagerly awaiting the next book."

> **—*RT Book Reviews*, 4 stars**

"Every dog has its day and there'll be plenty of days for Geri Sullivan and Pepe in this fun twist on the typical PI partnership."

> **—Simon Wood**, author of *Did Not Finish*

"Waverly Curtis has created a delightful cast of human and canine characters in *Dial C for Chihuahua*. Pepe never loses his essential dogginess, even as he amazes gutsy Geri Sullivan, his partner in crime detection, with his past exploits and keen nose for detail. I look forward to Pepe's next adventure!"

> **—Bernadette Pajer**, author of the Professor Bradshaw Mysteries

"Move over, Scooby-Doo, there's a new dog in town! *Dial C for Chihuahua* is a fun and breezy read, with polished writing and charming characters, both human and canine. If you like a little Chihuahua with your mystery, former purse-dog Pepe is a perfect fit!"

> **—Jennie Bentley**, author of the Do-It-Yourself Home Renovation mysteries

Also by Waverly Curtis

The Silence
of the
Chihuahuas

Waverly Curtis

KENSINGTON PUBLISHING CORP.

http://www.kensingtonbooks.com

KENSINGTON BOOKS are published by

Kensington Publishing Corp.
119 West 40th Street
New York, NY 10018

All Kensington Titles, Imprints, and Distributed Lines are available at special quantity discounts for bulk purchases for sales promotions, premiums, fund-raising, and educational or institutional use. Special book excerpts or customized printings can also be created to fit specific needs. For details, write or phone the office of the Kensington special sales manager: Kensington Publishing Corp., 119 West 40th Street, New York, NY 10018, attn: Special Sales Department, Phone: 1-800-221-2647.

Kensington and the K logo Reg. U.S. Pat & TM Off.

ISBN-13: 978-1-61773-064-1
ISBN-10: 1-61773-064-5
First Kensington Mass Market Edition: November 2015

eISBN-13: 978-1-61773-065-8
eISBN-10: 1-61773-065-3
First Kensington Electronic Edition: November 2015

10 9 8 7 6 5 4 3 2

Printed in the United States of America

Chapter 1

The veterinarian was a short man shaped like an egg, with a rounded torso that narrowed at either end to a bald head on top and tiny feet at the other. He wore rimless glasses and a white lab coat.

"Hello, I'm Norman Dodd," he said, holding out his hand. It was small and clammy. Nonetheless, I clung to it as he pumped mine up and down. I had never consulted a vet before about my Chihuahua, Pepe, but now I was really worried.

Pepe was one of a group of Chihuahuas who had been flown up to Seattle from LA, where they were being abandoned in record numbers. I had adopted him six months earlier and he had become my best friend and partner in my work as a private detective.

"Why are you here today?" Dr. Dodd asked, consulting the clipboard that the receptionist had placed on the counter in the exam room at the Lake Union Animal Clinic. Pepe sat on the metal table, his long ears perked forward, his dark eyes fixed on me. I wished I could tell what he was thinking. That was the problem.

"My dog stopped talking to me," I said. "About four days ago."

The vet had been running his pudgy fingers along the sides of Pepe's white flanks.

"What do you mean?" he asked. "He used to bark a lot, and now he's stopped?" He chuckled. "Some Chihuahua owners would celebrate!"

"No, it's not that," I said.

"Then what do you mean?"

"I mean he used to talk to me, but a few days ago he mysteriously stopped talking."

The vet's eyes narrowed. "Define talking!"

"He spoke," I said. "Words strung together into complete sentences. A bit of Spanish. Mostly English."

Pepe sat on the table, smiling up at me with those big dark eyes.

"What's wrong with you?" I asked, addressing him as I had many times during the last four days. "Why don't you speak?"

Dr. Dodd shook his head. "I think you've come to the wrong place, miss," he said. "You don't need a vet. You need a shrink."

I didn't tell him I had already consulted with my shrink. Susanna already knows about my talking dog, so when I told her he had stopped talking, she congratulated me. "So what do you think caused you to own your thoughts and feelings instead of projecting them onto your dog?" she asked with a happy smile.

"You don't understand," I said. "He was really helping me. I don't think I could have solved any of those cases without him." Pepe and I had been responsible for catching several murderers, kidnappers, and bad dogs while working for the private investigation agency run by Jimmy Gerrard.

"Geri, it has always puzzled me that you want to give credit to your dog. Why not acknowledge and celebrate your own accomplishments?"

"But that's wrong!" I said. Meanwhile, Pepe just sat there, on top of one of the many pillows in Susanna's office, seeming quite pleased with himself without saying a word.

"What's wrong with you?" I turned to him. "You always want to take credit for everything we do." My dog is a bit of an attention hound.

"Geri," said Susanna, "if I didn't think this was just a metaphor, I'd be very concerned about your mental state. If you persist in this delusion, I think you might consider in-patient treatment."

I saw Pepe flinch at that. Thank God, he was still registering his reactions, if not actually expressing his opinion. And like many dog owners, I could read my dog fairly accurately. "You don't want that," I said to him. "You don't want me to go away. They won't let you come with me."

"Do you want me to check into some possibilities for you?" said Susanna. "Or perhaps I should refer you to a psychiatrist?" Susanna had been licensed as a counselor in the state of Washington after she earned her MA, but she can't prescribe medication. It takes someone with an MD to diagnose and write prescriptions.

"I don't need a psychiatrist," I said. "My dog does!" I glared at Pepe. He looked a little worried. One ear quirked forward.

"Do you have referrals to dog shrinks?" I asked a

little loudly and defiantly, directing the words at Pepe, not at Susanna.

"I actually know several," said Susanna. "Dr. Mallard was very helpful when my cat started hiding under the furniture. He gave her some anti-anxiety medication and that cleared up her symptoms." She got up, went over to her desk and flipped through her Rolodex. She picked out a card and handed it to me.

"Thanks," I said, getting up, "I think I will look into that." I could tell by Pepe's expression that he was upset. Good! I was upset too. Maybe it would upset him enough so he would start talking.

I couldn't understand why he had stopped.

The irony is that I had spent the past six months trying to convince people, including my boss, Jimmy Gerrard, and my boyfriend, Felix Navarro, that my dog talked. They were just starting to entertain that possibility when he stopped. Now what? They would think I was crazy. Apparently everyone did.

The vet was talking again. "I'll check his vocal cords. See if there's anything causing problems in his throat. Perhaps he ate something . . ." He pried open Pepe's jaws and peered inside, waving around a little flashlight. "Nope. That all looks normal." He patted Pepe on the head. "I can't see anything that would cause him to stop barking. Of course, if you want, we can take some blood and do some tests . . ."

I saw the fright in Pepe's eyes, but I nodded. "Yes, I think that's a good idea!" If he wasn't going to tell me what was going on, I would do everything in my power to figure it out. But mostly I was terribly hurt.

I don't know if this has ever happened to you: your best friend suddenly stops speaking to you, won't return your calls, won't answer your questions about what's going on.

It had happened to me just a few weeks earlier and it was still painful. I had been working with Brad for more than five years, ever since we both graduated from interior design school. He opened a small shop where he refinished furniture he picked up at auction sales and then sold it to his clients. He let me use the back of the shop for my own thrift store finds and loaned me pieces I needed for my short-lived career as a stager.

Then suddenly, I couldn't get in contact with him. When I went by the shop, it was closed. When I called him, my calls went straight to voice mail. I was desperately worried about him and also confused. Had I done something wrong? I kept going back over the last conversation I had with him. We had been in the back of the shop surrounded by pieces of furniture in various stages of refurbishing. A stuffed owl looked over the scene from a perch on a grandfather clock. The skeletal remains of a Victorian sofa occupied one corner. A cracked blue-and-white Chinese vase sat on top of a mahogany drop-leaf table. Brad was at his sewing machine, stitching pink piping around an olive drab velvet pillow. It seemed like an ordinary conversation. We discussed whether or not he should agree to the color scheme his client Mrs. Fairchild demanded for her kitchen. Mrs. F wanted mint green and Brad recommended lemon yellow.

"Yellow can be such a harsh color to live with," I

had said. And that was the last thing I remembered from that day. Surely my opinion about paint colors had not been so outrageous as to cause the rift in our friendship.

I came back to the present. Dr. Dodd was staring at me, waiting for my answer.

"Yes, let's go ahead and get some blood work!" I said.

Pepe just stared at me with his big eyes. He wasn't talking but his message was clear: "Please don't do this to me!" But I was desperate. I needed to know what was going on. If anything was going to get him to talk it would be getting poked with a needle. He hates it. He began to tremble but still he didn't speak. When the vet sunk the needle into his little flank, he merely squeaked.

"We'll call you if anything unusual shows up in the results," the vet said.

We left the vet's office and went out into a typical September day in Seattle. The sky was grey and the air was full of moisture. Some might call it rain but it's more like a heavy mist. I had one more place to go. Since Pepe wasn't talking to me, I thought I would go visit my other silent partner, Brad, and see if I could get him to talk to me.

The Animal Clinic is on Eastlake Boulevard, just a few blocks from my condo. And Brad's shop is also on Eastlake, in the other direction down near the University Bridge. The drawbridge spans the man-made canal that connects Lake Washington to the east with Lake Union. It is Seattle's most urban lake, surrounded by houseboats and restaurants.

Pepe trotted ahead of me. He doesn't like rain, but he also refuses to wear the cute raincoat I bought for him. So he was just wearing his little turquoise harness as we headed down the street. His little white tail wagged from side to side, curved over his back like a comma. He seemed like just a happy little normal Chihuahua. If a Chihuahua could ever be normal. Maybe I would have to get used to the fact that my dog was no longer extraordinary. Maybe that was what was truly bothering me. It was either that or the distinct possibility that I was crazy.

We were still a block from the shop when I began to realize something was wrong. There was a piece of paper pasted to the front door. And as we got closer, I could see that it was a 3 DAY PAY OR VACATE notice. Not the sort of thing you want prospective customers to see as they go driving by.

Brad usually has a striking tableau in the window designed to catch the eye of passers by: maybe a chair covered in leopard print next to a red ceramic vase full of pampas grass on top of a black lacquered table edged with gold. Or a Victorian sofa upholstered in buttercup yellow underneath a chandelier made out of orange pill bottles. But it looked like he had been interrupted in the middle of changing the display. A purple armchair sat beneath a bare light bulb with a crate beside it. It wasn't even industrial chic. Just sad.

I ripped the paper off the door. Then tried my key in the lock, but it wouldn't turn. So I cupped my hands and peered through the window.

"What happened to Brad?" I asked Pepe, but he

didn't answer me. He just lifted his leg and peed on the tire of a white van parked in front of the building.

The telephone was ringing as we walked in through the front door of my condo. For a moment, I thought it might be Brad, calling to tell me what was going on. But that would be crazy, right?

I looked at the caller ID and it wasn't a number I recognized. The cryptic ID said "Forest Glen Clinic." I grabbed it up and said, "Hello?"

"Is that you, Geri?" said the female voice on the other end of the line. She sounded familiar.

"Who is this?" I asked.

"You've got to help me!" said the woman on the other end. Her voice was rising in pitch and intensity. "Someone's trying to kill me!"

And then there was a brief scuffle on the other end and I heard the dial tone.

"That's weird," I said to Pepe as he poked his head out from the kitchen door, clearly curious about what I was doing. "I think that was my sister."

Pepe's Blog: The Barking Detective

Welcome to my blog. I am Pepe Sullivan, the *numero uno* Sullivan in the Sullivan and Sullivan Detective Agency. I find I have a need to share my thoughts, as I have taken a vow of silence and am no longer able to communicate directly with my human partner, Geri Sullivan.

It is very sad as she was the first person ever to listen to me and I had much to say. But it seems that many of her friends and acquaintances think she is *loco*. They want her to go away to a place where they might retrain her brain so she cannot hear me, and that is unacceptable. So for now, I am silent.

Yet my insights and observations demand articulation and so I thought I would try this mode of self-expression that humans seem to find so appealing. Luckily, Geri purchased for me (well, to tell the truth, I ordered it myself using her computer), a lovely iPad that makes it possible for me to share my words with you. It has taken a little while for me to learn to manipulate the touch pad with my paw, but I have now trained the tablet to do as I wish.

It is possible that my silence will be good for Geri. She will have to develop her skills of observation and learn to trust her own judgment instead of relying on me. That will allow me to relax a little. It is hard for a little dog to be constantly protecting and directing his companion. Some days, I must nap for sixteen hours just to relieve my stress.

Chapter 2

What to do? I was so upset I couldn't think clearly. I would have called my boss, Jimmy G, for advice, but I wasn't speaking to him because of the way he had treated me on our last case. And of course, I usually talked things over with Pepe. He loves to give advice, whether I ask for it or not. But he wasn't speaking to *me*.

I looked at him. He looked at me, with those big deep brown eyes. I looked at the phone in my hand. And then I saw the redial button.

"Aha!" I said. "Thanks, Pepe." Although he hadn't said a word. But I think perhaps I was inspired by his confidence in me.

I hit the redial button and I heard the phone ringing on the other end.

"Forest Glen Spa and Clinic," said a female voice on the other end.

"Oh . . ." I said. "What sort of clinic?"

"We provide a variety of services," said the woman in a cheerful voice. "How can I help you?"

"I'm trying to reach my sister," I told her. "She just called me from your number."

"I'm sorry, but we cannot give out any information about our guests."

"Can you at least connect me to her room?"

"That depends. What is your sister's name?"

"Teri," I said. "Teri Sullivan."

"Just a moment." There was silence for a moment, and I was afraid we'd lost the connection. But the woman came back on the line. "I'm sorry," she said, "but we do not have any guests registered by that name."

"What?" I was stunned. "She just called me!"

"I'm sorry, but—"

"Are you sure?" I asked. "Maybe you checked under 'Terry.' She spells her name with an 'i.' Try spelling it T-E-R-I."

I don't think she even checked this time. "I'm very sorry, ma'am, but there is no one here by that name under any spelling."

"But—"

"I'm sorry I was unable to help you," she told me. And then she hung up.

There was no use protesting any further. I put the phone down. Pepe was still watching me.

"This is terrible," I told him. "I don't know what to do." My sister had disappeared twice in my life. Once when she was just a teenager and again during an earlier case I was working with Pepe. I was not going to let that happen again.

I looked at Pepe. Pepe looked at me. And suddenly, I knew. If he could speak, he would tell me we should go investigate. In fact, he would say, "*Andale*, Geri! There is not a moment to waste."

I turned on my laptop, and got the address for the Forest Glen Spa and Clinic. The website showed photos of what looked like a sprawling resort and said it offered "Holistic Healing in a Tranquil Setting." It seemed to be a treatment center for addictions and psychiatric illnesses disguised as a spa. Luckily it was located in the lush valley between Woodinville and Duvall, which was about an hour drive northeast of Seattle.

I took the quickest route to Forest Glen that I could think of: east across the Evergreen Point floating bridge, then north on the 405 freeway to the Woodinville exit. Once we had driven through that town, we continued east through the forested hills taking the highway toward Duvall.

It got more and more rural the farther we went. As soon as we dropped down into the valley, it was nothing but farmland as far as you could see: fields and pastures, all glowing a lush green on a grey day. I am always amazed that such pastoral settings still exist so close to Seattle and its urban sprawl.

Just before I crossed the Snoqualmie River, I saw a large wooden sign that read: FOREST GLEN SPA AND CLINIC—NEXT RIGHT. I turned and followed a narrow road that ran along the river, until it took a big bend to the right and my destination came into view. The buildings were hidden from the road by a long row of tall poplar trees that had probably been planted as a windbreak many years ago. Now the grounds had been landscaped with leafy, deciduous trees, rolling hills of closely mown grass, and flagstone paths that meandered between the main building and some smaller satellite buildings, all of them done in white stucco with red-tiled rooftops.

I parked in Visitor Parking, next to a large and graceful weeping willow tree. "This place is just gorgeous," I told Pepe. "It looks more like a luxury resort than a treatment center."

He didn't respond. That was beginning to seem normal to me. Sort of like my ex-husband right before our divorce.

I put Pepe's leash on him. He usually protests, but because he wasn't talking all he could do was give me a baleful look. Then we headed toward the main entrance at a slow pace as Pepe had to stop to put his mark on various tree trunks and shrubs. The big Spanish-styled main building had baskets of fuchsias hanging on either side of its rounded, oak entry door, their splash of vibrant scarlet-pink flowers contrasting nicely with the white stucco.

The foyer was dramatic with oak beam ceilings crossing high overhead and tiled stairs sweeping up to the upper floors on either side of a reception area, which was dominated by an ornately carved oak desk. The young man seated at the reception desk was in his mid-twenties at most. He had closely cropped blond hair that seemed ultra-blond set off as it was against his deeply tanned face and vivid blue polo shirt. He smiled as I approached, his perfect teeth almost blindingly white.

"Hello! I'm Justin," he said, rising from his seat. "How can I assist you?" His crisply pressed slacks were also white. He looked like he'd be more at home at a tennis club than at a clinic.

I hesitated. I had not come up with a story yet. I looked

at Pepe, wishing he would help me. The receptionist saw my gaze.

"Unfortunately, we don't allow dogs in our facility," he said.

"But this is my therapy dog," I said. "I need him because of my"—I lowered my voice—"disability." I knew that according to law they could not ask the nature of my disability. But they could ask to see the dog's certification. And he did.

"Can I see your paperwork, then?" Justin's voice was cool.

"I left it in the car," I said. But that gave me an idea. "I just came out here to check out the facility because my therapist recommended it. She thought if I saw it for myself, I would be more likely to check myself in. But I can't deal with any more stress. I guess I'll just leave . . ." I turned as if to go.

I thought I saw Pepe give me an approving nod. Perhaps I had learned a little bit about acting from watching Pepe's favorite telenovela, *Paraiso Perdido*. Although his favorite actress would have pressed the back of her wrist to her forehead while uttering those words.

"Oh no, that's not necessary," Justin said quickly. "We can arrange a brief tour. I'll just keep your little dog back here behind the desk with me."

"Or maybe we could just walk around by ourselves?" I suggested hopefully.

"Oh, no," Justin said. "We don't want to disturb our clients. Their privacy is very important to us. Our tours are comprehensive and well worth your time. Just a moment."

He put out his hands for Pepe, who backed away. I bent down to pick him up. "Now, don't bite the nice man," I said, hoisting him into the air. I hoped that would make Justin reconsider, but he didn't. He just picked up Pepe, holding him away from his body like people do when they don't want to touch something, and set him down on the floor behind the desk.

Then he hit a button for a walkie-talkie device that was pinned to his lapel. "Carlos," he said, "are you free to come to reception and guide a tour? Good." He turned to me. "You'll like Carlos. He is highly knowledgeable of our program, but quite respectful and discreet regarding individual needs."

As if by magic, Carlos appeared, emerging from a hallway off to my right. He was accompanied by a striking, raven-haired young woman. Both were dressed in the same blue polo-shirts and white slacks as the receptionist.

Carlos, who had caramel-colored skin and dark eyes, came up and offered me his hand.

"I am Carlos," he said, gazing deep into my eyes. "I'll be your guide today."

His grip was firm and he smelled like a warm, tropical night.

"And this is Lacey," he told me, introducing his female companion. "Lacey is one of our newer associates—she's in training to be one of our guides. I hope you don't mind if she accompanies us on the tour."

I nodded, although I was thinking it would be even harder to break away and do any investigating. Pepe would be disappointed in me.

"Shall we?" said Carlos, waving at the door.

"Enjoy your tour," Justin told me.

Pepe gave a muffled bark from behind the heavy oak desk.

After mentioning that the upper floors of the main building were devoted to office space for the fourteen doctors and twenty-two therapists on staff, Carlos explained that the west wing of the main building contained the spa whereas the east wing offered a pool and complete gym. "We can't disturb the people using the spa," he said, as he opened the glass door to the west wing to reveal a gleaming corridor. At the far end, a woman in a plush white bathrobe and fluffy slippers was just turning into a doorway, accompanied by an attendant, also in a blue polo shirt and white pants. I could see, even from a distance, that she was not Teri. She had the hunched back and shuffling gait of an older person.

"That guest is entering our salt scrub room," Carlos said. "We also have a mud room, a steam room, a sauna, several hot pools, a float chamber and, of course, as you would expect, rooms for massage and facials, waxing and mani-pedis."

"Of course," I said, weakly, having never had a mani-pedi. Maybe it was time.

Carlos swept back across the foyer to the other wing and ushered me into the large glassed-in room that contained a huge indoor pool. The pool was empty. The water glowed with a blue-green color, lit by underwater lights. The scent of chlorine filled the air.

At the far end of the pool, through a glass window, I could see a room full of exercise equipment. Carlos ticked off their various purposes as my mind wandered. I didn't think Teri would be working out, but what did I know about her life? She had run away from home when she was only seventeen and disappeared altogether when she was twenty. I had only seen her once in the intervening ten years, and then only briefly.

We left the main building by a back door and went out into the misty day. Carlos led me down a meandering path, pointing out the various buildings. "That one is Tranquility," he said, pointing to a two-story stucco building to our right. "And over there by the lily pond, you will find Harmony. Each is set up like a family home, with a dedicated kitchen and dining area, a lounge and separate bedrooms for the guests. And, of course, each is fully staffed at the appropriate level."

"Appropriate level." I seized on that phrase. "What does that mean?"

"Well," said Carlos, smiling happily, "our doctors do an assessment of your needs when you first enter the facility and decide what level of treatment and medication you might benefit from. Then we assign you to a residence."

I was wishing I had Pepe with me. He would be able to sniff Teri out and tell me if she was living in Peace or in Contentment. There was no one visible on any of the paths. When I asked about that, Carlos told me it was lunch time and no doubt all the guests were enjoying the fabulous gourmet meals prepared from fresh, organic ingredients that were purchased from local farms.

We had almost completed our circle of the grounds when the walkie-talkie pinned to Carlos's collar squawked. "Code Red in Serenity. Code Red in Serenity."

Carlos looked startled. "Oh!" he said. He turned to Lacey. "Can you take her back to the front desk?"

"I can find my way there on my own," I said. I could see the back of the main building. I could also see several blue-and-white clad employees running toward one particular building, set back in the woods.

"Oh, no!" said Carlos. "Lacey doesn't have the proper level of training to respond to this situation anyway. She'll go with you." He hurried off down the path.

"What does he mean by proper level of training?" I asked Lacey, who was staring after Carlos with a wistful look on her face.

"Oh, that's the most locked-down of the cottages," said Lacey. "Definitely the craziest people are in that one. So you need some special classes to know how to handle them." Then she stopped and looked at me, stricken. "Oh, I shouldn't have said that!" She clamped her hand over her mouth. Too late. The words were already out.

"So there are crazy people here?" I asked. I could see, even from this distance that the windows of Serenity were covered with wrought-iron grates. And I thought, as the door opened to admit the employees, that I heard muffled screams from inside.

"No, only guests," she stammered. "We're not allowed to use the term 'crazy,' even in jest. I could be fired."

"Don't worry. I won't tell anyone," I said as we turned away and headed back toward the main building. But I shuddered. Would I be locked up in Serenity if I told them I heard my dog speaking to me?

We were quickly back at the front desk where Justin looked harried. "Your dog ran off as soon as my back was turned," he said, looking at me accusingly.

"That's terrible," I said, but knowing Pepe it was to be expected. "I'll go look for him."

"No, you can't be out on the grounds right now," Justin said with tight lips. "We've got a bit of a situation. An unauthorized person tried to enter one of the cottages and we need to remove them." He looked at me sternly. "You see how hard we work to protect our guests. Once that situation is under control, I will send someone out to look for your dog."

But there was no need to do that, as within a few minutes, Pepe came trotting into the hallway. It was impossible to know where he had been. Had he been taking a swim in the pool? No, he hates water. Was he having a mani-pedi in the spa? No, it was clear he still needed to have his nails trimmed. Perhaps he was the cause of the disturbance in Serenity. I wouldn't put it past him.

"So where were you?" I asked as I carried him back to my car in the parking lot.

Unfortunately, he remained silent.

Pepe's Blog: Working with a Human Partner

My partner, Geri Sullivan, is a human and so she does not have the same skills I do. Her sense of smell is weak and she rarely gets down on the ground to investigate the plethora of clues to be found there. Yes, plethora. Just because I am a dog does not mean I have a meager vocabulary. Geri has not memorized, as have I, the various brands of tobacco products. She cannot tell from sniffing the pores of a perpetrator what they ate for breakfast. I can. But in the past Geri has been able to relay my findings to those in authority. Unfortunately, her insistence that I talk has landed her in a world of trouble. Several people were threatening to lock her up in a psychiatric facility, including her so-called counselor, Susanna. So I have taken a vow of silence in order to protect her. Which means I must watch helpless as she bungles along, trying to figure things out on her own. Just today we went to visit a fancy facility where she thought she might find her sister. She left discouraged.

But I know for certain that her sister is there. I managed to make contact with her and reassured her that Geri and I were going to rescue her. Unfortunately, my talking seemed to confuse her and she became quite agitated. Not only that, I happen to know there is a delectable smelling poodle bitch who accompanies one of the doctors to work. And I also know that a beet and bacon salad was served for lunch in Contentment. I sampled it and it met with my approval.

Chapter 3

When I got back home, there was a message on my home phone from Jay, Brad's partner. He said he was really worried by a message he had received from Brad and would I come right over.

So I got back in my little green Toyota with Pepe and raced right over to Jay's house. And it is Jay's house. He's the one who pays the mortgage. Brad has never made a profit in his interior decorating business. Brad is good at getting clients—better than I was—and his clients are pretty wealthy, though eccentric. But he buys extravagantly too. He's always snapping up deals at estate sales or prowling around second-hand stores. He'll plunk down one thousand dollars for a Victorian sofa, then let it sit in the back of his shop for years.

Brad's partner, Jay, on the other hand, runs a successful, high-end catering business, with more than forty employees on his payroll, and he's the one paying off the mortgage on the house they share on Queen Anne Hill. It's an old Victorian mansion decorated in Brad's favorite style: I'd call it baroque

Victoriana: red damask walls, gold tassels on the curtain tie-backs, gilded chairs, and lots of porcelain figures of birds. Jay, has a thing for birds. One room is a dedicated aviary where his pets—mostly parrots and cockatoos—fly around freely.

Jay came to the door with his favorite bird on his shoulder, a bad-tempered Quaker gray parrot. I flinched. My skin had been punctured by this creature's sharp beak more than once. I looked down at Pepe, who should have promised to protect me, but he had already trotted into the hallway and was sniffing around the edges of a wrought-iron umbrella stand that was shaped like an umbrella. An umbrella would have helped me defend myself against that parrot, but no one in Seattle ever uses an umbrella. We view it as a sign of weakness. But it helps us identify the out-of-towners.

"Geri! I'm so glad to see you! Come in! Come in!" said Jay, waving me off the front porch and into the crowded living room. I could see Brad's influence everywhere: the green Morris wallpaper, the gilt chairs striped in gold and green, the glittering gold lamé curtains, and the green velvet pelmet above them. Brad's style is way over the top, but it's recognizable and I suddenly missed my friend more than ever.

"What's going on, Jay?" I asked.

"I don't know," Jay said. "That's why I called you." He waved me to a seat on the mustard yellow velvet sofa and settled down opposite me in an armchair covered in green leather. Whereas Brad is blond and willowy, Jay has the bulk of someone who loves food and the reddish complexion of someone who loves wine. They couldn't look more unalike, but they've been together for over ten years. They fight all the time, but they love each other fiercely.

Pepe jumped up on the sofa beside me and stared at the bird on Jay's shoulder as if warning it that he would bite it if it came anywhere near me.

"Thanks, Pepe!" I said, patting him on the head.

"Your dog still talking to you?" asked Jay with a bit of a sarcastic twist in his voice.

"Ironically, no," I said. I was surprised and a little hurt that Brad had discussed my talking dog with his partner, but hey, that's what partners are for. I had discussed Brad's disappearance with my boyfriend, Felix. Felix told me to give him some time. Sometimes good friends, old friends, need a break, he said. I wondered if that was code and Felix needed a break.

"Brad thought it was cute," said Jay. His voice got sad. "It made him want a dog more than ever. I told him he couldn't have one. Do you think that's why he left?" His voice was now wistful.

"What do you mean left?"

Jay looked embarrassed. "Well, I hadn't seen him for a couple of days. I thought he was off on one of his little shopping sprees." It was true. Brad could take off to go check out an antique store in Arlington, a small town north of Seattle, and end up two days later two states away in Montana, buying the entire inventory of a taxidermist who was going out of business.

"Was he acting weird before he left?" I asked.

"Yes, he was jumpy and irritable. And when I asked him why, he just snapped at me." Jay flapped his hands in the air near his head to indicate how frazzled he was. That disturbed the parrot who flew up, circled around my head (I ducked) and then settled on a nearby lamp. "I thought he was getting cold feet."

"Cold feet about what?"

Jay's big brown eyes got sad. Almost as sad as Pepe's eyes when he wants something. "He didn't tell you, did he?"

"What? What are you talking about?"

"The wedding. Our wedding."

I was shocked. "You and Brad are getting married?"

Jay nodded. "On Halloween. But if he didn't tell you, his best friend . . ." His voice trailed off.

Pepe was sitting at my feet, looking at me. He seemed to be trying to get a message through to me. Oh, a message.

"You said he left some sort of message," I said. "What did it say?" I swear Pepe nodded his head. I could almost hear him saying, "Good work, partner."

"I'll show you." Jay got up and went out into the hall. He came back with an invoice, a bill for an armoire, on which was scribbled in Brad's loopy handwriting:

Crisis in the kingdom. Off to slay the dragon. Home soon.

I looked at it. I read it out loud for Pepe's sake.

"When did you get this?" I asked.

"I don't know," said Jay. "I just found it this afternoon. It was on top of the bureau in Brad's room. You know I never go in there."

I knew that Jay was horrified by Brad's messiness so they had separate bedrooms. Jay was a neatnik whereas Brad scattered chaos in his wake.

"Do you know there's a three-day Pay or Vacate notice at the store?" I asked.

Jay ran his hands through his tousled hair. "Yes, the landlord has been calling. He says Brad is six months behind on the rent. I told him I would send him a check, but he said he's tired of having to chase after Brad for the rent."

"Maybe Brad was referring to the landlord when he said he was going to slay the dragon?" I asked.

Jay brightened. "Could be. Never thought of that."

"Can you give me the landlord's name?" I asked.

"Sure," Jay got up and went out into the hall. We followed and watched him root around in a pile of business cards that lay in a silver tray on a curving sideboard with a marble top. A vase full of dried stalks of angelica stood beside it, each dried flower head like an explosion of fireworks "Here it is. His name is Samuel Morris. It says his office is in Bellevue. I believe he owns several small properties on Eastlake. My hunch is that he's getting ready to sell to a big developer and he'd be happy to see Brad out of there." Jay handed me a card. He looked at me with his bright eyes. The parrot looked at me with his bright eyes.

"Well, thanks," I said. "I'll let you know what I find out."

"Please do," said Jay. "I'm so worried about him."

"Why not call the police? How long has it been?" The note was undated.

"That's just it," said Jay. "I'm kind of embarrassed to admit that I don't really know when he disappeared. I mean sometimes he sleeps at the shop, so I just assumed he was there. You know how he gets when he's working on a project."

It's true. Brad once completely refinished a dining room table and reupholstered fourteen matching chairs in one all-night binge. When he was working on a project, he was obsessed.

"Well, when's the last time you saw him?"

Jay looked up into the air to the left of his head. I tried to remember from my research if that meant he was making something up or looking back at his memories. "Well, I know I saw him on Tuesday. No make that, Monday, because he came home really late and really drunk and I told him to go sleep in his bedroom."

"So he's possibly been missing for three days?"

"Well," Jay looked embarrassed. "Maybe. I mean, it's possible." He held out his hands. "You can see why it would be awkward to go to the police."

"I think you need to," I said. "They'll listen to you, since he's been gone for so long. They might even have a way to help you figure out when he was last seen. Do you know what bar he was drinking at?"

Jay frowned. "Probably the Cuff or the Manhole. Maybe Neighbors." He named several gay bars on Capitol Hill. "Those are the ones he frequents."

"Have you gone to any of them? Asked around?" I asked.

"It would be too humiliating. I don't know anyone any more," said Jay. "That's where we met—in a bar— but once I found Brad, I was done with all that. But Brad still goes out once or twice a month. He loves to dance and flirt and gossip. I thought that's all he was doing." He looked pensive for a moment. "But maybe he was looking for a way out. Maybe he ran off with some guy he met."

"Brad wouldn't do that to you," I said. "He loves

you. And you guys have been together for, what, ten years?"

Jay sighed.

"Oh, there is one other possibility," said Jay as Pepe and I went out the front door. "Brad always called one of his clients the dragon lady. Maybe he was talking about her."

"Ah yes! I know the one," I said. That would be Mrs. Fairchild. I had helped Brad deliver a hand-painted medieval-themed armoire to her house one day. After we had staggered upstairs with it, she decided the colors clashed with the curtains and had us carry it back down to the van Brad had rented.

We went out to the car. I looked over at Pepe who was watching me. "That didn't sound right, did it?" I said to him. He shook his head. "Something's fishy," I said. Pepe nodded. "Well, the good news is that I know where Mrs. Fairchild lives. And I know Brad was working for her. Let's go talk to her first."

Pepe nodded his consent.

But it wasn't good news that I knew where Mrs. Fairchild lived: in a luxurious fake Southern Colonial plantation house in the tony streets down below Volunteer Park. It wasn't good news that the front door, hidden from the street by an overgrown yew hedge, was open because that meant Pepe would go dashing into the house before I could stop him. And it wasn't good news at all, that when I followed him into the lemon-yellow kitchen, I found the dead body of Mrs. Fairchild lying on her kitchen floor in a pool of dried blood. The smell of fresh paint still lingered in the air. But it was faint under the stronger scent of what Pepe would say, if he could speak, was the smell of *muerte.*

Pepe's Blog: Sniffing the Scene

Good news, mi amigos! We found a dead body! There is nothing more exciting for a private detective than a murder investigation. Especially for a seasoned detective like Pepe Sullivan. I let my partner, Geri Sullivan, handle the more mundane aspects of the private eye business: the phone calls, the computer research, the driving from place to place, and the interviews with suspects and witnesses. She did pretty well interviewing the unpleasant man with the unpleasant parrot, but she did not seem to notice that he was lying.

A dog can always tell. You tell us you won't be gone long and then you disappear for hours, although I am not really sure about what an hour is. It seems an arbitrary period of time that involves having nothing to do between meals and walks and naps and tummy rubbing.

Unfortunately, I could not tell what he was lying about. Was he lying when he said he had not seen his partner for days? Or that he no longer went to bars? Or was he lying about not knowing the name of the dragon lady? Luckily, Geri knew where the dragon lady lived, so I was able to turn up the first clue in our case: a dead body.

Unfortunately, this discovery is not good news for Geri's friend, Brad, who she is trying to find. Because I could tell Brad had been in the kitchen. His smell—a nasty mixture of some kind of musky cologne mingled with paint remover and dust—was all over the body. But I did not tell Geri that. She will have to figure it out on her own.

Chapter 4

Pepe would normally have yelled at me to be sure I didn't do anything to contaminate the crime scene. Then he would have sniffed around, gathering clues and telling me what he found. But this wasn't normal at all. Instead I scurried out of the house, feeling nauseous, and threw up in the bushes in the front. Then I called 911 and stood on the front porch crying. Pepe disappeared—no doubt gathering clues, but ones he couldn't share with me.

I really wanted to talk to someone so I called my boyfriend, Felix. The call went straight to voice mail and I didn't bother to leave a message. Felix had been really distracted lately, and sometimes he wouldn't return my calls until the next day. Nothing makes a woman feel more vulnerable than leaving a message asking a man to call and then waiting and waiting and waiting for that call.

At least I didn't have to wait long for the police. A blue and white cop car, blue lights flashing and siren wailing, pulled up within minutes. The driver was a female police officer. She got out of the car and swaggered up to me.

"Are you the one who called?" she asked. Her strawberry-blond hair was short and tight on the sides, almost like a man's haircut.

"Yes," I said.

A young man—he looked barely old enough to have graduated from high school—emerged from the passenger side of the car. But he was wearing the slate blue uniform of a Seattle cop. "You called in a 187?" he asked eagerly.

The female cop frowned at him. "We don't use code with civilians," she said. She turned to me. "You reported a dead body?"

"Yes I did. It's in the kitchen."

"I see," she said. "Do you live here?"

"No."

"Do you know the victim?"

"No." It was not entirely a lie.

The two cops exchanged a glance that made me feel I was a suspect.

"I know her name," I admitted. "Mrs. Fairchild."

The female police officer spoke. "We'll go in and check it out. So which way is the body?" I stepped with them into the living room and pointed through the dining room towards the door of the kitchen.

"You stay out here and don't go anywhere. We need to talk to you some more," said the woman cop.

I didn't like the sound of that, but what could I do? Because I hadn't done anything, I shouldn't have to worry. But I did. I sat down on the living room sofa—which looked a bit like a giant bee since it was upholstered in yellow and black stripes—and wondered what happened to my dog. Just then he came slinking into the room. Probably scared away from the crime scene by the police.

He hates the police. I think he confuses them with the animal control officers who scooped him up off the streets of LA and put him into what he calls "dog prison." I have tried to point out to him that if he had not been in a shelter we would never have met, but so far he does not seem moved by that argument.

I picked him up and held him. He was shivering.

"What did you smell, Pepe?" I asked. "What do you know?" And just then, two men walked through the open front door. They did a double take when they saw me talking to my dog. So did I. I recognized them. So did Pepe. He barked.

The older detective, Larson, was balding and wore wire-rimmed glasses and a rumpled navy-blue suit, just like he had the first time we'd met. "Well, we meet again," he said.

At the same time, the two beat cops came out of the kitchen.

"You know this woman?" the female officer asked.

"Yeah, we know her all right," the other detective said. "Who could forget her and that nasty little dog?" Sanders was a tall black man with a shaved head, dressed impeccably in a camelhair sports coat and crisp tan slacks.

"Yeah, that's right," said Larson. "Claimed to be a PI. She was involved in another murder case a little over a year ago."

"For your information I am a PI," I told them, even though I had yet to be officially licensed. "And I just stumbled over this murder."

"Like the first time, huh?" said Sanders, very sarcastic.

"Yes," I said emphatically.

"So where you go, murder follows." That was detective Larson, also being sarcastic. He didn't give me time to reply, just quickly told the uniformed cops, "OK. Why don't you show us the crime scene?"

"Looks like the cause of death was blunt force trauma," said the younger cop quickly.

His woman partner gave him a chiding look. "But we'll leave the determination to the coroner," she said.

"What about her?" the young man asked. He was irrepressible in his desire to be doing something significant. "Should we cuff her?"

"She can wait out here until we're done," Larson said.

"Are you sure?" he asked. "I mean, if she was involved in another murder—"

"I don't think she's a flight risk," Larson told him.

"Yeah, but her dog sure is," said Sanders. "Bit one of our technicians last time around," he told the uniforms. "Then made a break for it. Had to put an APB out on him."

"On a Chihuahua," said Larson. They all shared a laugh at that.

I expected Pepe to comment on our situation, but he just stopped shivering in my arms and kept silent. His big ears rotated toward the kitchen where the cops were surveying the scene. I could only hear a low murmur of voices but he, no doubt, could pick up actual words. Still if he wasn't going to help me out, I needed to do something myself.

The living room was a hideous hodgepodge of styles. Here and there, I recognized Brad's work (the yellow-and-black sofa, for instance, and the huge gilt mirror over the fireplace, and maybe the blue-and-white Chinese vase in the corner full of dried pampas grass), but nothing really went together. The fireplace mantel was covered with little ceramic figures of peasant children. Two walls were olive green and one wall was turquoise; the remaining wall contained a mural of an indistinguishable nature scene. Was it a meadow? A forest? Were those nymphs frolicking in the woods? Or were those sheep making their way up a mountain trail?

I made my way over to look at the details and found myself standing in front of a rolltop desk. As I peered at the desk more closely, I saw that it had cubby holes organized and even labeled. One read BILLS PAID, another read BILLS TO PAY, another read PENDING.

I was curious about that last one, especially since it contained the most items. So I pulled out the handful of papers inside. Most appeared to be invoices from various contractors who had worked on her house, including a plumber, a carpenter, and a faux finisher. But seven of them were from Brad. They went back for months and included bills for furniture purchases, upholstery work, and the painting of the kitchen. She'd written across the bottom of all seven bills, "Not a penny until it's done right!"

I knew Brad had done a lot of work for Mrs. Fairchild. I didn't realize that she had not paid him for any of it. I couldn't help thinking about his fanciful note: "Off to slay the dragon." And then I thought: what if the cops saw these bills? Would they think it was a motive for murder? Would they think that Brad killed her?

I was just about to stuff them into my pocket, when the police came back into the dining room.

"What have you got there?" asked Sanders.

"Yeah," said Larson, looking past me at the open rolltop. "Going through the dead woman's desk, huh?"

Pepe barked at the cops and went charging toward them. I ran to intercept him and dropped the bills I was holding. Like toast always landing on the buttered side, a couple of Brad's bills landed face up.

"You're disturbing the crime scene," the female cop told me as Sanders came over and picked the bills up off the floor, then took the rest out of my hand.

"You could be arrested for that, you know," said the young male cop.

"Something important here?" asked Sanders, looking through the bills in his hand.

"No," I told him. At least they wouldn't know they came out of the PENDING file. On the other hand, the dates and the note on the bottom were pretty clear.

"Sure." He gave me a suspicious look, then told the uniformed cops, "Why don't you two put up the tape? Front door and back door. We don't want anybody else traipsing in before forensics gets here."

As they went out, Sanders told me, "Have a seat, Miss Sullivan. We need to take your statement."

Both the detectives sat across from me at the dining table. Sanders put the bills on the table as he took his seat and, of course, a few of Brad's bills were face up for all to see.

"Do you know the victim?" Sanders asked me.

"Not really," I said.

"What does that mean?" That was Sanders.

"I came here once with my partner, Brad, to deliver some furniture."

"Partner?" Larson gave that a bit of a leer.

"My business partner. Brad owns an antique shop. He does interior design and furniture restoration."

Sanders looked around the dining room which was, if possible, in even worse taste than the living room. It was ringed with china cabinets full of silver and gold tableware. The wallpaper was silver flocked. The tablecloth was a piece of intricate but stained white crochet work. His eyebrows lifted but he said nothing.

"So what were you doing here today?" Larson asked.

"Well, I came here trying to find Brad."

"What made you think he was here?" asked Sanders.

"I knew he was doing some work for Mrs. Fairchild."

"And why were you looking for him?"

I stumbled to come up with something plausible. I had just told Jay to report that Brad was missing. Would the police connect the two events?

"I haven't talked to him for a while and his partner was worried about him—"

"Another partner?" That was Larson, again with a leer.

"Jay is his life partner," I said. "His significant other. They're getting married."

"I see," said Larson, his expression betraying the same distaste for Brad's lifestyle as he had for my dog.

"And why did you think to look here?" Larson asked.

"She was the last client he was working with," I said, hating the way that came out.

"And these are his invoices," said Sanders, who had

been sorting through the papers. "Looks like she hadn't paid him for months." He handed them to Larson.

"Is it possible he came here to confront her about the unpaid invoices?" Larson asked.

"And it got ugly," Sanders went on. "Your friend Brad. He has a temper, doesn't he?"

I shook my head. "Absolutely not," I told him. "Brad's a sweetheart."

Larson rolled his eyes. "How can we get in touch with him?" he asked.

"Um."

"Um is not an answer." That was Sanders. He sounded like my seventh grade teacher.

"The truth is . . ." I hesitated, then decided I had to be honest. Pepe was shaking his head at me. Too bad. "Brad is missing."

Sanders sat up even straighter. "Since when?" he asked.

"I don't know for sure," I said. "Maybe a day or two? You'll have to ask Jay." I hoped that time frame would make it clear Brad could not have committed this murder. I hoped he really was on a buying binge.

"We may need to talk to you again," said Larson, closing his notebook.

"Yes," said Sanders. "We've got Brad's business address here," he continued, holding up one of Brad's invoices. "We'll go by there to look for him."

"There were other people she wasn't paying as well," I said, quick to defend my friend.

"You don't need to tell us how to do our job," said Larson, getting up rather stiffly. "You stay out of it, this time."

"Of course," I said, gathering up my dog and heading out the front door. But, of course, I wasn't going to do that. I had to try to find Brad before the police did. I headed straight for the shop.

I tried my key again, but it still didn't work. How was I going to investigate if I couldn't get into the shop? Luckily, the back door key did work. I was a little nervous as I entered the dim workroom, afraid of what I might find.

"Pepe, I hope you will let me know if you smell *muerte*," I said as he ran ahead of me. I couldn't bear the thought of finding Brad dead. But what other explanation could there be for his disappearance? I didn't buy Jay's thought that he ran off with another man. Brad was totally devoted to Jay. Or, at least, he had been.

Pepe disappeared into the gloom. I felt my way to the light switch and flipped the switch. No lights. Apparently the electricity had been turned off.

Some light filtered through the high dusty windows along the sides and I could see some familiar items: the big red-tail hawk with his wings outspread, which seemed to soar suspended by cords over the work area; the stuffed owl on top of the grandfather clock (Brad loves taxidermy); and the armoire, which we had carried up the stairs at Mrs. Fairchild's house. It was no longer painted olive green with red roses. It looked like Brad had stripped that off and was working on a new color scheme: sky blue with Pennsylvania Dutch designs of pink hearts and purple birds. Not Brad's style at all.

Pepe was standing in front of the armoire, his nose pointed at the doors, one leg lifted the way pointers do when pointing at a pheasant.

"What's in there, little man?" I said, coming over to him. Then I saw the note pinned to the door. It read "Dragon Lady." As I looked around the shop, I could see other notes pinned to other pieces of furniture. Every one of them read "Dragon Lady."

What to do? It made Brad look like a suspect. "I don't suppose the police will mind," I said, more to myself than to Pepe as I went around collecting them. He seemed to approve. His tail was wagging. But suddenly his demeanor changed. He looked at the front of the shop and started growling.

I poked my head through the velvet curtain that divided the front of the shop from the workroom in back and saw, through the big front windows, the big black sedan belonging to the two homicide detectives just parking outside.

"Time to leave," I said to Pepe. And we hightailed it out the back door. When we got home, I got another surprise. Felix was standing on my front porch, his arms full of bright orange gladiolas.

Pepe's Blog: Dealing with the Police

Remember that as a private detective, the police are not your friends. Too often they are trying to investigate the same case that you have been engaged to resolve. Your best bet is to keep silent, as I demonstrated when the police tried to take over the crime scene that I discovered. My partner, unfortunately, did not follow my lead and ended up giving the police some valuable information.

Intimidation may also work, especially if you are a fierce Chihuahua. But not if your partner picks you up and tucks you under her arm like you are some kind of small purse.

So then your next course of action is to get to the places and people of interest before the police do. I found many interesting pieces of scent evidence at the shop. I was trying to get Geri to open the cabinet because I could smell a pheasant inside of it. Probably stuffed but one never knows. And the pheasant had the distinct smell of the dead woman. But Geri thought I was pointing at the little signs. So it goes.

She went around removing the signs. That is one good thing about having a human partner as I am too small and do not have the opposable thumbs necessary to do some of the grunt work involved in detecting. On the other hand, humans are easily distracted. As soon as she saw the dog trainer with his arms full of flowers, well, that was the end of any investigating for several hours. Luckily, Felix had brought along Fuzzy, who had been my faithful assistant in a previous case, and I spent my time catching Fuzzy up to date on the elements of the case. While doing so, I uncovered a new detail I had missed. This is why it is essential to work in a team. I do miss being able to talk to Geri.

Chapter 5

I had never been so happy to see anyone. It seemed like nothing had gone right today. But I knew Felix would make it better.

"Oh, Felix!" I rushed up and threw my arms around him.

"I'm glad to see you, too," he said, trying to return the embrace while keeping the gladiolas out of harm's way. It wasn't entirely successful. One of the stems broke.

"I'm so sorry!" I wailed. "It's all my fault! Like usual."

Felix looked into my eyes and said, "Something's wrong, isn't it?"

That's Felix. So tuned in to my every emotion. Meanwhile, Pepe was scratching on the door while Fuzzy, so well-behaved, was merely sitting on the stoop, looking up adoringly at Felix. I thought that was a good idea.

"Yes!" I sighed. "Come on in. I'll tell you all about it."

And I did. He listened patiently while I rattled on

about the trip to the vet, the mysterious phone call, the trip to Forest Glen, my conversation with Jay, and the discovery of Mrs. Fairchild's body. I was too agitated to focus on anything practical so Felix took care of arranging the flowers in a vase, spooning out some food for Pepe and Fuzzy, and ordering a pizza when we both realized I hadn't stopped to eat.

The pizza arrived. Half goat cheese and pesto for me, half sausage and pepperoni for Felix and the dogs. We took it into the dining room because Pepe and Fuzzy were in the living room looking at something on Pepe's iPad, which sat on my coffee table.

Pepe had ordered it without my permission a few months earlier and it was one of his favorite toys. He could spend hours swiping across the pad with his paw, but he was very secretive about his activities, always shutting down the screen when anyone approached. Felix and I sometimes joked that he was looking at porn.

I snatched up the iPad before the dogs could protest. Pepe did, of course, with a sharp bark. Fuzzy just sat there quietly. She's a fluffy little terrier-poodle mix Felix adopted after she was abandoned. I swear he adopted her just to prove to me that he is really good at dog training. The only dog he can't train is my dog.

"What do we have here?" said Felix, poring over the iPad, which contained a bunch of squiggles. Pepe jumped around barking like mad. If he had been talking, he would have been saying, "Unhand that, you villain! That is mine!"

"I don't know," I said, bending over to look at it. The squiggles seemed to form some sort of random pattern: uneven rectangles connected by curving lines and interrupted by messy doodles. It reminded me of something, some place I had been recently.

"You know," I said, looking up at Felix, "I could swear this is a diagram of the grounds of the Forest Glen spa."

Pepe gave an excited, high-pitched yip.

"But what's all this crazy stuff going on here?" I asked, pointing to a messy section of the diagram all around the farthest rectangle. It looked like scribbling. I looked at Pepe and he looked at me with his bright eyes. Fuzzy looked at Pepe instead of at Felix.

I sighed. "If only Pepe would talk to me," I said to Felix, "I would feel so much better."

I headed for the dining room where the pizza waited. I set out my Fiestaware plates—the only good thing I got out of my marriage. Jeff didn't want them. He thought they were old-fashioned. No doubt he and his bride-to-be have registered for some fancy china with gold monograms.

Felix hesitated for a moment. I knew that believing my dog talked to me strained his credulity. Yet he had seemed to accept it. He set the iPad back down on the coffee table. Meanwhile, I dished up the pizza and Felix and I sat down to eat. We could see the dogs, both huddled around the iPad on the coffee table.

"I swear it's almost like they're talking to each other," I said, watching them with envy.

Felix laughed. "That would be something! Fuzzy has never said a word to me!"

"You don't take me seriously," I said.

"It's hard, babe," Felix said. "I mean, dogs don't talk." He saw the look in my eyes and quickly added. "Most dogs don't talk."

"But Pepe did!" I said. "And now he doesn't."

"But otherwise he seems normal?"

"Yes, but he's not talking," I told him.

"Yeah?"

"Don't you get it?'

"Sure, but—"

"But *what*?"

"Well—"

"Well *what*?"

"Geri," he said, then stated the obvious. "He's a dog."

It took a minute for his meaning to sink in. "Are you saying he doesn't talk? You said you heard him talk when we were at the ranch in Roslyn."

"I *thought* I heard him talk."

"So now you don't believe me!" I got up, grabbed my plate, took it into the kitchen. "You're just like all the others. You think I'm crazy!"

"I didn't say that," said Felix, getting up and coming after me. "Look, babe, there are a million reasons why he might have stopped talking."

"Now you're trying to humor me."

"Not at all," he told me. "Dogs are a lot like little kids. Pepe might just be acting out."

"About what?" I filled the sink with soapy water.

"Who knows? Could be anything. Maybe you've changed his food. Maybe he's upset about a favorite toy."

"I've been giving him the same food all along. And he's got his TV and iPad." I peeked around the corner at him. He was still hunched over the iPad, Fuzzy at his side.

"Maybe you've hurt his feelings somehow."

"I don't know how." I thought for a minute. "Well,

I do tell him to be quiet a lot, especially when he tells some of his outlandish stories."

"That could be it," Felix said, but he didn't sound convinced.

"What can I do, Felix?" I went back into the dining room and closed up the pizza box. There were still a few pieces left.

Felix followed me back into the kitchen. "I think I know how to help."

"Really?" I slid the pizza box into the bottom of my refrigerator.

"Yes, I know an amazing pet therapist in Laguna Beach. Her name is Caro Lamont. And she's coming up here for the audition for—" Felix broke off.

"Audition for what?" I asked.

"Oh, we can talk about it later," Felix said.

"No, really, come on. What?"

"Well, it just doesn't seem like the right time to talk about it."

"Why not?"

"Well, you're so stressed by this situation with Pepe. But I think Caro might be able to help you with him. She's really good."

"But you said she's in Laguna Beach . . ."

"She's coming to Seattle this weekend." He seemed sheepish.

"What for?" I knew something was up by the way he was acting.

"She's the consultant for a new reality TV show that your friend Rebecca Tyler is producing."

Rebecca Tyler is not really my friend. In fact, I suspected her of murder for the first few days I knew her. Once we got it all straightened out, she invited me and Pepe to participate in her reality TV show,

Dancing with Dogs. The first season hasn't aired yet, but I hear the networks think it has a lot of promise.

"What new reality TV show? And why would Rebecca be in Seattle?" The last I heard she was still down in LA working on the first season of *Dancing with Dogs.*

"It's called *Pet Intervention,*" said Felix. He actually seemed to blush a little. "They need an expert who can work with a lot of different kinds of animals that have behavior problems. And Caro recommended me." Felix has a background in working with animals in the film industry. He started his career working with big cats, until an accident on a set shattered his confidence. I sometimes wondered if he felt his current situation as a dog trainer in Seattle was a bit of a comedown.

"You'd be perfect for that!" I said. "That's such great news."

"Well, yes," he said, waving away my excitement with one hand. "I'm just one of many auditioning for the show. But if I got it, well . . ." His voice trailed off again.

"Well, what?"

"Well, I'd probably have to move to L.A. That's where they're filming."

"Oh." That could be a problem. Our relationship was really too new for us to move in together. And I noticed he wasn't asking me to move to L.A. And I wasn't asking him to stay in Seattle.

"What do you think?"

"I think it's amazing, Felix. I think you'll do great," I said, throwing my arms around him. And all the time I was thinking, I really need you here. I hope you don't get the job.

"Really?"

"When did all this happen?" I asked, thinking about how distracted Felix had been the last few times we were together and how he wasn't answering his phone.

"Oh, I got the first call a few weeks ago. We're doing the blocking tomorrow and shooting on Saturday and Sunday."

"And you didn't tell me?" I was dismayed. Maybe we weren't as close as I thought. I couldn't imagine not telling Felix news that big. Kind of like Brad not telling me he was getting married.

"Well, it didn't seem likely it would pan out. I guess I just don't think something's worth sharing until I have something definitive to say about it."

"Like my sister maybe calling me from someplace that's both a crazy hospital and a spa?" I asked. "I shouldn't share that with you until I know for sure if she's there and what it is that she's doing there?" I realized I was getting a little overly emotional but it was that sort of day.

"Geri, don't get upset!" Felix looked worried.

Pepe ran to the front door and started barking furiously.

"No, really, I mean, would you rather I figure everything out before I bother you by talking about it?"

"No, Geri, that's not what I was saying—"

Pepe's barking got even more frantic.

"What's wrong, Pepe?" I asked, even though I knew he wouldn't tell me.

Then my phone started ringing. I got up and went over to where my purse lay on the table in the hallway. Pepe raced from the front door to the sofa. He jumped up on the back of the sofa, so he could see out the window to the street, all the time continuing to bark. I dug my cell phone out of my purse and flipped it open.

"Geri Sullivan?" a man asked, his voice low and gruff.

"Yes," I said. I could barely hear him over Pepe's barking.

He said something else, but I couldn't make it out. So I went over to the sofa thinking I would grab Pepe. That's when I saw a large, black SUV with tinted windows parked directly in front of my condo. A man in a dark suit, with slicked back dark hair, was standing beside it talking on a cell phone.

"Your sister's name is Teri. Yes?"

I hesitated. Then I realized that the guy I was talking to on the phone was the same guy outside my house who was talking on *his* cell phone. "What business is that of yours? Who are you?"

"All I'm saying is: you need to stay away from her."

I swear he winked at me, then hung up and got into the driver's side of the SUV. I watched in shock as the car pulled out and sped away. I was so shocked I didn't even think to write down the license plate.

Pepe's Blog: Benefits of Not Talking

I must say, not talking has advantages and drawbacks. One advantage is that I am rediscovering my inner dog. It is liberating to just be a dog. When I heard those miscreants, no words could describe the primal instincts I felt. I barked and snarled and growled and barked. I was ferocious, wild, and free from the civilized constraints of language!

However, I was not so wild that I neglected my duty. I memorized the license number of the big SUV that was outside our house. I do not think that Geri thought to do so. And that leads us to one drawback about not talking: how will I convey this license number to her if I do not talk?

Aye, there is the rub, as the Bard would say. I stopped talking because people thought Geri was crazy because I talked. Now she is beginning to think she is crazy because I do not talk. But a vow is a vow and I am a dog of my word.

I could use some of the corny devices I have seen

on TV and the Internet. Writing letters in the sand. But how can I get Geri to take me to the beach? Hiring a skywriter to write the letters and numbers in puffs of smoke in the sky? Arranging for the fans at a Seahawks game to spell it out with flash cards?

Perhaps I will find the solution on the Internet. That is what it is for, *n'est-ce pas?* (And yes, in case you are wondering, I do speak French, having spent several weeks soaking up the sun on a beach in Cannes during the famous film festival.) Also a bit of Italian: *Ciao*, baby!

Chapter 6

Felix helped me calm down. He's always good in a crisis. Although I didn't appreciate the fact that he kept asking me if I had seen the license plate. It was true that when I tried to look back in my mind, I thought there was something funny about the number. Like maybe it was an official license plate, not the usual string of three letters and three numbers assigned to civilians. But that didn't make sense, either. The government doesn't send men in suits to intimidate private eyes.

Felix ended up spending the night and we reconciled some of our differences in bed, but when he left in the morning, after writing down the number for the Laguna Beach pet therapist, I was still puzzled about what to do next.

I decided finding out what was wrong with Pepe was my biggest concern, so I pulled up the number for Dr. Mallard. The receptionist wanted to know what was wrong with my dog. I couldn't tell her my dog didn't talk. So I told her my dog was acting very strangely.

"Like what?" she asked.

"Like he's usually very communicative about what he wants," I said, "and now he isn't."

"So he's withdrawn? Isolating himself?"

"Well no, he's not isolating himself." In fact, he was in the living room and I could hear the sounds of his favorite telenovela, *Paraiso Perdido*. "But he doesn't seem to have any interest in being around me."

There was a moment of silence. "So he's afraid of you?"

"Oh, no, not afraid of me. Just ignoring me. Sort of like a child sulking."

"Did you do something to him?"

"No, of course not!" I was indignant.

The receptionist was clearly puzzled. "Well, the doctor doesn't have any openings for several weeks but I will put your name on the waiting list, in case we get a cancellation."

"But—"

"That's the best I can do," she said firmly, "Dr. Mallard has a very busy practice." And she hung up.

My phone rang almost as soon as I set it down and I snatched it up, thinking maybe Dr. Mallard had a sudden opening in his schedule. But it was my sister. Not Teri. But my other sister, Cheryl, who lives with her dentist husband out in a subdivision on the east side of Lake Washington. How odd that she would call the day after Teri called me.

Without even thinking about it, I asked: "Did Teri call you too?"

"What? What are you talking about?" Cheryl sounded offended.

"Just that I thought she called me yesterday," I said.

"She sounded stressed out and frightened. I thought maybe she called you too."

"What did she say?"

"That someone was trying to kill her. And then she hung up. The call came from a clinic and spa out near Duvall."

I could almost see Cheryl shaking her head. "Geri, I think your new job is having a terrible effect on you. You're getting paranoid. When will you get a normal job and settle down?"

Cheryl is my older sister and she had to become a mother to me and my younger sister, Teri, when our parents died. She was only eighteen and we were sixteen and fourteen, respectively. It was a hard job and she has never let go of the task of trying to manage every detail of our lives. Teri managed to escape her relentless pressure by running away. I just tried to stay as far away from her as possible.

"I don't work for Jimmy G any more," I said.

"Well, that's good news," Cheryl said. "So do you have another job?"

"Actually, I'm freelancing," I said.

"As what?"

"As a private detective." Of course, Pepe and I didn't have any cases yet. Just a bunch of business cards that read Sullivan and Sullivan.

"You don't even have a license."

How did she know that? "I know but I'm signed up for the certification course. It's this Saturday." I had been waiting for this class, which was only offered twice a year, since I first started working for Jimmy G.

There was silence on the end of the line.

"So you're not coming to the wedding?" she finally

asked. "I was just talking to Amber and she said you had never RSVPed."

"You've got to be kidding!" Pepe could hear the tone in my voice and came running over to see what was up. "Do you really think it's appropriate for me to attend Jeff's wedding?" Jeff was the best friend of Cheryl's husband, Don, as well as, briefly, my husband.

"Yes, of course, it is," said Cheryl. "It shows you have no bad feelings toward him."

"But I do have bad feelings toward him." Jeff had divorced me after I put him through business school, which had qualified him to get a great job working for an insurance company, where he immediately hooked up with his secretary, Amber.

"It would heal a rift in our family," Cheryl said. "We could all hang out together again." Like the old days, when we had double-dated after I met Jeff at Cheryl and Don's wedding.

"No, thank you," I said.

"You could bring that guy you're dating," Cheryl said.

I knew she didn't approve of Felix, who had been gracious enough to accompany me to a tense Easter dinner at my sister's house on our very first date.

"His name is Felix and the invitation didn't say Plus One."

"So you did get an invitation!"

"Yes, but I threw it in the trash."

"Geri, think about it," said Cheryl. "We've only got each other now that Mom and Pop are gone. It would really mean a lot to me if you were there. And the kids have been asking about you."

Cheryl has two kids, Danielle and D.J., possibly the

two most obnoxious kids in the world, but I do take being an aunt seriously. And I hadn't seen them in months.

Cheryl continued, piling on the guilt: "Danielle is the flower girl and she looks so precious in her pink tutu. And D.J. will be wearing a little pink tux. He's the ring boy."

"I'll see what I can do," I said sulkily. I couldn't ask Felix since he was going to be filming. And I wasn't going to go to Jeff's wedding alone. Maybe I could find Brad and get him to go with me. He had accompanied me to my sister's house once before and had sworn he would never go back—he claimed the furniture gave him a headache—but if I found him and cleared him of the suspicion of murder, he would owe me big time.

"That's great!" chirped Cheryl.

"So you don't think that was really Teri that called?" I asked.

"Well, if you find her, invite her too!" said Cheryl with a dismissive tone in her voice. She clearly thought I was nuts. I guess everyone did.

"Pepe, what should I do?" I asked as he came scurrying into the kitchen while I was making myself a cup of tea.

He ran into the living room where *Paraiso Perdido* was playing. In this episode, Conchita was in jail because her angry ex-lover, Oswaldo, has framed her for a murder he committed. Conchita's little sister, Angela, commits a crime herself so she ends up in jail as well, smuggling in the evidence that Conchita needs to prove her innocence.

"That's not a bad plan, Pepe," I said as I watched the drama unfold while I sipped my second cup of Darjeeling. "But how would I get into Forest Glen?"

He gave a sharp bark.

"I wish you would talk to me," I said. "I miss our conversations."

Pepe just sat there looking at me. And that's when I realized that I could probably get into Forest Glen through a referral from my counselor. She had been suggesting I check myself into a facility ever since I adopted Pepe and he started talking to me.

I picked up the phone and left a message on her answering machine. Then I went to my computer and looked for information about the price of a week spent at Forest Glen. Nothing. Apparently you had to have a private conversation with one of their facilitators.

I called Forest Glen and scheduled an appointment for 3 p.m. for an assessment. The phone rang as soon as I hung up. It was Suzanna returning my call. I told her that I was considering checking myself into Forest Glen and that I had scheduled an assessment.

"Geri, this is wonderful!" Suzanna said. "I'm proud of you for taking this step."

"Do you think they will let me bring my dog?" I asked.

"You know, I can call them and make a referral. I will strongly suggest that Pepe is an integral part of your recovery and should be there with you."

"Thanks, Suzanna," I told her.

"Good. I'll phone Forest Glen right away. Does that sound good?"

"Sure."

"And do I have your permission to fax them your records upon request?"

When I agreed, Suzanna said, "Remember, even if things get a little rough while you're there, think about how great it will be to have a normal relationship with your dog again. Won't that be nice?"

"It sure will," I told her. Then we said goodbye and rang off.

Pepe seemed disappointed when I interrupted his TV watching. I was surprised to see he was no longer watching *Paraiso Perdido*. It took me a moment to realize what he was watching: *One Flew over the Cuckoo's Nest*. Nurse Ratchet filled the screen, a giant needle in her hand and a sinister smile on her lips.

"Very funny, Pepe!" I said, grabbing the remote and shutting off the TV.

Pepe's Blog: How to Communicate with Humans

I'm going to take a break for the moment from my usual advice on detecting to talk about a subject that is much on my mind these days: the clumsiness of communicating with humans. I had forgotten how obtuse they are. They seem to require the most obvious clues before they are able to discern what we want. We must escalate to a sharp reprimand of a bark, a lively dance in front of the food dish, or a vigorous scratching at the front door to get their attention to attend to our basic needs.

I am trying to communicate through the television shows I choose and these blog posts, but my partner remains clueless, seeing the television simply as a vehicle for mindless entertainment. For instance, she likes to watch something called *Downton Abbey* and cries over the perils of life as a maidservant in a mansion. I have much more entertaining stories about my life as a servant; for instance, the time when I was employed as an assistant concierge at a hotel in

Cabo San Lucas. Those tourists could get very irritable if a little dog did not deliver the right brand of tequila for their margaritas.

Until recently, I was able to use words with Geri because she had the ability to hear me. Now that I am reduced to the same communication channels as other dogs, I often get frustrated. Geri tries hard. I can see that. She is so eager to please. It is one of the things you must love about humans. That and their loyalty.

All in all, what would we do without them?

Tips for Managing Humans

- Behavior modification is the most effective way to train your human. I learned about it when Geri's animal trainer boyfriend tried to use it to train me. It involves rewarding only behavior you like and ignoring behavior that displeases you. For instance, when your human says, "Do not eat the cat food!" just continue eating the cat food. (For some reason, manufacturers of food for pets seem to think cats deserve a richer, meatier diet than dogs. Does that make any sense? Cats do nothing but lie around in the sun all day and sleep, whereas dogs go for many walks and chase squeaky toys.)

- Speaking of squeaky toys, you can train a human to toss one for you by dropping it at their feet. They will eventually realize that you want them to throw it for you. Bring it back to them if you want to continue the game.

Sniff it and then walk away if you are tired of the game. Or pick it up and stash it somewhere out of reach of your human playmate.

- I used behavior modification to train Felix. When he wanted me to do something, I ignored him. He finally gave up and now he devotes all his time to Fuzzy. Fuzzy is not the brightest penny in the fountain but Fuzzy is a good sidekick for a detective dog like me.

- The best sidekicks are a bit dimwitted. Think Doctor Watson. I won't say that's why I chose Geri to be my partner but I will say this: if your sidekick is a bit slow, is always asking questions, and needs constant instruction, then your brilliance shines by comparison. Think Sherlock Holmes. Think Pepe Sullivan.

Chapter 7

I headed back to Forest Glen after packing a few items in a suitcase—some clothes for me, some treats and his iPad for Pepe. I thought we might not be returning home for a while.

We arrived at Forest Glen a few minutes before my scheduled appointment. I was pretty nervous. Pepe, on the other hand, seemed calm. But he immediately lifted his leg and peed on my Toyota's right rear tire. I couldn't tell whether he was just marking his "mobile territory" (as he called it when I first got him) or demonstrating his displeasure over our current circumstances.

"Ms. Sullivan!" said Justin as we walked in. He frowned when he saw Pepe trotting beside me. "Dr. Lieberman will be doing your assessment, but he's running a bit late. That should give you plenty of time to fill out the necessary paperwork."

He handed me a clipboard with four or five forms attached to it. As I took it, I said, "I hope it's OK that I brought my dog."

Justin tried to smile. "As long as he behaves," he said.

I figured I should start playing it up now that I was here, and told him, "Pepe says he will be *muy bueno*."

"Your dog speaks to you?" he asked, his eyebrows shooting up.

"Of course."

"Of course," he said, his bright smile returning like an expression he could paste on and off his face at will.

"Are there any questions on these forms that my dog should answer?" I asked.

"Uh . . . I don't think so," he said, his smile staying in place this time. "But if there are any questions for your dog, I'm sure Dr. Lieberman will ask him. He's very thorough."

"Good."

"Well, have a seat." He gestured toward a grouping of black leather chairs across the way. "I'll call the doctor and let him know you're here."

"Thanks," I said.

I chose to sit in one of the Stress-less Recliners since I was feeling somewhat stressed. I wasn't used to pretending that my dog spoke. I was used to pretending that my dog *didn't* speak. But it had gone pretty well so far; I just had to calm down and get through the paperwork. Pepe, on the other hand, seemed surprisingly calm; just lay quietly on my lap, soaking up the sunshine that came through the tall arched window behind us.

The paperwork was pretty standard—much the same as I'd filled out for Suzanna when I first started seeing her: personal history, medical history, etc. When I came to the blank for insurance information,

I balked. I didn't really want my provider thinking I was nuts. So I wrote in "private pay." I had enough in the bank to cover a short time at Forest Glen (I hoped) and it would be more than worth it to find and protect my sister.

"Ms. Sullivan!" It was Justin heading my way. "The doctor will see you now."

"Thanks." I stood and handed him the clipboard. Justin didn't even look at it, just said, "Follow me. I'll take you up to Dr. Lieberman's office."

Pepe and I followed him up the stairs to the second floor where he knocked on a door marked "Intake." The door opened, and a tall, grey-haired man, with tortoise-shell glasses, wearing a crisp white shirt and yellow tie, beckoned me inside. Once through the door, he offered me his hand, introduced himself as Dr. Lieberman, and motioned me to a green leather chair opposite his desk.

"A pleasure to meet you, Ms. Sullivan," he told me, looking through the paperwork Justin had handed him. "How are you today?"

"I'm fine," I told him. "My dog hopes you're doing well, too."

"Ah, yes." He glanced at Pepe, who had jumped up onto the other chair, then at the paperwork, then back at Pepe. "This must be Pepe, yes? It's a pleasure to meet you, as well, little pup."

"He says *gracias*."

"*Da nada*," said the doctor, evidently understanding Spanish. "So what would you say is the reason you are here, Miss Sullivan?"

"Well, I hear my dog talking to me."

He looked thoughtful. "And this disturbs you?"

"Well, no, actually Pepe is very helpful." I looked at Pepe. I knew what he would say. He would say that he was more than helpful. In fact, if I was to be honest: "I think he actually sees me as his assistant."

The doctor was silent.

I dug around in my purse and pulled out one of our business cards and handed it to Dr Lieberman. "In fact I'm pretty sure he thinks he's the first Sullivan in Sullivan and Sullivan."

Dr. Lieberman set it down carefully. "And how does that affect you?"

Finally someone was going to get to the root of the Pepe business.

"Well, you know all my life I've been the second fiddle. My older sister was the responsible one and my youngest sister was the wild one so I sort of faded into the background. I'm loyal."

Pepe nodded.

"And I'm quiet. I like to help other people. When my husband—ex-husband—wanted to get an MBA, I quit school and got a job as a secretary so we could pay our bills. Then when he graduated and got a good job at an insurance company and was supposed to put me through art school, he dumped me instead. For his secretary!"

"That must have been upsetting," said Dr. Lieberman.

I nodded. "Yes, but then I adopted Pepe and I got a job as a PI and I was enjoying that. Because I was helping people. But then Pepe stopped talking. Just when I needed him."

"And you feel you need his help?"

"Because I need to rescue my sister—someone is

trying to kill her—and find my partner who's disappeared."

"So tell me more about that."

"Well my dog was talking to me and then one day he stopped. And he hasn't said a word since."

"No, I mean about your sister and your partner."

"Well, Teri called me and said someone was trying to kill her. And the call came from inside—"

Pepe barked.

I stopped. I couldn't tell the psychiatrist that I only wanted to get into Forest Glen to find my sister.

"From inside?" Dr. Lieberman prompted.

"From, um . . ." Darn! This is when I really needed Pepe. He was always so good with coming up with schemes. "She sounded like she was inside a boat!" I said, not being able to come up with anything better.

"A boat?"

"Well, it was all hollow and echoey." Oh dear, maybe he really would think I was crazy. "And I thought I could hear seagulls." I improvised wildly.

Dr. Lieberman scribbled some notes on his piece of paper. "And your partner?"

"Brad! He disappeared about the same time this old lady got murdered and we found her lying in a pool of blood in her kitchen and it was painted lemon yellow."

"And that was significant because?"

"Because I told Brad that lemon yellow was too harsh a color."

More scribbling on the part of Dr. Lieberman. "Well, I can see why you would be upset," he said at last, taking off his glasses and placing them on his desk. "It sounds like you're under a lot of stress."

I nodded vigorously.

"And I think you could definitely benefit from our services. The question is how quickly can we get you in?"

"Yes, that's the question," I said. "I brought a suit-case with me." I was relieved. Apparently acting crazy was beneficial in some situations and this was one of them. "And my dog."

"And how do you think your dog feels about stay-ing here with you?" Dr. Lieberman asked.

"Why don't you ask him?" I said.

Lieberman fixed his gaze on Pepe and asked, "Would you mind that, pup?"

Pepe gave a deep sigh that shook his little frame, then laid down and rested his head on his front paws.

Quickly, I interpreted. "He says he doesn't mind at all. In fact, he'd be happy to stay here with me and work on his issues."

"Very well," said Lieberman, smiling warmly at both of us. "We will admit you to our program as soon as possible."

"As soon as possible?" I asked. "Not today?"

"I need to consult with my colleagues to come up with a treatment plan. Your case has some"—he glanced over at Pepe who had jumped down and was sniffing around the room—"unusual components. Once we determine the proper level of treatment, then we have to wait until the right space becomes available."

"I wish I could stay here," I said wistfully. Not only was I eager to find my sister, but I wanted a good excuse for not attending Jeff's wedding.

"Do you feel like you would be a danger to yourself or others?" he asked.

"Maybe to Amber," I said.

"Who's Amber?"

"My ex-husband's fiancée. They're getting married this weekend."

"And you think you might do something to hurt her?" Dr. Lieberman's brow furrowed.

"Not really," I said. Pepe snarled. "But my dog might."

"And what would your dog do?" he asked.

"Well, the first time he met my ex-husband, Pepe peed all over Jeff's expensive Italian loafers."

"I see." More scribbling on the papers. "So your dog acts out your feelings."

That was an interesting interpretation. I thought about Pepe's brave attacks on marauders and murderers in our previous cases. If he was acting out my feelings, then maybe I was braver and more aggressive than I thought. "I suppose that's true," I said.

Pepe gave a sharp bark. I think he was saying that I carried out his wishes rather than the other way around.

"Do you think you can control him for a few days until I can get you some help?" Dr. Lieberman asked.

I looked at Pepe. He looked at me.

"Why don't you ask him?" Dr. Lieberman suggested.

"Do you think you can be good for a few days?" I asked Pepe. Then I realized that was the last thing I wanted him to be. Dr. Lieberman had totally confused me.

Pepe growled softly.

"He says he'll try," I said, "but he's not sure he can handle all of the stress."

"Well, I have your number. I will try to get your

case expedited and I'll give you a call as soon as space is available."

It seemed like that was the best I was going to get from Dr. Lieberman. In fact, he seemed to be in a hurry to get rid of me. Maybe he had another intake.

As Pepe and I headed back down to the lobby, I paused at the landing of the stairs and looked out the tall arched window at the various buildings.

"My sister might be in one of those buildings," I said, "but how will I know which one?"

Then I remembered the map Pepe had drawn on his iPad. I pulled it out of my backpack and booted it up. Sure enough the design he had drawn corresponded to the landscape in front of me.

"And you know where she is, don't you?" I asked him.

Pepe yelped again. I put the iPad on the ground and he stepped on the farthest square to the right, which represented the building closest to the woods, the one called Serenity, which Lacey had said contained the craziest people.

I realized that the mass of scribbles that surrounded the one cottage were meant to depict the woods.

"We could sneak through the woods and get close to Serenity!" I said.

I could practically hear Pepe saying: "Finally!"

"Let's go check it out!" I said. Pepe's tail was wagging furiously. "I'm getting pretty good at speaking dog, aren't I?" I asked him as I slid the iPad back into my bag and followed him down the stairs.

I could almost hear him saying: "Not as good as I am at speaking human," but then again, he didn't really talk.

Pepe's Blog: Humans and Dogs: A Comparison

I stopped speaking because everyone thought my partner, Geri, was crazy for thinking that I talk. Now she is pretending that I speak when I do not. She is putting words in my mouth. I fear she may be going *loco*. She actually growled at the doctor at the insane asylum.

And he was talking to me as if I do speak. He knew I was not speaking, and was *muy* patronizing. I think the shrink is a little *loco* too.

Plus, I could smell Geri's sister in that office. It was a faint scent but it was clear. Does Doctor Lieberman know they are related? I heard him get on the phone as soon as we left the room. He told someone that he had some security concerns.

But then Geri finally recognized I was using my iPad to communicate with her. She deciphered the map I drew. What joy! We are finally working as a team again. Now if only she will notice that we could gain access to that one cottage by sneaking up on it through the woods.

Pepe's Advice

- Never expect humans to act like dogs, even though humans often think that dogs should act like humans.

Chapter 8

"Let's see if I can park closer to that area," I said, starting my old green Toyota, the most beat-up car in the parking lot, and pulling over to a row of parking spaces along the river and in the shade of the poplars. The sign said they were reserved for the staff.

I turned off the car and studied Pepe's map some more. "If we go behind the poplars," I murmured, "we should be able to approach the cottage without being seen."

Pepe's tail wagged energetically. I imagined him saying: "Right on, partner! I will lead the way." And as soon as I opened the car door, he scrambled across my lap, jumped down, and disappeared into the undergrowth.

I looked around, saw no one stirring in the parking lot, and followed him. A small dirt path led between the trunks of the poplars to an even smaller trail in the grass, which ran alongside the river. When the river took a bend toward the right, the path went with it, but Pepe veered to the left, and led me through a glade of giant ferns and under the wide-spreading branches of a magnificent old red cedar. From this sheltered shade, we could see out across a short stretch of lawn to a cottage with grated windows and barred doors.

We could also see a golf cart drawn up behind the back door. Two men wearing grey uniforms and heavy tool belts sat in the cart. Maybe they were supposed to be working on the yellow hydrant that popped up out of the ground like an unsightly mushroom a few yards outside the door. If so, they weren't very effective. One guy was smoking a cigarette while the other guy kept his eyes on the cottage. They both wore radio transmitters. I could hear them squawking with static.

Before I could figure out what to do next, Pepe had taken action. He's like that: impulsive. He went running toward the cart, barking furiously. I was furious myself. In the past, we would have planned our attack together. What was I supposed to do?

One of the men jumped out of the cart and tried to grab Pepe.

"What the hell?" said the other guy, getting out as well. He threw away his cigarette.

Pepe danced around their heels. This is a good strategy for a Chihuahua. I didn't have a good strategy myself.

"Oh, look, it's that Chihuahua," said someone inside the cottage and the back door opened. A heavy-set woman in a white nurse's uniform came out onto the concrete pad that served as a stoop. She looked just like Nurse Ratchet, but she wasn't holding a giant syringe, just a pair of handcuffs.

She didn't seem startled to see the men in the maintenance uniforms.

"It's that dog again!" she said. "Where did he come from?"

"I don't know," one guy said. As he bent over to grab at Pepe, I saw that he had a gun in his belt. Pepe danced out of his reach and dashed through the open door.

"Darn it! Now I've got to chase him down. Do you suppose he's a security risk?" The nurse laughed, but it was a sinister laugh.

"I don't know," said one of the men. "Seems unlikely he's carrying a bomb."

"You never know," she said. "Last time a dog came in here—and I swear it was the same dog—one of the patients insisted she knew the dog and the dog was talking to her."

Oh, joy! I could hardly believe it. Pepe wasn't talking to me, but he seemed to be talking to someone else. I just had to get into Serenity so I could find this person.

"Maybe he has a walkie talkie attached to his collar," said the other guy. "Go find him and we'll check him out!"

The nurse went back inside and a few minutes later came back out with Pepe in her hands, wriggling and trying to get loose.

"He didn't get far!" she said.

"Did you check him out?" one of the guys in uniform asked.

"Yes, he's clean!" said the nurse. "But the tag on his collar says he belongs to G Sullivan."

The two men looked at each other. "That's not good," said one of them.

"Seems like a security breach," said the other. "I'm going to contact headquarters."

I shivered in the bushes. It seems like these guys recognized my name. Could they possibly be the men who were trying to kill Teri?

The nurse turned her head. "Phone's ringing. I've got to get that," she said. She set Pepe down on the ground and he made a beeline for the bushes.

I swear I heard him say, "This way," in a whisper. And then he trotted off to the left, leading me down a maze of rabbit trails that took us through stands of salal and giant horsetails until we finally emerged by the main building. Looking out over the campus, I could see several blue-clad employees all rushing toward the cottage closest to the woods.

"What have we done?" I wondered aloud.

"Established that your sister is in Serenity," I thought I heard Pepe say. But when I looked down he had trotted off toward the car. Was I really just imagining his talking all along?

There was a ticket on my windshield. Apparently I owed Forest Glen eighty dollars for parking in an unauthorized space.

"Well, that went pretty well," I said to Pepe as I crumpled up the ticket and threw it into the back seat. He just curled up in the passenger seat, gave a deep sigh and went to sleep.

I had no one to talk to as I headed back into town. Was Teri really in danger? Or did she just think she was? She was, after all, in the most locked-down of the cottages. Maybe she was paranoid. The men with the guns had not tried to kidnap her or shoot her. Instead they seemed to be in cahoots with the nurse, who seemed to have some sort of connection to Forest Glen. Unless she was an imposter who was going to smuggle Teri out in a body bag. Or in those handcuffs. Whatever it was, I needed to get back into Forest Glen and I needed to get in soon as possible.

But first I thought I would stop by and talk to Samuel Morris, Brad's landlord. His office was in Bellevue—I had looked it up online—and I could find out what was happening with the rent. Maybe I could even bring us up-to-date with a payment.

Samuel Morris operated out of a small storefront, sandwiched between a car rental office and a pho restaurant, in a small strip mall on the edge of Bellevue. Bellevue thinks of itself as Seattle's more modern, more glamorous little sister but this part of Bellevue was more like the white trash cousin's trailer.

Blinds covered the front window admitting only a few strips of light into the dim interior. A grey metal desk heaped with papers stood against a wall. A folding screen blocked the view of the back of the narrow room. In its messiness and shabbiness it reminded me a bit of Jimmy G's office. For a moment, I actually missed my old boss. Then I reminded myself of his treachery.

"Hello? Is anyone here?" I called out. I heard mumbling in the back and then a man walked out from behind the screen. He was a short man with a shiny pink pate and a fringe of white hair around his ears. He wore a pair of dark-rimmed glasses and a shabby grey suit that was too big for him.

"What do you want?" he asked in a mumble.

"I'm here to see Samuel Morris," I said.

"Who are you?" He looked me over with suspicion in his eyes.

"I'm Geri Sullivan," I said. "I'm a friend of one of your tenants."

"Which one?"

"Bradley Best," I said.

He didn't seem to recognize the name. So I rattled off the address instead: "3121 Eastlake Boulevard in Seattle. You just posted a three day, pay or vacate notice."

"Oh, that building!" he said. "That one's a pain in the tuchus. I'm about ready to tear it down."

"Hey! You can't do that," I said. "We run a business there."

He looked me over with a frown on his face. "You're not on the lease."

"No, I'm not," I said. "I work for Brad. He sent me to find out how much we owe. We want to make a payment."

"Brad already knows what he owes," said Mr. Morris. "He was supposedly bringing it over three days ago."

"Really? What day was this?"

"I think it was Tuesday."

The day Brad disappeared. "And how much was he bringing?"

"Twelve thousand dollars," said Mr. Morris.

I almost fell over. "What?"

"He was six months behind," said Mr. Morris. "Rent's two thousand a month."

I was shocked. "And you think he was bringing you the whole amount?" I didn't see how Brad could come up with that much money.

"Yeah, he was supposed to be here at 2 p.m. Tuesday but he never showed up. I even stayed late. My wife, Gloria, she wasn't too happy with me because dinner was cold by the time I got home. He never showed up. He never called. And I haven't heard from him since."

"Well, neither has anyone else," I said. "Maybe he was mugged on his way here," I added. "That's a lot of cash."

"He was supposed to bring me a cashier's check," Mr. Morris said.

"Or on his way to the bank!" I could practically see Pepe nodding. This was making sense. Although it really didn't make sense that Brad could come up with twelve thousand dollars in one day.

Mr. Morris squinted his eyes. "So are you going pay me now?"

"Well, I can't pay you the whole amount," I said.

Mr. Morris made a sound of disgust.

"I can give you a check for three thousand," I said, pulling out my checkbook. I would just tell Brad that he owed me free storage space for a year.

"That's not going to cut it, sweetheart," said Mr. Morris. "My lawyer has already filed the eviction papers. Unless the rent is paid in full by the end of the month, your boss is going to be out on the street."

He looked me over carefully.

"If you know anyone that wants to rent a nice shop on Eastlake Boulevard starting October first, send them my way."

Pepe, who had been sleeping on the floor, jumped up. I saw the gleam in his eyes. I knew what he was thinking even though he wasn't speaking. He was thinking Sullivan and Sullivan Detective Agency.

Pepe's Blog: We Found an Office!

Amigos, excellent news. The one who likes to stuff dead animals and display them in bizarre poses is going to lose his lease and my human partner and I are finally going to be able to open our detective agency. It will be like in all the books. Gorgeous bitches will appear in the doorway, asking me to follow their faithless mates. Geri can answer the phone, which is a skill I have not yet mastered, and go out for sandwiches (I will eat them but cannot pay for them), and drive me to our various appointments (another skill I have yet to learn).

Together we will be an unstoppable team.

Chapter 9

When my cellphone rang an hour later, the caller ID said it was Jimmy G on the phone. I hadn't talked to 'he-isn't-my-boss-anymore' (HIMBA, for short) in quite a while. I still hadn't forgiven him for betraying me on the last case we'd worked on together and didn't think I ever would. Not if Pepe and I actually opened our own agency.

So I let the call go to voice mail. But I was curious about what Jimmy G had to say, so I did listen to his message:

"Hey, doll! Jimmy G, here. Pick up the phone, huh? Jimmy G knows you're still steamed at him, but an old client of yours, a Mrs. Snelling, wants to talk to you. Won't talk to yours truly, only you. Says it's an emergency."

I didn't know anyone named Snelling and thought it was just a ploy by HIMBA to try and get back in my good graces.

Then my phone rang again. And again. Same caller each time. When it rang for the third time in a row, I finally answered it.

"What do you want?" I asked.

"Look, doll, Jimmy G's sorry about what happened, and—"

"So?"

"—and he doesn't blame you," he continued. "But this is a separate issue. This old broad, Snelling, keeps calling and—"

"I don't know anybody named Snelling."

"Wait a minute. It's not Snelling, it's Nelson."

"I don't know anybody named Nelson, either," I told him. "You're just trying to—"

"Hold on; let Jimmy G think," he interrupted. "Snelling . . . Nelson . . . *Snelson!* That's it. *Snelson!* What a wacko name."

"Mrs. Snelson? Are you sure?"

"Yeah. Dame lives over in the Gladstone Retirement Home. Same one you and your rat-dog helped with the big mutt that wouldn't stop pooping in her garden."

"Well, why didn't you say so in the first place?"

"Tried to. Look, can you help Jimmy G out here?"

I didn't answer right away. I was thinking about our first case for Jimmy G. He had sent us out to help Mrs. Snelson identify the dog who was pooping in her garden. Kind of humiliating, really, but we solved the case, and obviously the old lady was grateful. Because she wanted us back.

"So," I finally said, "what's Mrs. Snelson's problem this time?"

"Don't know. She wouldn't tell Jimmy G. Said she would only talk to you."

"That's too bad," I said. "Because I don't work for you anymore."

"But Mrs. Snelson said it was serious. Also she said

she would pay our normal rates, plus a thousand dollar bonus when the case is solved."

"That's nice, but—"

"Pretty please, doll," he implored me.

I knew something serious was going on, because Jimmy G never used "pretty please" about anything.

"OK, here's the straight skinny," he continued. "Jimmy G's in a fix. He hasn't had a case lately, and there's a certain type he owes dough to."

"Sorry to hear that," I told him. "But like I said, I don't work for you anymore."

"Yeah, but it would be just a one-time only thing. There's plenty of stuff Jimmy G would do over if he could, but . . ."

As he went on trying to explain his past actions, I found myself thinking about Jeff's upcoming marriage, and me not wanting to attend my ex's wedding alone under any circumstances—even the one I'd just thought of.

"OK," I told HIMBA. "I'll do it, but only under one condition."

"Oh! Copasetic!" The relief in his voice tinged every syllable of the words. "Jimmy G's your main man when it comes to conditions—any conditions—every condition! What is it?"

"You have to attend a wedding with me."

"That's it? What a snap! Maybe you'll even catch the bouquet, doll."

"There is one other condition," I told him.

"There's always a catch," he said, much more subdued.

"I might be working under your license until I get my own, but this is my case. I handle it the way I want to handle it. I'll split the fee with you, and the bonus, fifty-fifty." All I'd gotten in the past was a salary, often late. "Half for you, half for me," I added.

"OK," he agreed. "Half of something's better than all of nothing, like they say. So, tell Jimmy G about this wedding—when and where. Jimmy G will be there with bells on his toes!"

I filled him in about the time and place for Jeff's wedding. Before we hung up, he told me how good it was for us to be working together again.

Except for his delusion about us working together, the conversation with HIMBA had gone fairly well. All I still had to deal with was my ex-husband's wedding, and Mrs. Snelson, who could turn crotchety at the drop of a hat. I didn't know which would be more problematic.

I was tempted to rush right over to the Gladstone. It was exciting to be back on an official case. I didn't realize how much I had missed it. And Pepe seemed eager to go when I told him about our assignment, dancing around in circles and barking.

But then my phone rang again.

"Sullivan and Sullivan," I said, thinking it would be fun to use my business name because I was (almost) officially in business for myself.

"Geri Sullivan," said a deep, male voice. "We told you to leave your sister alone. If you don't do what we ask, we will have to take drastic measures!"

"Who is this?" I asked, walking over to the window. But there was no dark sedan outside and no man with glasses. And there was no answer from the voice on the phone either. I was listening to a dial tone.

"That's weird, Pepe," I said, shivering a little. I still

talked to my dog even if he didn't talk to me. I looked at the phone. "Who could that be? Should we go see if they're outside?" Probably not the smartest idea, but, you know, that's always what the heroine does in the movies. Goes down the stairs into the basement even though she knows she shouldn't. Besides I expected Pepe to protect me.

I got him fitted into his little turquoise blue harness and clipped a leash to the rings in back and off we went. He charged down the steps and out toward the street as if he were tracking a particularly interesting scent, but then he just dawdled as he usually does, sniffing under a juniper bush, circling around a telephone pole, leaving his mark on grass and bushes and tree trunks and hydrants all down the block.

I didn't see any sign that anyone was watching me and Pepe didn't seem to find anything but an interesting scent under the rhododendron across the street, so we headed back home. My phone was ringing again as we entered. I snatched it up after removing Pepe's leash. He bolted for the living room.

"Sullivan and Sullivan," I said hesitantly. Better to sound like a business than a woman alone in her tiny apartment with her tiny dog.

"Geri, it's Felix!"

"Oh, hi!" I was surprised.

"It sounds like you were expecting someone else."

"Not really," I said quickly. "What's up?"

"I'm over at Rebecca Tyler's. We just finished setting up for tomorrow's shoot. She invited me—and some of the other cast members—to stay for dinner and I said I was going to go by and see you. She told me to invite you."

"Oh, that would be great!" I looked at the living

room where Pepe was working away on his iPad. "I had a busy day. I totally forgot to pick up anything to eat."

"I'll tell her you're coming. And bring Pepe. Rebecca says that Siren Song wants to see him."

"Is her dog talking to her now?"

Felix laughed. "You'll have to ask her yourself."

Pepe's Blog: Dames and Detectives

I am at my wit's end. Sometimes my partner can be so dense. I was trying to show her where someone was standing and watching our house, hidden behind a rhododendron bush, but did she get down and sniff the ground where I indicated? No, she did not.

I can only hope she will find my blog. I leave the iPad open on the coffee table but she so seldom sits down beside me to watch TV and so she doesn't see it. One problem with the large size of the screen is that I cannot easily move it around. Perhaps I should cleverly knock it over when she is walking by. She will bend down to pick it up, and voila! She will see my blog.

Meanwhile, Geri informs me that we are invited to a party and I will be reunited with my first love, Siren Song. I say first love, because being a detective dog means that I meet many beautiful dames, as Jimmy G would put it, and a detective dog cannot play favorites. Every dame might be dangerous. That is just the way it is for detectives.

Chapter 10

Rebecca's house was not far away. Just up the hill and across the freeway. She lived on Capitol Hill on a street known as Millionaire's Row because it contained the mansions of some of the early business owners in Seattle. Rebecca's house was a huge white extravaganza with two stone lions on pedestals.

I had a nostalgic flashback as we pulled up, remembering the first time I had driven to this address. I had just adopted Pepe and he was talking to me, an amazing reality that I didn't fully appreciate at the time. In fact, he helped me find the address. Now he stood beside me, his back feet on the passenger seat, his front paws pressed to the window, gazing out but not saying a word.

Luis answered the door. He's Rebecca's bodyguard, or personal assistant, or boy toy. I'm not sure which. Maybe all three. He used to be the gardener until Rebecca's husband got killed.

Pepe took off running down the hall as if he owned

the place. So typical of Pepe. That was how we first got involved in Mr. Tyler's murder: Pepe found the body by running in through an open front door, just as he had at Mrs. Fairchild's house.

"Everyone's downstairs," Luis said, beckoning me through the hall. I glanced at the living room to my right where we had found the body. It was completely redecorated, which made sense. I would want to redecorate, too, if my husband had bled to death in my all-white living room. Now the walls and furniture and draperies were all gold and russet tones, creating a warm and inviting feel. Rebecca must have hired a designer to redo her house while she was in Los Angeles. I wish she had thought to hire me, but I had never really worked as an interior designer, despite going to school to learn the trade. You need a lot of wealthy clients, like Brad has, and I just never had access to people with that income.

As we went down the hall, I also noticed a whimsical chandelier, hung with pink crystals, and a playful curvy white cabinet with a pink marble top. It didn't seem at all like Rebecca's taste. I always think of her as severe and formal. Maybe she was lightening up.

According to Luis, the party was in the basement, only he called it the media room. I could hear laughter and ice tinkling in glasses and the low buzz of conversation as we descended the stairs.

The last time I was in the basement at Rebecca's it was the dog training room. But it had been transformed. Gone were the rubber padding and the boxes full of sparkly dog clothes. Now the sparkles were all in the mirrors that hung on the walls in gilded frames and the gold ropes around the red velvet curtains and the gilded low tables scattered among the plush red velvet settees.

I spotted Felix talking to a group of men and headed in that direction. Felix saw me coming and his eyes brightened.

'You look great," he said, coming forward and giving me a subtle once over. I had put on a Forties dress that I bought at a thrift shop. It had a wild pink and red rose pattern with a tight bodice and a full skirt. I was glad I had taken the time to wash and blow dry and tame my curly hair and put on some make-up. A bit of red lipstick can go a long way. "Where's Pepe?" he asked, looking around.

"I don't know." I was puzzled too. Usually Pepe is right by my side. But nothing Pepe did was usual any more. "I see you brought Fuzzy." The little white poodle-terrier mix was right at Felix's heels. "She doesn't let you out of her sight."

"Caro says she has abandonment issues," said Felix with a laugh.

"Oh, Caro! That's the pet therapist you told me about," I said.

"Yes, she's right over there!" He pointed at a gorgeous redhead in a slender lime green linen dress who was in the center of a group of men over by a marble-topped table spread with appetizers. "Come on, I'll introduce you."

"I think I need a drink first," I said.

"Right this way!" said Felix, ushering me over to a bar that was tucked in the corner. The bartender wore a vest and a fedora and the bottles of liquor were all made of cut glass. They sparkled in the light of a flotilla of votive candles.

Felix ordered a negroni, which surprised me because he doesn't drink. I ordered my usual: chardonnay.

The negroni arrived in a martini glass. It was a pretty red color, with an orange twist. It looked a bit like a grown-up cosmo. Felix cradled it in his fingers but didn't take a sip. I clutched my wine glass and looked around the room.

"I'm shocked by all the changes," I said. "This doesn't seem like Rebecca's taste at all."

"Rebecca mentioned that she was working with a decorator to shift the atmosphere in the house."

"Shift the atmosphere?" I asked. "Are you sure that's what she said?"

Felix nodded.

"That's the way Brad would describe what he does." Brad sees home decoration as a spiritual and energetic process. He's been known to decorate rooms based on the color of the chakras and cleanse negative energy by smudging a room with sage.

"Maybe she's working with Brad."

"I don't think so," I said. "I'm sure Brad would have told me."

Felix was silent. And I could guess what he was thinking: Brad didn't tell you he was getting married and Brad didn't tell you why he disappeared, so maybe he wouldn't tell you if he was working with Rebecca.

I sipped my wine while Felix pointed out various people who were involved in the filming of the pilot for *Pet Intervention.* I recognized one of the gaffers from *Dancing with Dogs* and commented on that.

"I'm surprised that your brother isn't here," I said to Felix. I had met Tavio a few months earlier when he was working on a werewolf movie that was shooting on location in the Pacific Northwest woods.

"Oh, he's coming in tomorrow," Felix said. "In time to start shooting the actual segments."

"So how does it work?" I asked.

Felix looked a bit nervous. "They're going to present each of us with the same problem dog. Then film us as we figure out what's going on and provide training. We won't be able to watch each other's work and they haven't told us yet about the type of dog or the problem. I guess they'll make the decision about who to feature after they view the film."

Caro slipped away from the group she was in and headed our way. She had an empty martini glass in her hand.

"I was just heading for the bar to get another drink," she said.

"Taken care of," said Felix, handing her the negroni. She thanked him with a pretty smile.

Felix introduced us. "I was just telling Geri about the concept for the show," he said.

"I wish they would tell us ahead of time about the dog's problem," said Caro. She was even more gorgeous up close: the lime green dress showed off her curves and her tanned legs and strappy gold sandals. Definitely a Southern California kind of vibe. "I usually know what's going on before I show up to work with a client."

Felix nodded. "I guess they want to give us each the same chance to succeed or fail."

"Have they chosen the dog yet?" I asked.

They both looked at me puzzled.

"Because I've got a dog with a problem," I said.

Felix gave me a warning look.

"Oh, really," said Caro. She had a slight drawl, maybe Texas. "Tell me about it."

"My dog used to talk to me and now he doesn't," I said.

"Oh!" She looked surprised. She glanced at Felix, who raised his eyebrows and tilted his head, as if to say, 'Go figure!' "Felix told me you have a Chihuahua, I think."

"Yes, a lovely Chihuahua," I said, suddenly nervous. "He's very well-behaved."

Felix cleared his throat.

"Well, OK, he's not well-behaved, but he's sweet-tempered."

Felix rolled his eyes.

"OK, he's a bit arrogant. He thinks he's in charge of everything," I said.

Caro laughed. "You just described the typical Chihuahua. Those little dogs always act much bigger than they are." She smiled. "So what's his problem?"

"He used to talk to me, and now he doesn't," I said, taking a quick sip of my wine.

"Like he used to bark and now he doesn't?" Caro asked.

"No, he used to talk to me. In complete sentences. In English. Well, sometimes he speaks Spanish. And occasionally French. And even a bit of Italian." I realized I sounded completely crazy. I took another sip of my wine. "Plus sometimes he quotes the bard."

Caro looked horrified.

"Shakespeare!" I added hastily.

Caro stared at me. Then she laughed. She had a really pretty laugh, like little bells ringing. "Oh, I see, you're joking! A dog that quotes Shakespeare! That's great!"

"No, he really does quote Shakespeare," I said. I looked at Felix for help. "You said you were going to tell her about my problem with Pepe."

Felix looked embarrassed. "It's a little hard to explain," he said.

"You said you heard him talking!" I waved my empty wine glass at him, hoping he would notice it was empty.

"I *thought* I heard him talking." Felix said.

"Fine! I get it! You think I'm crazy!" I said.

"I don't think that's crazy," said Caro. "I can see it's important to you to be able to communicate with your dog."

"So you do believe dogs talk?" I asked eagerly.

Caro laughed again. "I've never heard one speak English," she said, "but I'd like to. Maybe we can get together after the show wraps. I decided to extend my stay." She glanced at Felix again. Was there something going on between them? Was this why he had been so hard to reach over the last few weeks?

"That would be great," I said. It looked like I was going to have to get my glass of wine for myself. I excused myself and marched over to the bar.

I decided to try a negroni, curious about what Caro was drinking, and ordered one from the bartender. The party was picking up steam. The talk was louder. The laughter was shriller.

My drink arrived. It had a strange bitter flavor and the color was an almost neon red. I wasn't entirely sure I liked it. But I kept on sipping it, savoring the unusual flavor.

Just then Rebecca Tyler spied me and came rushing up to me. She's a tall, elegant woman with long dark hair and a long tanned face. She wore a tight cocktail dress. Silver with a pleated top, it showed off her cleavage, which was bountiful. It looked like maybe she had had some work done in LA.

"Geri!" she said, giving me two quick air kisses on either side of my cheeks. "It's so good you could come. We love Felix on the set. He's such an asset. He knows so much about production. I guess that's what happens when you grow up in a show business family."

It's true that Felix had grown up in LA where his father worked as a lighting tech and his mother was a costume designer.

"I'm surprised you're filming up here," I said, "with all the talent in LA."

"Well, Felix said it was hard for him to get away," Rebecca said. "And besides I needed to come up here and supervise the work being done on the house." I could tell she was trying to frown but her forehead did not even ripple. "Unfortunately my interior decorator seems to have vanished."

"I noticed you were making changes," I said, taking another sip of my drink. "Who did you hire?"

"Oh, I thought he would have told you," Rebecca said. "It's someone you know. I think he said you worked together. His name is Todd or Tad or . . ."

"Brad?" I said. "Bradley Best?"

Rebecca nodded. "Yes! That's it. He approached me. Said he heard from you that my house needed a makeover. At first, I was offended, but then when he explained, about the need to shift the energy, I got it! He had some great ideas and, as you see, he did do some work. But then he just disappeared. I haven't been able to get a hold of him since I paid him."

"You paid him?"

"Yes he showed up a few days ago, said it was urgent. He needed money to pay his landlord. I paid him in cash. He went off and I haven't been able to reach him since."

"How much did you pay him?"

"Ten thousand dollars."

Pepe's Blog: Dames Are Distracting

Bitches can be so distracting. My only thought when I first rushed into the Tyler residence was to find my old flame, the dog of my dreams, the luscious and delicious and odiferous Siren Song. And she was just as lovely and smelled as sweet as I remembered.

But even as we were circling around each other, sniffing butts, I knew that I was shirking my duty as a detective. Because there was some odor in the house that I had passed by in my hurry, and it was relevant to another case.

Yet, the spell that siren Siren Song cast upon me was a powerful one and soon I had forgotten all about our case, and even Geri. That is until the food arrived. Seafood. Very popular in Seattle. It is strange how humans like this food that is only good for cats. And dogs who have not been fed for many hours.

Chapter 11

Our conversation was interrupted when the sushi arrived. Rebecca had ordered takeout from one of the fancier sushi restaurants in town, and the spread, set up on a mirrored sideboard, consisted of more than thirty different white boxes, each containing a pile of artfully created rolls. A stack of gold-rimmed plates materialized near the end of the sideboard along with a heap of gold-colored linen napkins, and the guests queued up to help themselves to the feast.

As the guests filled their plates, they wandered over and found seats on the settees. A happy buzz soon filled the room, the happy buzz of people talking and eating.

I was one of the last to get any food. I hung back still feeling irritated by my conversation with Caro and Felix. He should have defended me. Also, I was worried about Pepe, but I discovered I didn't have to worry about him when I finally made it to the buffet. He had positioned himself under the sideboard and was eagerly nibbling at any scraps that fell to the ground.

When I had filled my plate with some classic California rolls and a crispy salmon roll, there were few seats left in the room and I felt like that kid who is new at school, facing the daunting social jungle of the lunch room.

"Over here, Geri!" said a cheery voice, and I saw Caro in a group that included Felix, seated on a fancy sofa against the wall at the far end of the room. "We saved a place for you."

Pepe followed me and I took that awkward middle seat on the sofa between Caro and Felix. I tried to balance my plate on my lap while Caro introduced me around. I didn't know the man sitting in the chair across from Felix—Caro said he was the director— but I did recognize the vividly dressed woman sitting across from me. Miranda Skarbos.

We met on the set of *Dancing with Dogs*. Miranda is a famous pet psychic and she enhances her image by dressing like a gypsy. Upon this occasion, she was wearing a full black skirt, embroidered with flowers in red, blue, and green, and a dusty pink top made all of ruffles that fluttered whenever she moved. Her dark black hair was pinned up into a messy bun high on her head.

After a few minutes of catching up, Miranda said, "Caro says that Pepe has a problem."

Yes, he did have a problem. Besides not speaking, he had bad manners. He was tapping my leg with his paw while staring up at my plate. Begging. Of course, Fuzzy, who was at Felix's feet, was lying down with her head on her paws and her eyes closed, like a good dog.

I nodded. I couldn't speak since my mouth was

Pepe's Blog: Get Your Blog Posts Read!

Some police departments use psychics to help them solve crimes. Perhaps this is useful for them, given their tendency to rely strictly on science and rationalization. A dog has so much more information to use to solve crimes: scent and intuition, empathy and energy. We have no need of psychics, who, perhaps, now that I think of it, are simply humans who are more like dogs than other humans in their ability to sniff out clues in body language and energetic exhalations.

During a previous case we worked with a famous pet psychic known as Miranda Skarbos. Her efforts to "read" me have been, for the most part, inaccurate. She does score a good hit every now and then, but "frightened?" Ha, Pepe Sullivan is never frightened. Wary, perhaps. And she was certainly closer at guessing what was going on in my life than either Felix (please! Spending more time with him! Geri needs to spend more time with me!) and Caro Lamont (who

seems like a nice enough lady but all of her advice
was for Geri, as it should be, because we all know
that there are no bad dogs, only bad owners). But I
digress.

As I wandered back through the house on my way
home with Geri, my mind now occupied with crime
rather than Siren Song, I smelled that haunting smell
again and realized where I had smelled it: on the
body of Mrs. Fairchild. The same person who had
killed Mrs. Fairchild had also been in Rebecca Tyler's
house. I need to let Geri know this. She needs to read
my blog. How do I get her to read my blog?

I will have to do some research on Search Engine
Optimization to see if I can get my blog to move to
the top of results when people search for "dog detectives." But would Geri ever search for a dog detective
when she has me?

Chapter 12

It seems unfair that after his advice Felix didn't come home with me. But he did have a good excuse. An early morning shoot, 7:00 a.m. to be exact. He walked me and Pepe to my car and told me that whenever we spend the night together, he never wants to leave, wants time to stand still so we can stay in bed forever, and that was why he couldn't spend the night with me. He was afraid 7:00 a.m. would come and go and he'd miss the shoot.

That was so romantic. And so was the kiss and the embrace that followed as we leaned up against my car. I think I almost persuaded him to change his mind. Until Pepe starting barking furiously from inside the car. I might point out that Fuzzy was standing quietly by Felix's side. Well, I did point that out when I got in the car with Pepe, but he didn't seem to care.

I don't know why he was so impatient to get home because all he did when we arrived was go straight into the living room and turn on the television. I have a couch potato for a dog.

* * *

The next morning, I was up early but not as early as Felix, and calling Mrs. Snelson to set up an appointment.

She picked up on the first ring. "Hello?"

"Mrs. Snelson," I said. "This is Geri Sullivan, I—"

"I'm so glad you called," she said rapid-fire, sounding tense. "It's getting worse—"

"What's getting worse?" I asked.

"The situation." She was whispering into the phone.

"What situation?"

"I can't talk about it on the phone. I really need to talk to you in person."

"I can come by this morning if it's urgent." Jeff's wedding wasn't until 3 p.m., so I had plenty of time.

"It is! How soon can you get here?"

"Say about ten?"

"Yes. Ten is fine. And be sure to bring your dog."

"My dog?" That was strange, I thought. Mrs. Snelson didn't like dogs.

"Yes. He was good luck last time. With any luck this time, he'll have somebody to bite."

"Bite? Who?"

"I have no idea." Her voice quavered. "That's why I need your help."

"OK," I told her. "I'll bring Pepe along."

"Good. I'll see you soon." And she hung up.

Mrs. Snelson lives at the Gladstone, a seven-story concrete building designed for housing seniors. She has one of the coveted ground floor apartments, coveted because those units have patios and a little bit of earth around the edges for planting. That had been the problem when we first met Mrs. Snelson: a roaming dog had been pooping in her flower beds. Pepe and I had been able to identify the culprit and get him locked up.

Parking is always difficult around the Gladstone because it's just a block away from Green Lake, one of Seattle's most beloved parks, especially for the mile of trail that circles the lake and is always thronged with walkers, dog-walkers, joggers, roller skaters, skate-boarders, and strollers. And even more crowded on a beautiful September Saturday. The air was cool but it wasn't raining. As sometimes happens at the end of September, summer seemed to have reappeared and everyone was out enjoying the sunshine.

I finally found parking several blocks away and Pepe and I strolled back toward the Gladstone, its imposing concrete silhouette hard to miss in this neighborhood of elegant single-family homes with their manicured lawns and carefully pruned shrubbery. All except one. As we came in sight of the Gladstone, we spotted the same scruffy rental house that we had noticed on our first visit: directly across the street from Mrs. Snelson's patio. And in the front yard was the dog we had sent away for his crimes: Bruiser.

He was an imposing beast, with a huge, thick head and a muscular frame. At first, I jumped at the sight of him, worried that he could snap up a tiny white Chihuahua in a single bite. But then I saw that he wore a heavy chain attached to his collar, the other end looped and padlocked around a tree in the front yard. His endless pacing had worn away the grass in a circle around the tree so he laid, with his head on his paws, at the edge of a circle of bare brown dirt. And as we went by, he merely lifted his massive head and sighed.

It was a heartbreaking sight.

Even Pepe, who likes to bark at bigger dogs to let them know he's *El Jefe*, did not utter a word. Of course, he hadn't been uttering a word for quite a while. And maybe he never had.

Mrs. Gladstone's apartment was easy to identify. The beds around her patio were full of dahlias and chrysanthemums in shades of red, yellow, and orange. And her vegetable patch held tall ears of corn and other vegetables, including what I took to be a monster Zucchini plant (the kind that took over our garden when I was a kid) that spread out in all directions like some green monster about to devour everything around it.

I figured since Mrs. Snelson was expecting us, I'd just knock at the sliding door on her patio. We couldn't see inside as the drapes were drawn, and when there was no response, I knocked again.

"Leave me alone!" It was Mrs. Snelson's voice, high and shrill on the other side of the drapes. "Go away!"

"Mrs. Snelson," I said. "It's Geri Sullivan."

Pepe barked.

"And Pepe Sullivan," I added.

The drapes opened and there was Mrs. Snelson. She looked rather disheveled. She was still in her bathrobe and fuzzy slippers, her white hair sticking up all over her head.

"I'm so glad it's you," she said, pulling the sliding glass door open. She had a butcher knife clutched in one hand. "He's been here again," she whispered as we stepped into her apartment.

"Who?" I asked, thinking that this was so unlike her—she was a feisty old lady who had always been in command, not the nervous and scared type at all. Pepe took one look at the knife and darted past her into the dim interior.

"Some man, some damnable man!" said Mrs. Snelson. As soon as I stepped inside, she slammed the sliding door shut, then quickly pulled the drapes closed.

"Can you put the knife down?" I asked.

Mrs. Snelson looked embarrassed. "Oh, sure." She went into the kitchen and laid it on the counter.

"What man?" I asked. "What are you talking about?"

"I'll show you," she said. "It's in my bedroom."

She turned and led the way into her bedroom. Pepe was there before us, his little front paws up on the side of the bed, his nose up in the air and quivering.

"There!" said Mrs. Snelson, pointing to her bed, which was made up perfectly: a green-and-pink-and-blue floral patterned comforter spread carefully across it, and the two perfectly fluffed pink pillows arranged just so at the head of the bed.

"What?" I asked, not seeing anything but the well-made bed.

"There!" She stalked up by the pillows and pointed at the nearest one. "There! Don't you see it?"

I did notice a small, dark shape laying on the pillow. Moving closer, I realized it was a foil-wrapped piece of chocolate, like you might find on your pillow after checking in to a fancy hotel.

"I do see it," I told her. "How did that get there?"

"I left it so you could see," she told me. Then she picked it up and threw it across the room, where it bounced off her dresser. "I was in the shower and I thought I heard something in the bedroom. When I came in to get my clothes, there it was! My bed already made up and that chocolate on my pillow! The same as yesterday."

"That's so . . ." was all I could manage.

"And this time, there was a note, too," she said.

"A note?"

"With the chocolate! Here, I'll show you." She took a small piece of paper off of her nightstand and handed it to me. Written in a lovely, but slightly shaky longhand, it read:

> Roses are red,
> Violets are blue,
> I'm totally head,
> Over heels over you.

"Goodness," I said. "It seems you have a suitor."

"I don't want a suitor! I gave up on men long ago. Men are pigs!"

"Why don't we go sit down somewhere? I need you to fill me in on everything that's been happening."

"Yes," she said, seeming a little calmer after venting. "Yes, let's do that." I followed her into her dining area. "I'm sorry," she said, "I'm usually not the type to fall apart like this. I haven't even put the coffee on yet, I was so upset. Sit down at the table, and I'll make us a pot."

I took a seat at the Early American maple table. Pepe jumped up onto another chair and gave me a look. Not sure how to interpret it, I took my notebook out of my purse. As Mrs. Snelson finished with her coffeemaker and joined us at the table, I said, "Let's start from the beginning. How did all this begin?"

"With a garden gnome," she replied, running her hands back through her hair.

"A garden gnome?"

"Yes. It appeared under my zucchini last week. Cute little thing, long red cap, white beard, blue coat—well, you know, a garden gnome."

"I take it that it wasn't yours, right?"

"No. I thought one of my friends put it there, then didn't give it another thought until a female garden gnome appeared beside it the next morning."

"I didn't know they made female garden gnomes."

"Well, they do!" she snapped. "Anyway, I was sure my friends were playing tricks on me, but when I asked them, they said they didn't know anything about it."

"I see."

"The next day, there was a note attached to the male gnome. It was written, just like today's note, on a small note card."

"What did it say?"

"It said: Roses are red, Violets are blue, I so love, sharing this garden with you."

"Oh . . ."

"That's when I knew something was wrong. I don't know why some man would be after me. Considering they can have their pick of any of the women here. You know, there's ten women for every man here at the Gladstone."

"I didn't know that," I said.

"Men die younger than women," she said matter-of-factly. She got up and went over to the coffeemaker which had clicked off. "And so most of the women here are widows. They're looking for another husband. They run after the men, fawn over them, flirt and . . ." Her voice trailed off. She took two mugs off a row of mugs hanging from hooks on the wall. "Well, the men get swelled heads about it, think they're hot stuff. " She poured the coffee into the mugs. "Not me. I don't need a man any more. I'm better off without them. What is that saying about fish and bicycles?" she asked as she brought the full mugs over to the table.

"A woman without a man is like a fish without a bicycle," I murmured.

"Exactly!" said Mrs. Snelson, setting the mugs down on the table. Mine was decorated with violets and said "Happy February Birthday."

"Mrs. Snelson," I asked, "why are we whispering?"

Mrs. Snelson leaned in. "For all I know, this stalker has planted a bug in my apartment and is listening to everything I do." Her eyes gleamed.

Was she maybe just imagining things? Had she made her own bed and put the chocolate on her pillow and then forgotten it while in the shower? Mrs. Snelson seemed as sharp as a tack, but maybe she was in the early stages of dementia.

"Have you talked to the management? Have you called the police?"

"Well, no," said Mrs. Snelson indignantly. "I'm not a helpless old lady. I intend to handle this myself." She picked up the butcher knife from where it was lying on the counter and waved it in the air. "I just need your help identifying the perp."

"What do you intend to do to the, um, perpetrator?" I asked.

"I intend to teach him a lesson!" she declared, a

maniacal glint in her eyes. Maybe I really needed to help find this guy and warn him to stay away from Mrs. Snelson. I would be doing two people a favor.

"How do you think he's getting in?" I asked. Pepe jumped down from the chair and went over the front door. "Do you think he has a key?"

Pepe gave a sharp bark, evidently confirming my theory.

"I don't see how," said Mrs. Snelson. "I had my lock changed after the first time it happened. I claimed that I dropped my key in the toilet and flushed it away!" She looked at me as if for approval.

I nodded. "Very clever!" I said.

"Of course, I had to pay the stupid fifty dollar fee for losing a key," said Mrs. Snelson. "You would think they would figure that old people would lose their keys all the time but, no, they try to get money out of us any way they can."

"Right," I said, trying to steer the conversation back on track. "So, the, um, perpetrator could not have a key to your apartment . . ."

"Unless," said Mrs. Snelson, "he's in cahoots with the management."

I nodded, secretly thinking she really was going batty. How to reassure her that no one could get into her apartment?

Pepe was still over by the door lifting his little paws high in an exaggerated movement. Then he sat down and licked the little pink pads of his feet.

"What's he doing?" Mrs. Snelson asked, watching this pantomime.

"Aha!" I said. "Thanks, Pepe!" I turned to Mrs. Snelson. "It's a trick we learned from watching old detective shows on TV."

'What is it?" she asked. I could see she was getting into the idea of catching the perpetrator in the act. She looked all around. "But keep your voice down!"

"We're going to lay a trap," I said, whispering. "We just need some flour."

"I have that!" she said, springing up from her seat and going over to the cupboard where she pointed at a full bag of all-purpose whole wheat flour on one of the shelves.

"Perfect!" I said, motioning her back over to the table. Pepe crept close to us. "Tonight, when you go to bed, sprinkle some in front of the door." I looked at the garden. "You should also sprinkle it in front of the sliding window to the patio."

Mrs. Snelson's eyes lit up.

"And in the morning, you'll be able to see if anyone has crossed the threshold."

"We might even be able to get a shoe print!" whispered Mrs. Snelson fiercely. "Then all I have to do is compare it to the shoes of the men who live here!"

"Yes!" I said, giving her a high five. Only she didn't seem to realize what that was. She just frowned at the sight of my raised hand. So I dropped it in my lap.

"Excellent work!" Mrs. Snelson said. "I'm very happy with the way your dog thinks!" She patted Pepe on the head. He looked longingly at the cookie jar. "You and your cute companion. I think you both deserve a treat."

She went over to the cookie jar and brought out two freshly baked enormous snickerdoodles. She put Pepe's on the linoleum floor and he gobbled it down in a minute. I dunked mine into my cup of coffee and finished it off almost as quickly.

We went back out the way we had come, exiting

through the sliding door and admiring the two gnomes. Mrs. Snelson had separated them, putting the female gnome in the corner near the door, and the male gnome at the edge of the property peering in. We stood for a moment on the patio, looking out across the green lawn. Bruiser was still lying in the dirt, gazing up at us.

"I see Bruiser still lives across the street!" I said.

"Yes," she said sharply. "The animal control officers gave the dog back to his owner. I can't imagine why. The poor thing is out there day and night, chained to that tree, even in the rain."

"At least he isn't running loose in the neighborhood," I said.

"Yes, but I almost wish he was," said Mrs. Snelson. "That is no kind of life, even for a dog."

Pepe's Blog: Shoes or Underwear?
A Dog's Dilemma

Sometimes a detective does his job and the results are not satisfactory. Long ago, Geri and I helped solve a dastardly crime involving a villain by the name of Bruiser who terrorized an old lady and chased innocent children. The perpetrator went to jail and all was right in the world.

Except that Bruiser is now out of jail and suffering an even worse fate, if that is possible. The sight of that beast shackled to a tree, well, it makes my blood run cold. A dog must run and a dog must chase and a dog must poop. Those are things a dog must be free to do. I will make it my mission; I shall not rest until Bruiser is free.

Meanwhile, in the case of the garden gnomes, I know Geri thinks Mrs. Snelson is becoming senile. Anyone who can make snickerdoodles as good as hers is definitely not senile.

The truth is that a man has been in Mrs. Snelson's apartment and in her garden. I could identify the man immediately if we could arrange for a lineup as they do in the police shows. Perhaps the trick with the flour will work. If Mrs. Snelson obtains a shoe from each of the men in the building, we will have a shoe line-up. If we cannot tell from the flour on the shoes—and if I were the perpetrator, I would be sure to provide a different pair of shoes—I will be able to tell by smell. Shoes are the most deliciously smelly item worn by a person, although I am also fond of underwear.

Chapter 13

It was still early when we left the Gladstone and I thought I should take advantage of my freedom to go check in with Jay. After all, at any moment, Forest Glen might call me—I was still hoping it would be *before* the wedding—and I'd have to dash over there and check myself in.

I got onto Highway 99 and headed south. Where the highway hit downtown, at the sign of the Pink Elephant car wash, I took a right, heading to Queen Anne. In a neighborhood full of fabulous houses, Jay and Brad's house was the most original: the outside painted purple with lime green trim. Topiary trees lined the walk and a fantastic juniper dragon sprawled across the front lawn.

I parked my little green Toyota on the street and hurried up the front walk. The doorbell chimed inside, a sonorous tone, like a gong.

A few minutes later, the heavy door swung open. Jay stood in the doorway, frowning at the sight of me and Pepe on his doorstep.

"What are you doing here?" he asked.

"I wanted to find out if you had heard from Brad," I said.

"No!" He almost snapped at me. "You're supposed to be finding him." He lowered his voice to a whisper and looked over his shoulder. "Before the police do."

"Have you reported him missing to the police?" I asked.

"Yes, he has," said a familiar voice, and I saw Detective Sanders come into the hall from one of the interior rooms. "Look who's here!" he said, directing his voice toward the occupant of the room. And his partner, Larson, appeared in the doorway.

"Just who we wanted to see," Larson said. He waved me and Pepe into the room. Pepe growled at him as he went by and I saw Detective Sanders flinch. They were meeting in the room that Jay and Brad called the bird salon. Brad had done it up with framed Audubon prints all over the blue-flowered walls, blue and white curtains imprinted with a pheasant motif and, with what I thought was a rather macabre sense of humor, an oil painting over the gilded fireplace which displayed a brace of dead pheasants. A huge gold cage in the corner of the room contained a bevy of little finches whose soft cheeping filled the room.

Pepe went over and studied them with the look of a scholar.

"If only those birds could speak," I said to him. I know it seems absurd, but Pepe actually had a conversation with a cat once. So it seemed possible he could talk to finches.

"Sit down, Miss Sullivan," said Detective Larson. He was all business.

"I'm on my way—"

"This will only take a few minutes. We want to know what you've found out about Brad's whereabouts."

"Yes, I want to know too," said Jay. He looked at the policemen nervously, "Since I'm paying you to find him."

"I haven't found Brad, if that's what you want to know," I said.

"But," said Sanders, who had remained standing near the doorway with his arms crossed as if to prevent me from leaving, "you have learned something."

"Well, of course I have," I said, goaded into admitting something I shouldn't have by Jay's lack of confidence in me.

Pepe gave a sharp bark.

"Out with it!" said Larson.

"Yes, please tell me what you learned," pleaded Jay.

Pepe gave another bark. I knew what he was trying to tell me. He had said it often before. "A good detective does not reveal information unless he receives information in return."

"You already know this," I said. "Mrs. Fairchild owed Brad a lot of money and he needed it to pay rent. He was falling behind."

"Yes, we've talked to the landlord," said Sanders.

"Then you know that Brad told him he was bringing over the full amount he owed," I said.

The two detectives looked at each other.

"When was this?" Jay asked in anguish.

"I believe it was Tuesday," I said.

"The day Mrs. Fairchild was killed," intoned Larson.

"What? What are you talking about?" Jay looked alarmed.

I looked at the detectives and they looked at me.

Finally Sanders spoke up: "We're working a homicide case. Brad's name came up in connection with it since he was working for the woman, a Mrs. Fairchild."

"So you're not following up on a missing persons case?" asked Jay.

"It seems likely there's a connection between the murder and your partner's disappearance," said Sanders.

"What do you mean?" asked Jay.

"We just found his car. It was parked about five blocks away from the murder scene."

"You did?" That was me.

"Yes, in a parking lot at Volunteer Park." That used to be a cruising spot for gay men. It still was a place where someone might meet for a brief encounter. "Do you have any idea how it got there?"

I saw Jay's face cloud over. Again, he was considering the possibility that Brad was out screwing around.

"Maybe he wanted to visit the Conservatory. Or the Asian Art Museum—Brad is a big fan of Japanese art."

"Yeah. We thought of that," said Larson with a sarcastic tone in his voice. "But that doesn't explain the blood on the steering wheel. Or the bloody hammer on the floorboard."

"Whose blood?" I asked.

"Good question," said Sanders, giving me a sharp look. "It will be a few days before we get it tested."

"It puts him in the vicinity at the time of the murder," said Larson. "And in possession of the murder weapon. And now that we know he was trying to collect money for rent, it gives him a motive."

"You think he killed her?" asked Jay in a voice full of anguish.

"Maybe he finally lost it. The old woman was a piece of work," said Sanders. "We've talked to some of the contractors who were working on the kitchen. Apparently she never paid any of them. Several of them had to file suit to get anything out of her."

"So Brad could have done that too," I said.

"But he was desperate." That was Larson. "He needed the money right then."

"He already had most of the money he needed for the rent," I said.

"And how do you know that?"

"I know another one of his clients. She had just paid him on that morning."

Sanders flipped open his notebook. "We need to know the name of this client."

"I'm not sure—" I started to say, but Jay interrupted.

"Geri, if you know something that will help them find Brad, you need to tell them."

"But what if—"

"What if he actually killed Mrs. Fairchild?" Sanders was quick to jump on that.

"That's impossible!" said Jay. "You don't know my Bradley. He could never hurt a living thing. He carries spiders out of the house. And he hates conflict."

"So you two never fight?" asked Sanders.

"When we do," Jay said, "I'm the one who blows up. Brad is more likely to give me the silent treatment."

I looked at Pepe. Maybe that's what was going on. He was punishing me for something.

Jay went on. "He learned it from his mother. She's really good at guilt."

"So he has mother issues," said Larson. "Maybe he took out his rage at his own mother on Mrs. Fairchild."

Jay moaned. "I don't believe it."

"Of course he didn't kill her," I snapped at Sanders. "Don't listen to them!" I told Jay. "There's some logical explanation and I will find it. I promise you that."

But meanwhile I did give Rebecca's name to the detectives, at the same time warning them that she was going to be extremely busy this weekend as she was filming a new reality TV show called *Pet Intervention.*

I headed home to change into my wedding attire although I wasn't really sure about what one should wear to the wedding of one's ex. Something sexy to make him regret tossing you aside, but nothing so sexy as to come across as desperate, especially given that I would be attending the wedding with Jimmy G.

I asked Pepe for help, laying out my choices on the couch. Pepe put his paw on a black-and-white print dress with a plunging neckline, a small waist and a full skirt. I liked the idea of black-and-white for a wedding. It would send a business-like message, as in, I'm here because I have to be, which is how I endured the weary years of working at the waste treatment center while married to Jeff.

I checked myself out in the mirror and liked what I saw. My dark hair was a cloud around my shoulders and the dress created the illusion of an hourglass figure.

"*¡Guapa chica!*" I thought I heard Pepe say. Was it possible he was speaking again?

"What did you say?" I asked him.

But he just stared at me, his brown eyes shining.

Before I left the house, I called Felix. I had been so wrapped up in my work that I forgot this was an important day for him. He didn't answer the phone, but I left a voice mail telling him that I hoped his day went well and just mentioning that I was on my way to my ex-husband's wedding in Bellevue. "I wish you could have gone with me," I said. "But since you were busy, I asked Jimmy G to be my date."

Pepe looked at me. I could practically hear him saying: "Not a good idea."

"Probably not a good idea," I added on my phone message.

The truth of that statement became absolutely clear when I arrived at the wedding venue, a country club at the edge of a golf course at the edge of Bellevue, and spied Jimmy G, leaning against the hood of his red Thunderbird in the parking lot, smoking a cigar. Normally Jimmy G likes to dress like a caricature of a Forties detective, with a fedora, suspenders, and houndstooth sports jackets. But he had really outdone himself for this occasion: he was wearing a red fedora with a foot-long pheasant feather stuck in the brim and a shiny grey, double-breasted, gabardine suit with wide shoulders and huge lapels that was a size too big for his lanky frame. The baggy pants were held up by his usual red suspenders.

"Hey, doll," he said as I approached him with Pepe at my side. "You're pretty as a picture today." He held out a red carnation that matched the one in his buttonhole. "Jimmy G got you a corsage."

"For heaven's sake, boss!" I said. "This is a wedding. Not a prom!"

Jimmy G's expression fell. He's almost as easy to read as Pepe. His big brown eyes got sad and the edges of his moustache matched the downward curve of his mouth. "Sorry, doll," he said, turning away. "Jimmy G's never been to a wedding." He stuffed the red carnation into his pocket. "Or the prom," he muttered.

"Hey! It's a thoughtful gesture," I said, wanting to cheer him up. "I can find a place for it."

His whole face brightened and he pulled the flower out. The spicy scent filled the air. "Here, let Jimmy G pin it on you!" He was aiming for the spot between my breasts, with a sharp pin raised in one hand and his eyes all bugging out.

"No way," I said, grabbing the pin and the flower out of his hands. "I think I've got the perfect place for it."

I bent down and tucked it into Pepe's harness. I didn't need to use the pin, just bent the flower's flexible stem through the loops at the top. The colors clashed, since the harness was turquoise. Maybe that's why Pepe didn't seem to like it, at all. He kept turning around to look at it. Or maybe he was trying to smell it.

"Tell me you don't like it, and I'll take it off," I said, taunting him.

"Jimmy G doesn't like it," said Jimmy G.

"Not you!" I said. "I'm trying to get Pepe to talk to me again."

"The rat dog speaks?" asked Jimmy G as we headed toward the building. It was long and low, made of dark wood with lots of tinted glass windows. A flight of shallow steps led up to a bank of glass doors which were flanked by wicker baskets of white gladiolas and chrysanthemums.

Other people had been pouring into the building as we talked. Most of the women, both young and old, wore long elegant evening gowns that looked like they would be perfect for the red carpet at the Academy Awards, whereas the men were attired in tuxedos. Jimmy G and I would stand out like sore thumbs.

I almost turned around and ran. And probably that would have been the smart thing to do. But just as I contemplated it, my sister Cheryl came barreling out of the front door. She was wearing a hot pink strapless dress with a skirt that seemed to be made of torn toilet paper bits. The tight fit around the torso made her look flabby around the stomach and her breasts, squashed upward by the bodice, looked like they might spill over the top of the neckline. I suddenly felt OK about my outfit.

"Oh, thank God, you're here, Geri!" said Cheryl. Her breasts wobbled as she reached forward to embrace me. She hitched the dress up, tugging at the neckline with both hands, then glared at Jimmy G who was ogling her.

"Matron of honor dress," she explained to me. "You should see the bridesmaids dresses! And who's this?" She gestured at Jimmy G.

"My boss, Jimmy G," I said. "Jimmy G, this is my sister, Cheryl."

"Honored, to be sure," said Jimmy G with a stately bow. "Jimmy G wishes he had another favor to bestow, but as you see, G has already donated it to decorate the dog."

Really, I could not believe Jimmy G's language.

Where did he come off sounding all British and proper? And why did he point out Pepe to my sister who hates dogs?

"Geri, you can't bring your dog to a wedding," Cheryl said.

"He could be the flower dog!" I said, pointing to his red carnation corsage.

"There's no such thing as a flower dog!" declared Cheryl.

I tried to get her back on track. "You said you needed my help!"

"I do!" she wailed. "It's Amber. She's having a meltdown. Crying hysterically. Says she can't go through with it. I remembered that you had a meltdown, too, on your wedding day. Maybe you can talk some sense into her. Convince her that marrying Jeff is the best thing she could do."

I didn't point out to her that marrying Jeff was the biggest mistake of my life.

Pepe's Blog:
Checking out the Crowd

For a detective, there is nothing more advantageous than a large gathering of humans. For instance, a wedding or a funeral. Even a dinner party will do. One can find out much by watching their interactions. They slap each other on the back and clasp paws (a mere parlor trick for dogs) and sometimes even embrace. But they never sniff butts, a quick way to determine age and readiness to either mate or fight, nor do they sniff skin, which can reveal a great deal including where they have recently been, what they have eaten, and what sort of mood they are in. Mostly they jabber in that quaint but complicated language of theirs. Fortunately, as a student of languages, I have learned to translate from English to Canine.

Geri's sister seemed to be asking her for help calming down a distraught bride. But actually she was plotting to get rid of Geri. If I had to guess, it was because she did not want anyone to know they were related. Perhaps because of Geri's companion. She trotted Jimmy G off to count chairs in the reception space.

But I was on to her schemes and I also could smell the reception dinner as it was being warmed up in the adjoining dining room: roast beef, one of my favorites. No way I was going to let Cheryl get between me and roast beef.

Another thing I learned quickly, from scent, not words, is that the bride was furious. Very furious. And it had something to do with another female. Could it be that she was going to attack Geri? I must be on my guard.

Chapter 14

Cheryl pointed Jimmy G in the direction of the reception hall and grabbed me by the arm, dragging me over to a little room off the lobby. A gaggle of young women wearing sparkly tiaras and short hot-pink dresses even more hideous than Cheryl's were gathered outside the door. Some were crying. One of them was bent over, hyperventilating. The others were encouraging her to take deep breaths.

"It's OK, Tiffany. Just keep breathing!" they said.

"What's going on?" asked Cheryl.

"She threw us out of the room!" one of them said.

Cheryl beat on the door with her fist.

"Leave me alone!" shrieked a voice from inside the room. I shuddered when I heard it. It didn't even sound human.

"Geri is here to talk to you!" Cheryl said firmly.

"I don't want to talk to anyone!" shrieked the voice.

Pepe barked once, twice.

"What about a flower dog?" I said, bending over to pick him up.

The door opened an inch. I held up Pepe wearing his red carnation. He stuck out his long pink tongue and licked the nose which was just visible in the narrow crack. There was a weird giggle from inside the room, then the door opened just wide enough to admit me and Pepe, then slammed shut behind us.

Amber was not just having a meltdown. She was having a nervous breakdown. She was still wearing her wedding dress—a frothy concoction with a skirt composed of ruffles and pick-ups and pleats, and a bodice embellished with beads and sequins and crystals. But she had torn her wedding veil into little tiny pieces and now the bits of lace and netting were scattered all over the room. A champagne bottle sat in a silver cooler on the table.

"Want some champagne?" she asked me. I could tell by her voice that she had been drinking more than her share.

"Sure!"

"Drink up!" she said, hoisting the bottle to her lips and taking a hefty swig, before handing it to me. "Sorry no glasses!" She giggled and pointed to the wall. "I smashed them all!"

I was glad I was still holding Pepe. I did not want him to get any glass in his tender little paws. I set him down carefully on one of the chairs before taking the bottle away from her. It appeared to be empty.

"What's going on, Amber?" I asked.

"Want more bubbles!" she said, grabbing the bottle out of my hands. She frowned when she realized that it was empty.

"I think you've had enough," I said primly, then realized I sounded just like my sister, Cheryl. I never wanted to sound like my sister, Cheryl. "Oh, hell," I said. "Let's get some more!"

I stuck my head out the door. "We need another bottle of champagne in here," I said.

"*Pronto!*" added Pepe.

"*Pronto!*" I repeated.

"He's got the right idea," said Amber.

"What? You can hear him?"

"Of course! He said '*pronto!*' So cute the way he speaks in Spanish." She kissed him on the top of his head.

Someone from outside handed in a bottle. "Can we come in now?" asked a girlish voice.

"No!" I said and slammed the door.

Amber wrestled the bottle away from me and had the cork out in a minute, aiming it at the door. "Take that, Jeff!" she said. "And just be glad this is a champagne bottle and not a pistol!"

She took another swig out of the bottle and the champagne poured down her chin and dribbled onto her dress.

"You're going to ruin your dress," I said, trying to take the bottle away from her, but she wouldn't let go.

"Don't care!" she said. "Not getting married anyway."

"You have to get married . . ." I started to say, thinking of the guests, the invitation, the money spent on caterers and florists and bakers and wedding dresses.

But then Pepe interrupted. "You don't have to get married," he said.

Amber chuckled. "It's so cute, the way you pretend to be speaking for your dog," she said. "Are you a ventriloquist?" Because she was drunk, it sounded more like ven-trill-o-quish.

"No, my dog really talks," I said calmly. "Although

I don't know why he's talking now. He hasn't been talking to me for weeks."

"When the occasion arises, I rise to the occasion," said Pepe.

"Ha, ha! That's what I like about you, Geri," Amber said. Let it be known that Amber has never liked me. And she's made that clear on the few times we actually had to be in the same room together. "What I don't understand is why you ever married Jeff?" She said his name as if it was a dog turd.

"Yes, I wonder about that too," said Pepe.

"I know," said Amber, now forlorn. "He's such a jerk."

"Absolutely." I was happy to pile on. "He's a chauvinist. He thinks women should be seen but not heard."

"He's a control freak. Everything has to be the way he wants it," said Amber.

"He buys cheap shoes and passes them off as Italian imports." That was Pepe who had actually peed on those shoes so he should know what he was talking about.

She picked up Pepe and put him on her lap, her tears falling on his head. As Pepe does in moments of great emotion, he licked her face. That made her cry even harder. Pepe is such a comfort to a crying woman. Unlike Jeff.

"So why are you marrying him?" I asked.

"I don't know!" she wailed. She looked up at me. "Do you think I should?"

I felt helpless. Cheryl had given me an assignment. I was supposed to coax Amber out of the room and down the aisle. But I felt sorry for her.

"If he treats you the way he treated me," I said,

"you'll be miserable. He'll cheat on you with the first—"
I stopped, aware that Jeff had cheated on me with
Amber.

"He already is cheating on me, she said. "With one
of my bridesmaids. I caught him with Tiffany in the
back of the limo, just a little while ago. He tried to tell
me it was his last fling before he got tied down! He actually called me his ball and chain!" She picked up
her bouquet, a tasteful arrangement of pink Stargazer
lilies and white chrysanthemums, and threw it at
the wall.

"That's despicable," said Pepe. "What a *cabron*!"

"Why are you talking now?" I turned on him.

"You're right. I've known all along he was no
good for me. I just let myself be carried away because
everyone said he was such a great catch." Amber was
actually starting to make sense.

"A woman needs a man about as much as a fish
needs a bicycle," I said.

"Quick!" she said to me. "I've got get out of here.
Trade dresses!"

"What?"

"Yes, give me your dress. I can't leave here in a
wedding dress." She picked up her cell phone. "Yes,
I need a cab. At the Bellevue Country Club. I'll be
wearing a black and white dress. Thanks!"

"Amber—"

"Come on!" she said, reaching around to pull
down the zipper on her wedding dress. In a minute
she was down to her lacy bra and panties. She tore off
the pale blue satin garter that held up her white
stockings and tossed it into the melting ice in the
champagne bucket. "This feels so good!" she said,
prancing around the room in her underwear.

"But Amber—"

"I'm walking out there, either dressed like this, or wearing your dress. I'd rather wear your dress," she said. Her voice had a new confidence.

Reluctantly, I removed my dress, and just as reluctantly put on the abandoned wedding dress which was drenched with champagne. Meanwhile Amber slipped out the side door which led into the front office. I watched her through the windows as she got into a yellow cab and the car drove down the drive. What was I going to do? My sister was going to kill me!

And that's how I ended up walking down the aisle, preceded by my little flower dog, in Amber's wedding dress to the horror of all the assembled guests. But it was worth it for the look on Jeff's face.

Pepe's Blog: Wedding Fantasy

I am not a sentimental dog but I must say that Geri looked *magnifico* in that wedding dress. I even allowed myself to daydream for a moment about her walking down the aisle. I could picture Phoebe and Fuzzy and Siren Song as bridesmaids, wearing matching rhinestone collars, and I, of course, would be best dog, standing at the aisle, watching Geri with pride. But who would be standing next to me? Ay, there's the rub! For no man is good enough for my Geri.

Certainly not that idiot Jeff who was gaping at her as I trotted down the aisle and the Wedding March played in the background. At least he had the good sense to declare that the roast beef would not go to waste.

Tip

- A detective needs to be well-fortified for the rigors of the job. Whenever roast beef is available, one should take advantage.

Chapter 15

It would have been funny if it hadn't been so embarrassing. As I marched down the aisle, the organist started playing the wedding march, not realizing that I wasn't the bride. Pepe trotted ahead of me. A rustle ran through the assembled guests.

"That's not Amber," said a young woman to my right, seated in the section reserved for the bride's family.

"That's a dog!" somebody on the groom's side of the room exclaimed.

Meanwhile, the bridesmaids rushed in behind me, all flustered because nobody had told them the "bride" was about to enter. One of them grabbed the train of my wedding dress and followed along as I moved closer to the altar. The rest scrambled past me to take up their positions in front.

"What's going on?" said Cheryl, who was standing at the front of the quickly assembled line of bridesmaids. "Why are you wearing Amber's wedding dress?"

Jeff stepped forward. "Where's Amber?" he asked.

"It's a long story," I told him. "But the short version is she's gone. She doesn't want to marry you." I can't tell you how much satisfaction it gave me to say that to him. If only I had been so smart when I was getting married to him.

"What?" Jeff's eyes went wide with disbelief (evidently because he was the one who always did the leaving, like with me, and it was a shock to find himself left). "Why?"

"I would have to guess it had something to do with her catching you boffing Tiffany in the limousine," I said.

"Oh my God!" gasped one of the bridesmaids. She was a stunning redhead whose low cut neckline displayed a lot of cleavage. She staggered a little and one of the other bridesmaids had to reach out to steady her.

"You cheated on my daughter?" said an older gentleman in the front row, with his arm around a gorgeous blonde. Must be Amber's dad. And Jeff's boss. "And I was going to make you a partner in the firm as a wedding present."

"Sir, I can explain . . ." said Jeff, looking over at the bridesmaid who had turned a bright pink.

"You can forget it," said the older man. "You're fired!"

The assembled crowd was silent. They could hear every word we said. The acoustics were fantastic. And, if I wasn't mistaken, the videographer was catching the whole thing on tape.

The minister seemed to be confused. "Are we ready to begin?" he asked.

"No," I said. "No one's getting married today."

"We could get married again," Jeff suggested. I

heard one of the bridesmaids gasp. Pepe gave a short, angry bark. "What about it, Geri?"

I couldn't tell if he was joking or not but there was no way I was going to say *yes*. I tossed the bouquet to the buxom bridesmaid who I suspected was Tiffany. She caught it, then turned a bright pink, almost the same color as her dress. "Find someone else foolish enough to marry you. I won't make that mistake twice."

Jeff had the good sense to realize that the best way to salvage the situation was to invite everyone to enjoy the appetizers and cocktails being served next door.

"Well, folks, guess I won't be putting on the old ball and chain today after all," he announced. "I'm still a free man!" he added, full of bravado. "And we've already paid for the food and drinks. So let's celebrate!"

After a few minutes of confusion, everyone filed out of the ceremony space and into the lobby of the building where black-clad servers were passing trays of salmon puffs and teriyaki chicken strips.

Amber's signature cocktail, of course, was a Cosmo, and I helped myself to one at the bar. If I spilled a little on the wedding dress, well, it didn't matter. Amber probably wasn't going to use it.

The guests buzzed around me, talking in little knots and casting suspicious glances my way, but no one dared to approach me except Cheryl, "What did you do to Amber?" she asked.

"I didn't do anything," I said.

"You were supposed to convince her to marry him," she said.

"I tried," I replied. "But we decided she was a fish and she didn't need a bicycle."

"Are you drunk, Geri?" Cheryl asked, sniffing me suspiciously, just as she used to do when I was in high school and she was my guardian.

"Not yet, but I intend to get there," I said, tossing down my Cosmo. I set the empty glass on a nearby table.

Jeff had disappeared along with most of the bridal party. Amber's parents were missing as well. My niece and nephew, Danielle and D.J., were running around the room, trying to catch Pepe, who looked terrified (he's afraid of children—claims they're worse than cats). Danielle wore a dusty pink dress, the same color as the bridesmaids', but hers was floor length and had a big satin bow in back. D.J. was attired in a pink tux—poor boy. He was still carrying the pillow he was supposed to present to the groom at the time of the exchange of the rings. He kept throwing it at Pepe.

I rushed over and rescued my dog.

"*Gracias*!" panted Pepe as I patted his back. I laid him against my shoulder with his little head resting on my collarbone. I could feel his heart beating rapidly.

"Did you speak?" I asked him.

"Congratulations!" It was HIMBA strolling up to me, smelling like cigar smoke. "Jimmy G didn't realize you were the one getting married today."

"I didn't get married," I snapped. "Did you miss the whole wedding debacle?"

Jimmy G looked embarrassed. "Jimmy G was out in the parking lot having a little nip. They don't carry Old Grandad at this fancy bar." He waved his hand at the flashy country club bar, all silver and black leather and mirrors.

"So you missed all the drama," I said.

"Plenty of drama in the parking lot," he said.

"Really? What?"

"Hit and run."

"Really?"

"Yeah. The police are out there now."

"When did this happen?"

"Just about the same time the cab came by to pick up the young woman in the black and white dress. Thought it was you for a minute."

"This is what I was trying to tell you, Geri," said Pepe, "but those children had me on the run."

"So what happened?" I asked again. "And why are you talking now?"

"Because you asked Jimmy G what happened," said Jimmy G.

"Because Jimmy G already thinks you're crazy," said Pepe.

"OK, so what happened?" I asked again.

"There was this big, black Suburban idling at the back of the lot. When the cab pulled up and the young woman got in it, the Suburban shot out of the parking spot, clipped another car coming around the corner, and took off. Almost seemed like he was trying to follow the cab."

"Why would he do that?"

"Don't ask Jimmy G."

"You said 'him.' Did you see who was driving it?"

"No. It had those tinted windows all the way around. Jimmy G couldn't make out the driver."

Suddenly I got it.

"Kidnappers!" said Pepe.

"They were after Amber!" I said. "Or, actually, they were after me. They thought Amber was me because she was wearing my dress. Oh my God! Amber's in danger!"

Pepe's Blog: Time to Talk!

Yes, I had to break my vow of silence to get Geri to realize what was happening. I heard the squealing of brakes and the crunch of metal while I was running around trying to get away from those children, but I was unable to communicate in that loud room until Geri scooped me up and held me close. It is so nice to be held close, especially when one has been in danger, as I was at the sticky hands of those undisciplined children.

Geri is quick while Jimmy G is not. Another reason why we should be working on our own. She put it together within minutes and she took immediate action.

The police were called and would soon be on the scene but every detective knows the police are slow, whereas we are fast because we are not constrained by the law. Geri and I are good at car chases. I hope this turns into one.

Chapter 16

At that moment, the doors to the wedding space were thrown open. The guests began pushing through the double doors. Pepe and I followed behind them. I had to find someone who would know where Amber might be heading.

The room had been transformed for the banquet. Uplighting turned the walls a bright pink. Huge centerpieces of pink carnations and Stargazer lilies centered the round tables. The chairs were covered with white linen, finished off with pink bows. At the far end, a DJ, a slim black man wearing horn-rimmed glasses, was setting up his supplies for the dancing, which would apparently take place in the big open space in the middle. A spotlight picked out the fancy initials J and A in the center of the floor.

I rushed around the room, bumping into people who were trying to figure out their table assignments. I didn't see Amber's parents and Jeff was nowhere in sight. I spotted Cheryl, settling the kids at a side table. She was tucking a big pink napkin into the collar of DJ's pink suit. I was threading my way through the tables, aiming for her table, when Jeff and one of the bridesmaids appeared in the doorway.

The DJ, seeing them, announced, "And welcome for the first time, as husband and wife, Mr. and Mrs. Jeffrey Johnson." Apparently no one had informed him of the change in plans. He put on a swoony waltz. Jeff and Tiffany stood awkwardly in the middle of the floor. Then, ever a gentleman and an idiot, Jeff offered her his hand and they set off galloping around the floor. It didn't seem like they knew how to waltz. It looked more like a polka.

I ran up to them and tapped Jeff on the shoulder.

"What?" he asked. "Cutting in?"

"No, I'm not cutting in. Amber's in danger. When she left here, someone followed her. I need to know where she would go."

Jeff looked puzzled. "That's a good question." He turned to the bridesmaid. "What do you think?"

Tiffany shrugged at first, then twisted up her pink pouty lips as she thought hard. "If she's really leaving you," she said at last, "she'd have to go home to get Party Girl. Amber would never take off without her Chihuahua."

"Amber has a Chihuahua?" I asked. I was surprised. I guess she did have good taste after all. Except for the name.

"Wedding present," said Jeff, seeing my surprise. "We picked her out at the animal shelter last week." Maybe he wasn't so bad after all.

"Well, we've got to get over there. She's in danger."

"Both of them!" said Pepe, quivering in my arms. "Party Girl too!"

"What?" Jeff asked.

The music stopped playing an instant before I

repeated myself. "Amber's in danger!" I yelled at the top of my lungs.

"What?" said somebody behind me. It was Cheryl, my sister, with her husband, Don, at her side.

"What did you say about Amber?" asked Amber's dad, as he pushed into the middle of the room, followed by the young blonde. I guess she was his wife, which would make her Amber's stepmother. She looked about the same age as Amber, but that was thanks to some work she had done on her face, which was frozen in a perpetual smile.

"Someone's been following me," I said. "They must have thought Amber was me because she was wearing my dress."

"You and your stupid job," scolded Cheryl.

"We've got to find her," I said.

"Good Lord," said Amber's dad. "This is all your fault!" He glared at Jeff. I didn't tell him that it wasn't entirely Jeff's fault. It probably was mine. The bad guys were after me, not Amber.

"This is serious," Jeff agreed. He seemed excited at the prospect of rescuing his runaway bride. "Let's go!"

"But where do we go?" asked HIMBA who had come up behind me.

Jeff gave us the address of the house in Bellevue that he had bought after our divorce and we all headed out to our respective cars. I wanted to drive my car, but Jimmy G insisted he could get us there faster. And it was true. I was having trouble even walking, trying to manipulate the huge skirt of the wedding dress.

We hadn't gone very many blocks in Jimmy G's cherry-red T-bird convertible before people started honking and waving at us with big smiles on their faces. Good grief, I thought, realizing what they were looking at. They must have thought HIMBA and I had just gotten married!

Jimmy G loves to drive but he's not the best driver in the world. Still he's fast. I'll give him that. So we arrived at the address first. As I tried to crawl out of the car in the bulky wedding dress, Amber's dad and stepmother showed up in a silver Mercedes, followed shortly by Jeff and Tiffany, who emerged from the chauffeur-driven limousine. Judging by her tousled hair, they might have been getting frisky again. Cheryl and Don followed in their big beige SUV.

The house was a really boring low-slung rambler with grey siding and a few pathetic rhododendrons in the front yard. My twenties brick condo has twice the charm and twice the personality.

But I barely had time to make this assessment because the front door was wide open. I went running into the house, holding up the increasingly bedraggled skirt of the wedding gown with one hand.

The scene inside was one of chaos. I could tell there had been a struggle. A suitcase lay on the living room floor with colorful clothes spilling out of it. Looked like Amber had packed for a tropical vacation. A bright red bikini. A white mesh tunic top. A ruffled pink-and-white gingham blouse. A big lime green leather purse lay sprawled beside it. I knelt down to root through it and found Amber's wallet, her phone, and a sandwich bag containing doggie treats.

Pepe went right to work sniffing all around the living room. Jeff and Tiffany went running into the bedroom. Amber's dad and stepmom headed for the kitchen. Cheryl and Don scoured the back yard. I don't know where HIMBA went.

"Party Girl is missing," said Tiffany, returning to the living room and breaking into tears. "That poor creature!"

"Where's my daughter?" asked Amber's father, coming back in from the kitchen.

"I don't know," I said. "I have no idea who would do this."

"You must have been sticking your nose into something that was none of your business," said Cheryl indignantly.

"But I'm not involved in anything . . ." I stopped. I thought about Teri and her plea for help. I thought about Mrs. Snelson and her stalker. Then my cell phone began ringing. I dug it out of my purse.

"I can't believe you're going to take a call at a moment like this!" said Cheryl.

"Hello?"

"Is this Geri Sullivan?" said a gruff male voice.

"Um, yes."

"Well, we need to know where your sister is."

"Which sister?" I asked shakily, trying to buy time.

"Teri Sullivan!" said the voice.

"I don't know!" I said.

"Well, that's too bad," said the voice, "because we have a hostage. We're willing to make an exchange. We don't want this useless bitch. Say hello bitch!" I heard a shriek and then a breathy voice. "Geri, this is Amber. Please do whatever they say. They're going to kill me and Party Girl!" And she burst into tears.

I started shaking.

The voice came back on the phone. "We'll exchange this useless piece of trash for your sister, Teri.

This transaction has to take place within the next twenty-four hours or this useless bitch and her useless dog will die."

"Can you repeat that?" I asked.

"You heard me the first time." And the caller hung up.

I was shaking when I faced the assembled crowd. I didn't really know what to say. "That was someone who says he's holding Amber hostage."

"We can pay. We'll pay whatever he wants!" declared Amber's dad. He looked at Jeff. Jeff nodded vigorously. "How much do they want?"

"They don't want money," I said. "They want my sister, Teri."

That was a conversation stopper.

Don started to say, "Well, that's good news. We just have to get Teri. . . ." He trailed off as Cheryl glared at him.

"They're going to kill her!" I said.

Jeff groaned.

Tiffany shrieked.

"Not Amber," I said. "Well, maybe Amber."

Amber's father moaned.

"But certainly Teri if they get their hands on her."

"But why?" asked Cheryl.

"I don't know," I said. "And anyway, I don't know where Teri is."

"I thought you said she called you!" Cheryl pointed out.

"Yes, but I haven't been able to track her down," I said. "Surely you're not suggesting we exchange our sister for—"

"Your ex-husband's new wife," said Don.

"She's not his wife," I pointed out.

"Soon to be wife," said Jeff firmly. "I know she'll come to her senses."

Tiffany gave a little sigh.

"We've got to go to the police!" That was Amber's dad.

"That's a great idea," I said.

"Maybe they can canvas the neighborhood. See if anyone saw anything. Maybe someone got the license plate. Meanwhile, I have something I need to check out. Give the police my phone number and have them call me!"

I was pretty sure that Forest Glen held the key to Teri's whereabouts. And if they weren't going to admit me, I was going to admit myself. Couldn't be that hard, could it? All I had to do was act really crazy. I thought I would have a good head start if I showed up in a wedding dress. And with Jimmy G.

Pepe's Blog: Sniffing the Scene Part 2

You must give humans credit sometime for their ability to change. I would not have thought Amber, a spoiled and superficial young woman, ever gave a thought to anything but her own comfort. But in her moment of great stress, she tried to protect her Chihuahua, who goes by the unfortunate name of Party Girl. However, the evildoers—there were two of them—seeing her great devotion to her pet, decided to use that as a way to lure Amber into their clutches. And rather than run away she fought for her dog.

Amber and Party Girl, though they worked together most excellently throwing clothes (Amber) and snapping at ankles (Party Girl), were no match for the villains, who carried them both off shrieking and barking. I tracked their scent to the curb where their vehicle had been parked. It did not smell familiar. I was willing to bet my detective credentials that this was not the same car that I spotted outside of our *casa* just two days earlier. Likewise the scent of the bad guys was also new to me.

What to tell Geri? How to tell her? I still did not like to encourage her to talk to me in public. It was OK with Amber who was so drunk no one would ever believe her if she said she heard me and it was OK with Jimmy G who no one would ever believe ever. But around other people and the police, it was important for her to appear to be professional. Luckily, Geri took me to the one place where I could talk as much as I wanted.

Chapter 17

"Jimmy G, let's go!" I said, marching back out to the curb. I thought about changing out of the wedding dress, but the quick glance through Amber's suitcase had convinced me that she didn't have anything I could wear.

HIMBA trotted along obediently. He smelled like an ashtray.

"What were you doing?" I asked, thinking about how everyone else had searched the place.

"Jimmy G was cogitating," he said. "Best way to solve a crime!" And this is the man who is supposed to be training me in my field.

"And what did you conclude?" I asked, trying to keep the sarcasm out of my voice.

"Jimmy G concluded that his lighter was out of fluid and it was a good thing he found this book of matches on the front porch," he told me.

"Book of matches?" I let my sarcasm show this time. "Is that the best you can come up with at a time like this?"

Instead of being insulted, he smiled like the Cheshire

Cat. Pulling the wide matchbook out of his pocket, he proudly held it up for me to see. "It's not any ordinary book of matches. Take a look, doll."

I glanced at the matchbook. It advertised some place called The Broadway Bowl and Pool Hall. "So?" I asked. "Why should I care about bowling and playing pool?"

"It's not what's on the outside that's important; it's what's written on the inside." He flipped the matchbook open and showed me the inside cover. "Take a gander at that."

A phone number was written on the inside. I almost said, 'So what?' Then it dawned on me. "That's *my* cell phone number!" I blurted.

"So it is," said HIMBA, still smiling ear to ear. "Good bet whoever grabbed Amber dropped this when they hauled her away. That is, unless the young lady liked to bowl and play pool."

He was right. I couldn't picture Amber as a bowler or pool shark. Besides, she didn't even smoke as far as I knew.

"So," said HIMBA, still puffed up with pride. "Your old boss did good, huh?"

"What to do? What to do?" I asked myself aloud. I had to find Teri, but I also had to help Amber. "I can't be in two places at once," I said.

"Don't know which two places you're talking about," said HIMBA. "But Jimmy G can do surveillance on the bowling alley/pool hall, if you want. Meantime, all we have to do is wait for the ransom request. Might give us two ways to get our mitts on these kidnappers."

"We already got the ransom request," I said, "while

you were smoking. And they want my sister, Teri, not money."

"That's peculiar," he said.

"I have to find Teri," I told him. "I'm sure she's at Forest Glen."

"That fancy schmancy nut-house?"

"Yes. I need you to take me there. And I also need you to back me up. I need them to admit me so I can find her. They didn't have room for me the other day, but I'm going to act really crazy so they have to take me. If you come in with me and say I've worked with you for a long time, but I've gone nuts, it will help."

"Well, you do talk to your dog," HIMBA said.

"Then after I get into Forest Glen, you can go check out the bowling alley/pool hall and try to get a line on Amber's kidnappers."

"Boy, you sure need a lot of help from the boss you ditched," he said with a gleam in his eye. "This mean you're working for Jimmy G again?"

"No."

"Oh . . ." He paused, then continued. "Well, there oughta be some kind of prod quo quid involved."

"That is *quid pro quo*," Pepe said, correcting him.

"I know what he means," I told my dog.

"So how about we be partners, then?" HIMBA went on.

"Partners?" I asked. "As in the detective agency?"

"Sure. Something Jimmy G's been mulling over for a while."

"*Full* partners?"

"Well . . ." He hesitated. "Jimmy G was thinking more like a seventy-thirty split."

"Fifty-fifty," I told him.

"Hey!" Pepe interjected. "What about Sullivan and Sullivan?"

"Shhh!" I told him

"*Ay caramba*!" he said. "I finally start talking again, and now I am told to be quiet. This is turning into a lose–lose proposition."

"Sixty-forty," countered HIMBA. "Final offer. Jimmy G's glad to help you out, doll, but he does have other fish to fry."

"OK," I said against my better judgment. I really needed his help and was secretly pleased at becoming partners in the agency. Cheryl couldn't scoff at my job any more if I was a partner in a detective agency.

"Deal," he said, spitting on his right hand and offering it to me.

"Why did you spit on your hand?" I asked.

"That's the old-fashioned way they used to seal the deal," he told me.

"I'm not spitting on my hand, let alone touching yours with spit on it."

"We'll just take it on trust, then," he said. "Jimmy G will have the partnership agreement drawn up ASAP."

"Fine," I said. "We'll take it on trust."

"Fat chance," said Pepe.

"We need to get going," I said.

"To the funny farm, right?" Jimmy G turned the key in the ignition. "Where is it, exactly?"

I gave him the directions to Forest Glen.

"I just can't figure out why anyone would want to hurt my sister," I mused as we took off.

"Perhaps because of the murder she witnessed," said Pepe, who was in my arms.

"So you're talking again, for sure?"

"It does not matter if Jimmy G thinks you are crazy," said my dog.

"That's why you haven't been talking?"

"*Sí*, I wanted to protect you from yourself," he said. "But now it does not matter. Because it will be a good thing if the people at Forest Glen think you are loco. And your sister is there!"

"Teri really is at Forest Glen?"

"*Sí*, I smelled her the first time we were there. She is in the cottage called Serenity, the one at the edge of the woods."

"Are you talking to yourself?" Jimmy G asked.

"No, I'm talking to my dog," I said. "He's finally talking to me again."

"Good thing we are heading for a loony bin," said Jimmy G, stepping on the gas, as he headed toward a freeway onramp.

"Also, I wrote down the license number of the car outside our casa," Pepe said. "It was a government-issued license. Federal. I saw a similar car the last time we were at Forest Glen."

"So you think the Feds are looking for Teri? Why?" I asked. But as I asked, my heart sank. Teri had been mixed up in some seriously illegal activities when she was younger.

"I do not know. That is what we must determine," said Pepe.

Soon we were zipping along on the 520, heading for Woodinville. It was too noisy to talk to Pepe. I just clutched him close to me (Felix would be furious that I was transporting him in a car without protection for him in case of an accident) and tried to keep the wind from blowing my hair into my eyes.

We finally got off the freeway at the Woodinville exit, and got onto a winding road that took us past some huge housing developments like the one my sister Cheryl lived in, alternating with stands of the few patches of forest still remaining out here in the suburbs of Seattle.

I thought about the last time I had seen my sister Teri. She was living under an assumed identity. She told me she was hiding from some gangsters who had committed a murder back in the late 1990s, which she had witnessed when she was a young woman dancing at a strip club they owned. She had been on the run ever since. Pepe and I had stopped the hit man hired to take her out, but she had disappeared again. Was it possible they had found her again? And what was she doing at Forest Glen?

Those were questions I could answer only if I could talk to her and I was determined to do that.

When we arrived at Forest Glen, HIMBA left the car in front and we marched straight up to Forest Glen's reception desk. We must have been a sight— him dressed like he'd walked out of some forties noir movie, and me in a wedding dress holding a Chihuahua.

I recognized Lacey sitting at the reception desk wearing a bright blue polo shirt. "Wow!" she said, rising to greet me. "Did you get married, Miss Sullivan?" She studied my wedding dress and I figured she was noticing its bedraggled condition because her eyes got narrow and her lips scrunched up. "Congratulations," she said half-heartedly.

"No, I did not get married," I said.

"Oh . . ."

"Tell her you are *loco*," said Pepe.

"My dog wants me to tell you that I'm crazy," I told her.

"Oh!" she said again. She gave Pepe a frightened look.

"You are on the right track," Pepe told me. "You are very convincing in your pretend *loco*-ness. Add something else to spice it up a bit."

"My decorating partner is missing and a client of his was murdered and the police think he did it and somebody's trying to kill my sister and she's missing and this old lady in a retirement home has an unwelcome suitor after her and I told her to put flour on the floor by her front door and I only took her case because," I pointed at HIMBA beside me, "'He Who Isn't My Boss Anymore' wanted me to take it and I said I'd do it only if he went to my ex-husband's wedding to Amber with me and—"

Lacey cut me off, addressing a question to HIMBA. "And who are you, sir? Are you a friend?"

"No," he said. "Jimmy G is her boss, even though she doesn't seem to realize that. She has definitely gone off the deep end. Thinks Jimmy G is going to make her a partner."

I paid them no attention and kept on going. "But Jeff boffed one of the bridesmaids in the parking lot and Amber won't marry him now and she's been kidnapped because they thought she was me and they'll kill her unless I trade her for my missing sister and my dog has started talking to me again and I'm being followed and spied on and threatened and—"

"So you're feeling paranoid," said Lacey. I saw her reaching for the phone.

"Of course," I told her. "I'm having a nervous breakdown *and* I'm paranoid!"

"Tell her I am also in that agitated state," said Pepe. "That will surely get some action."

"So is my dog!" I said.

Pepe put on a show; he fidgeted and looked around nervously, like he was seeing danger everywhere, and said, "Tell her that paranoid *perros* can be *muy* unpredictable."

"Paranoid *perros* can be *muy* unpredictable," I told her.

"Let me call someone who can help you," said Lacey. "You just need to be patient." She glanced around nervously. Apparently they did not want someone really loco cluttering up the beautiful front lobby. "I'll show you to a waiting room and contact the doctor on call."

"He better hurry!" I said.

"*Pronto!*" said Pepe.

"I'm not sure how long I can hold it together!" I added as Lacey waved us into a little office alongside the reception desk. I noticed that she locked the door. Through the little window (which was intermeshed with wire to keep crazy people from breaking it), I watched her scurry back to the desk and pick up the phone, all the time darting nervous glances in our direction.

I paced back and forth, trying to act crazy but actually feeling pretty crazy.

"Jimmy G should leave and go check out the clue," said Jimmy G.

"Well, you can't now!" I snapped. "They've got us locked in here."

"Jimmy G doesn't like being locked up," said

HIMBA, getting up and trying the door. It was true. He couldn't budge it. He rattled the doorknob and pounded on the door. Lacey seemed to get increasingly agitated.

Luckily, a few minutes later a white-coated doctor came hurrying down the stairs. It was Dr. Lieberman. He held a whispered consultation with Lacey who was pointing at us and talking rapidly, then opened the door and stepped into the waiting room.

"Dr. Lieberman," I said. "I'm having a major meltdown. I need to be admitted."

He looked me over thoughtfully. "Why, Miss Sullivan . . . Why are you wearing a wedding dress?" He glanced over at Jimmy G.

"No, I didn't get married and no, I'm not getting married," I told him. "Especially not to HIMBA."

"She says she's having a nervous breakdown and she was acting paranoid," said Lacey from behind him.

"I'll be the one to make those determinations, Lacey, not you," Lieberman told her sternly. She nodded and went back to the front desk.

Dr Lieberman then addressed me again. "As it happens, Miss Sullivan, I came in this morning because we had a Situation and because of that we have an unexpected opening. So I actually can admit you immediately."

That didn't sound good. What sort of Situation would cause an unexpected opening? I wasn't sure I wanted to know. I just wanted to get in and find Teri. "That's wonderful," I said.

Dr. Lieberman swiveled to look over HIMBA. "Who is this?"

"He's my boss," I said to Lieberman. "He was nice enough to drive me here."

"Yeah, she's nuts," said HIMBA, still trying to help me out.

Dr. Lieberman sighed. I bet he was thinking that Jimmy G was probably as nuts as I was. "Well, we can take it from here, sir. Although I would like to have your contact information. I assume you are willing to be her emergency contact."

"Actually, it should be my boyfriend, Felix," I said, then wondered what Felix would do if he got a phone call saying I was in the loony bin. Maybe I should call him myself. I would do that and try to explain what was going on as soon as I was settled.

It took a lot longer than I thought. HIMBA left with a wink of his eye, an awkward hug, and a promise to check up on me the following day. There were endless forms to fill out and information to provide. They took away my phone because, as Dr. Lieberman said, "we want our patients to focus on recovery without having to worry about what's going on outside of Forest Glen." They put a plastic arm bracelet on my left wrist with my name on it, I guess, in case I got so crazy I forgot my own name. I got increasingly agitated as I was thinking about Amber in the clutches of the kidnappers and Teri being hunted by men who were willing to kill a woman and her Chihuahua to get what they wanted. But finally, Dr. Lieberman gave me a little blue pill that he said would calm me down and had Lacey walk me over to Serenity.

Pretty soon I was feeling very tranquil indeed.

Pepe's Blog:
Locked in a Room

Geri was feeling tranquil thanks to whatever medicine the doctor gave her. She curled up on the bed in the room they assigned her and drifted off to sleep. But I was not tranquil. No, indeed. For it was clear to me that the room had previously been occupied by her sister! (Human siblings have remarkably similar scent profiles.) But how was I to find out what happened to her since I was locked in the room, along with Geri. They seemed to fear her when they should have feared my wrath.

From time to time an attendant peered in the little window in the door and then went away. The smells of dinner drifted under the crack in the door. I could smell hamburger and French fries, and that reminded me that due to all the consternation at the wedding I had never been able to sample the

roast beef, which had smelled so divine. My stomach
growled. I growled at the edges of the door. And that
finally woke Geri up. At first, she seemed confused
about where she was, but I was able to straighten
her out.

Chapter 18

I woke up disoriented, lying on a bed in a strange room with a dim light filtering through the window. It seemed to be dusk, and I was covered with a soft chenille blanket, a bright blue color, the color of the Forest Glen employees' polo shirts. I was still wearing a wedding dress. I tried to sit up but felt surprisingly rubbery, as if my limbs weren't connected to my brain.

Pepe sat beside the bed, watching me with his big brown eyes. "Ah, finally, you are awake," he said. "We have much to do!"

"Where am I?" I asked, gazing around the room. It was bare except for a bedside table.

"You are in the *casa loco* where you wanted to be," he said. "But now we must get out of here."

"Why?"

"Because your sister is no longer here."

"What? Teri was here?"

"Yes, in this very room. We must get out there." He wagged his head toward the door, which had a window in it. I could see light behind it. "Find out what happened to her."

"So you are talking to me now?"

"As long as you are in the casa loco already, it will not matter," he said.

I struggled to stand. It was a bit difficult, what with the wedding dress and whatever pill was making me feel so calm and happy. After the craziness of the last few hours, I appreciated it. Finding Teri seemed important, but I was confident I could solve all the problems of the world.

I noticed a call button by the bed and pushed it. Nothing happened for a while so I pushed it again. A few minutes later, a red-haired nurse, buxom and broad-shouldered, appeared in my doorway. She said her name was Joyce.

"I see you're finally awake, Miss Sullivan," Joyce said, coming in and briskly rearranging the pillows on the bed. "Would you like some dinner? It was just delivered. We didn't know what you would like so we just ordered—"

"No!" I interrupted her. "I need some information about my sister. My dog tells me she was here. In this very room. Is she still here?"

Joyce looked alarmed. "Your dog talks to you?"

"Of course, I talk to her," said Pepe. "We are partners."

"He's my partner," I said. "I'm a private detective."

Joyce smiled a weak smile. "How very interesting," she said. "So let me get your dinner—" She turned to go.

"No! You can't leave," I said. "You have to tell me about my sister—"

"The one your dog said was staying in this room?" she said. An amused tone had crept into her voice.

"Yes, my dog is always right!" I said.

"Finally, you admit it!" said Pepe.

"How lucky for you," she said with an even bigger smile. "Especially since he can talk."

"I'm serious!" I practically shouted. "I've got to find my sister. If I don't find her, the kidnappers will kill Amber and even though she's about to marry my ex-husband—or maybe she's about to ditch him, I'm not sure—I can't let that happen!"

"Don't forget Party Girl," said Pepe.

"And they've got Party Girl too!" I said.

The nurse's smile slipped a little. "Well, truly I am sorry these matters are troubling you," she said. "Dr. Lieberman wrote up an order for more medication." She looked at her watch. "I can give you something that will help relieve your anxiety."

"I don't want my anxiety relieved!" I insisted. "I want to find my sister. Was she here? Teri Sullivan? Did she stay in this room?"

Joyce's lips compressed. "Even if she was here, I couldn't tell you that," she said primly. "Confidentiality is one of our most prized commitments to our patients."

I didn't give up. "We don't look that much alike. She's taller and skinnier and her hair is frizzier and has a slight reddish tone to it."

I saw a shadow cross the nurse's face. "I'll fetch that medication for you, Miss . . . She checked the name on the door. Again I saw that something troubled her. "Miss Sullivan," she said. She closed the door with a bang and I heard her footsteps hurrying away.

I tried the door, but the door was locked.

"Now what?" I said to Pepe, sitting down on the edge of the bed. "She knows something, doesn't she?"

"*Si,*" said Pepe, "and if you would be quiet, I might be able to hear what she is saying." He had his head pressed down to the crack in the door. I tried to be patient, watching his ears twitch slightly. Finally I couldn't stand it any longer.

"What is going on?" I asked.

"You do indeed need to take an anti-anxiety pill," said Pepe. "There is nothing either of us can do shut up in this room. We need to get out and roam about and to do so, you must stop acting *loco.*"

"You're beginning to sound like Cheryl," I said, "and that is not good."

"Ah!" said Pepe. "Already the treatment is working. You are getting in touch with the source of your problems with authority."

"I don't have problems with authority," I snapped. "I have problems with dogs who tell me what to do."

"Do you realize how *loco* that would sound?" said Pepe. He looked around. "Suppose the room is bugged."

I looked around too, although I didn't know what I was looking for. "Just tell me!" I pleaded. "And by the way, did I mention how much I appreciate the fact that you are talking to me?"

"No, you did not," said Pepe gravely. "I am glad to know that."

"So?"

"So the nurse was very concerned. She told someone else that you knew something about the previous patient, but she did not use Teri's name. She said there must be a leak."

"Did she say where Teri is now?" I asked.

Pepe shook his head. "No, she did say it was a good thing that she was moved. I assume she was talking about Teri."

"Moved where?" I wondered. "To another cottage?"

"She did not say," said Pepe. "Perhaps you can bribe her. That always worked in Mexico with *la policia.*"

"But I don't have any money," I said. I realized that I had surrendered my purse along with my cell phone when I was admitted.

"Then I think since they are so insistent on confidentiality that you need to get out of here and go mingle with the other patients who are eating dinner right now in the dining room," said Pepe.

"Other patients?"

"Yes, there are at least four other residents in this cottage. Unfortunately, from what I can tell, they are all very crazy. But that may be good for us, as they can tell us things the staff will not."

"But how do I—"

The door opened and Joyce came back in carrying a glass of water and a pill in a plastic cup. "Here's the medication I mentioned," she said. "It will help calm you down. It sounds like you have had a stressful day."

"I don't want to take a pill!" I said.

"Geri, remember our strategy!" said Pepe.

"But I will," I continued. "I know you know what is best for me." Obediently, I took the offered glass of water and pinched the pill up out of the cup. I tried to conceal it in my cheek and swallow the water without swallowing the pill, but I got confused and before I knew it, the pill was down the hatch too.

Joyce smiled.

What was in that pill? Would it knock me out for

another twelve hours? If so, it would be too late for Teri. And for Amber. And for Party Girl. I needed to act fast.

"What about dinner?" I said. "I'm so hungry."

"If you're feeling a little better," Joyce said, "you can join the others in the dining room."

"Mission accomplished," said Pepe.

"But your dog can't go with you," said Joyce. "And"—Joyce frowned at my attire—"you'll need to change out of that gown. Let me get you one of ours."

She was back in a few minutes with a terrycloth robe in what I was coming to think of as Forest Glen blue. I noticed there was no belt, just Velcro fasteners. I wriggled out of the wedding gown, which was wet and stained, and Joyce bore it away, apparently fearing that I could harm myself with a wedding dress. I wasn't sure how. She returned with a pair of comfy blue slippers. I put them on and shuffled out to the dining room where I was introduced to the others.

Greg was a tall, pale man with bony joints and big haunted eyes. He didn't say a word, but he did look frightened when he saw me. Nicole was barely out of her teens. She had short, pink hair. She must have been anorexic because she was all skin and bones and she toyed with her food, moving it from one side of her plate to the other. Frances was her opposite, almost morbidly obese, with unhealthy-colored grey skin and rolls of fat around her chin. I saw her eyeing Nicole's food enviously. We each had a tray in front of us, which contained a hamburger on a limp bun, a heap of French fries, some carrot coins and a bowl of what looked like applesauce.

"Hi, everyone! I'm Geri," I said. They looked up and then looked back down without saying a word. I sat down at the one empty place at the big round table. "My parents named me and my sisters Cheryl, Geri, and Teri so we would all sound alike," I said, hoping the mention of the name Teri would spark a response. Nothing.

"Greg doesn't talk," said Nicole helpfully.

"Ha! That's just like my dog," I said. "He wasn't talking either. Until I ended up here—"

"They let you have a dog?" Nicole asked.

"Well, he's part of my problem," I admitted. "I think he talks to me. Of course, he doesn't. Or at least that's what they tell me."

"What kind of dog?" asked Frances.

"A little white Chihuahua," I said.

Frances looked at Nicole and Nicole looked at Frances.

"What?" I asked. "Have you seen him?"

"A dog like him," Nicole said. "Came into the cottage the other day and Carrie got all excited about it. Said the dog looked just like her sister's dog. Swore the dog talked to her."

"Carrie?" I asked.

"Yeah, she was in the room you're in now, until—"

Nicole and Frances both shut up as Joyce came back into the room. "Nicole," she said, "if you don't eat more than that, you're going to have to go back into the hospital. Try and see if you can at least drink the Ensure."

"That's for old people," said Nicole. But she picked up the can, which was on her tray and shook it, then popped the tab on the lid. She took a tiny sip then put it back down again.

"You need to drink more than that if you're going to meet your goals for this week," said Joyce in a cheery voice. She turned to me. "I didn't get your paperwork yet from the main office. Do you have any dietary restrictions I should know about?"

"Well, I am a vegetarian," I said, poking at the hamburger patty with my fork.

"In the future you can have a garden burger on hamburger days," Joyce said in a happy voice. "For now, maybe you can just eat the bun."

Frances grumbled under her breath. "They should be feeding us sirloin steak for the prices we pay to be here."

"What is that, Frances?" asked Joyce in the singsong voice of a kindergarten teacher.

Frances refused to repeat her comments.

Joyce hefted an extra tray of food from the rolling cart and sailed off with it.

"Where's that going?" I asked.

"There's one guy who never comes out of his room," said Frances with her mouth full. "Nicole thinks he's a werewolf."

"I saw him one day when the door opened," Nicole said with relish. "He was totally naked and his body was covered with red scratches. Plus we can hear him howling at night."

I shivered. I really wasn't prepared to be locked up with truly crazy people.

Nicole noticed my distress. "You know we are the most locked down cottage," she said proudly. "We're the craziest of the crazy."

I was starting to feel a bit floaty and woozy and I needed to get information fast. "So what can you tell me about Carrie?" I asked after sampling a few of the French fries. Although they were lukewarm, they were pretty good. I realized I hadn't eaten anything since breakfast.

"Totally nuts!" said Frances, waving one pudgy finger around her temple.

"Not like us!" Nicole cackled. She slid some carrots off her plate and into her napkin.

"What way was she nuts?" I asked.

"She thought someone was after her," said Frances, leaning in and whispering, then looking all around. "Kept saying they were coming to get her. Jumped at every noise. Freaked out at the sight of strangers. A classic case of paranoid schizophrenia."

"Like you would know," said Nicole.

"Hey," said Frances, "when you've been in here seven times like I have, you'll know what I'm talking about." She turned to me. "She claimed a little dog came running in to give her a message."

"What did the dog tell her?" I asked.

Frances gave me a pitying look. "Dogs don't talk," she said.

"Right!" I said with a forced laugh.

"The sad thing is she couldn't accept the diagnosis. Kept insisting she was really in danger. Refused to take the medication." Frances wagged her head toward the door through which Joyce had disappeared. "They don't like that here."

"So what happened to her?" I asked. "Why isn't she here now?" My words came out slurred. My tongue felt so thick I could barely move it. I choked down a bite of the carrots.

"One day she was here. The next morning she was gone. No explanation," said Frances matter-of-factly. She scraped the bottom of her applesauce bowl with her spoon, then swapped her empty bowl for Nicole's full one.

I thought back to what Dr Lieberman had said about a Situation. "Did she freak out or something?" I asked.

Frances shrugged. "If she did, we didn't hear nothing. Course they give us stuff to make us sleep through the night."

"Men with guns," said Greg in a somber voice.

"What?" Nicole looked at him with big eyes.

"What?" Frances stopped with a spoonful of applesauce halfway to her mouth.

"Men with guns," said Greg. "They took her away."

Pepe's Blog: If She Had Only Listened

My partner has been rendered dopey by the medicine she was given by the nurse. She was babbling about men with guns while she took me outside to, as she puts it, "do my business," although how mere bodily functions could be equated with income producing activity I do not understand. As soon as we got back to the room, she fell onto the bed and started snoring away. And she did not even have the courtesy to bring me a scrap of the hamburger that was served for dinner. What is a dog to do?

I had to sneak out of the room when the night nurse came in to check on Geri and make my own way to the dining room where I found a stash of fresh carrots and cold French fries wrapped in a napkin tucked behind a cupboard. Not sufficient for a dog with a mission but it would have to do.

Once my hunger pains were somewhat eased, I sniffed around and caught the scent of the men who had taken Teri away. There were two of them and they had come in the back door. Someone else, a woman, perhaps another nurse for her shoes smelled of bleach though her sweat smelled of deception, walked with Teri from her room to the back door. That was where the trail ended for me, as I could not escape through the locked back door. Nor could I get back into Geri's room. So I did what any good detective would do. I went to interrogate the night nurse about the events of the prior evening and found her in the office at the front of the cottage, chuckling over a video about cats(!) she was watching on a computer screen. If only I had my beloved iPad with me.

But she refused to answer my questions. Instead she scolded me for making a racket and stuck me back in the room with my sedated partner. Sadly, my full belly inclined me to similar slumbers so I jumped up onto the bed and curled myself into Geri's arms. And the next thing I knew it was morning.

Chapter 19

I was startled awake by a piercing scream. And then the sound of a struggle. Judging by the dim light filtering through the window it was just before dawn. How could I have fallen asleep when both Amber and my sister were in jeopardy?

Pepe apparently felt the same way. He flew at the door, barking and scratching at it with his little claws, but, of course, that was ineffective. I tugged at the knob, but it was locked from the outside.

Pepe stopped suddenly and turned on me. "*Silencio!*" he said. "We must not let them know you are here."

"What? Who?" I asked.

"Back!" he said, blocking me from the door with his little body. "Let me listen!"

I heard voices but I could not distinguish what they were saying. A male voice and a female one. It sounded like the woman was pleading for her life. I looked around wildly for a weapon but, of course, the room had been cleared of anything that could possibly be used as a weapon. All I had was a bright blue terrycloth bathrobe and a pair of fuzzy slippers. I slipped into the bathroom, thinking perhaps there was a water glass I could shatter and use as a weapon, but no, all I could find was a cup made of flimsy plastic like those you find in hotel rooms.

Pepe came running into the bathroom. "This is most serious, Geri," he said. "The man wants to know where to find Teri Sullivan or Geri Sullivan. It is only a matter of time before the nurse breaks down and gives him the information he needs."

"Do you think she knows where Teri is?" I asked eagerly.

"No, for certain, she does not. When she says so her voice is sincere. But," he said with an ominous tone in his voice," she does know where you are. Although she has not yet told him."

"There must be something we can do," I said, going back into the bedroom and looking around desperately. There was a button on the wall that said "Push in an Emergency." I had only a moment to wonder what would happen. Would it light up in the downstairs office where the nurse was being assaulted? Or in the main building and bring some other staff running? Wouldn't the nurse have a similar button in her office and why hadn't she pushed it?

I pushed the button repeatedly.

The sound of the argument escalated. The nurse was shrieking. The man was shouting. And then the air was split by a horrible howl, followed by a scream of agony, followed by a wailing, keening sound. And then all was silence.

I had never felt so helpless in all my life. I darted over to the window and tugged on it, but it wouldn't budge farther than an inch. But that inch might be enough to send Pepe for aid. "Do you think you can get out?" I asked him.

"Indeed, I am designed for just such an occasion," he said, eagerly jumping up into my outstretched hands. But just as I was about to shove him through the crack, we saw several people with flashlights approaching the cottage. Surely we were about to be rescued. I hugged Pepe close, cradling him in my arms, hoping the staff would arrive in time to save me.

I could hear loud voices in the cottage. Then the thump of footsteps. Someone pounded on my door.

"Who is it?" I asked in a squeaky voice. The door knob rattled.

"We'll come back for you later," the voice said and went away.

"All clear!" I heard someone say.

"The police are on their way," I heard someone else say.

Looking out the window, I could see a crowd gathering around the cottage. Several men in suits. Several employees in the blue polo shirts. A nurse or two in pale blue scrubs. A doctor in a long white coat. An emergency vehicle with flashing red lights pulled up onto the grass and some dark-blue clad EMTs clattered into the building.

A short time later, Dr. Lieberman appeared in my doorway.

"Oh, good," he said, running a hand through his hair. "You're safe." He shook his head. "But we've got to get you out of here. You're a liability to our safe operation and you apparently gained entrance here by falsifying your condition."

"I falsified nothing!" I said indignantly. "I do hear my dog talking to me."

I looked at Pepe, but he said nothing.

"You are actually a private detective who is trying to find Teri Sullivan," he said. "By pretending to be her sister."

"I am her sister!" I said.

"We don't have a Teri Sullivan here, and," he lowered his voice, "if we did, she would no longer be here but someplace far safer."

"Is that a hint?" I asked desperately.

"I'm not at liberty to reveal anything," he said primly. "I'm here to deliver you to the police. They want to take a statement."

"What happened downstairs?"

"You'll find out soon enough."

I shuffled downstairs in my fuzzy blue bathrobe and slippers with Pepe in my arms. He was shivering, poor little guy. I thought at first it was due to the traumatic events of the night but soon remembered that he hates the police.

A young woman in pale blue scrubs was sitting on the sofa talking to a policeman who sat beside her taking notes on a notepad. "He saved me, for sure! That guy was going to kill me."

As I passed the office, I saw that it had been trashed. There were papers all over the floors, blood splashed on the walls and a chair overturned.

"What happened?" I asked Dr. Lieberman again.

"We're still trying to figure that out," he said. He gripped me by the elbow and steered me out the front door.

"Geri!" said Pepe. His nose was twitching rapidly. "Look!"

I looked and saw a man in handcuffs beside a police officer who kept a wary eye on him. He was naked, although he had a blanket wrapped loosely around him. He must be the crazy guy who was supposed to be locked in his room, the one Nicole thought was a werewolf. He had long blond hair which flopped over his face. As we passed by, he looked up, and I saw, to my shock, that I knew him.

"Brad!"

"Do you know this man?" Dr. Lieberman brought me to a halt. That gave me a chance to look Brad over thoroughly. He was covered with blood and I could see a long scratch on his arm. He had light blond stubble on his chin and his hair was matted. I had never seen my business partner naked or unshaven or with his hair uncombed. But still there was no doubt. Brad was the werewolf of Serenity.

"Sure. That's my business partner, Brad Best," I said, peering at him closely. "Don't you know his name?"

Brad got a wild and fearful look in his eyes. He shook his head and held one finger up to his lips. His wrists were encircled by handcuffs.

"No," snapped Dr. Lieberman, "and he wouldn't tell us."

"But surely the police . . ." I looked at the blue-clad officer guarding Brad.

"They couldn't get any information out of him when they found him wandering around Volunteer Park, naked and covered with blood. They thought maybe he was the victim of a hate crime. He was transported to Harborview for evaluation and then they shipped him over here," said Dr. Lieberman, hustling me past him. "Maybe they'll do a little more investigation now."

"Did he attack the nurse?" I asked, shuddering. Maybe Brad really had killed Mrs. Fairchild, and then gone mad with guilt.

"No." Lieberman was thoughtful. "Actually he saved her life. An intruder had entered the cottage and was threatening to kill her." He pointed toward the aide car with the flashing lights. I could see a large body on the gurney inside.

"Do we know who that was?" I asked. "Or why he was here?"

"The police have not yet been able to identify him," said Dr. Lieberman, hustling me down the path. "He has no ID and he's unconscious. Serious head wound. But we do know why he was here."

He pushed me down the path towards the main building. It was much colder out here in the country than in the city. I shivered in the chilly night air and quickened my steps.

"Geri, can you let me down for a minute?" asked Pepe.

"Sure," I said, "but why?"

"He was trying to get to you," Dr. Lieberman said in a stern voice.

"A call of nature," Pepe replied. I realized he had not been outside for many hours.

"Of course," I said. I lowered Pepe to the ground and he went scampering off towards the nearest tree, which was just barely visible in the darkness. The paths were illuminated with lights set about two inches above the ground, but the rest of the grounds were full of shadows. Here and there, I saw the lights on in distant cottages.

"What do you mean he was trying to get to me?" I asked.

"According to the nurse, he told her that he would shoot her unless she turned you over to him."

I shuddered.

"That's when your friend intervened. We still don't know how he got out of his room. He was locked in for his own safety and the safety of others in the cottage."

Dr. Lieberman hustled me along and we soon approached the back door of the main building. Pepe was nowhere in sight.

"I can't go anywhere without my dog," I said.

"We're not waiting around for him," said Dr. Lieberman. He entered a code on the numeric pad by the back door. A green light flashed and he turned the handle. "He's caused quite enough trouble as it is."

There was a man waiting in the corridor on the other side. He did not wear a uniform. He did not wear a bright blue polo shirt. Instead he was dressed in a dark suit. I could tell by the way his suit jacket flared out over one hip that he was packing a gun.

"Here she is," said Dr. Lieberman. "Get her off my property. She's done enough damage."

Pepe's Blog: Where There Is One Villain ...

I was taking some private time to mark my territory and leave aromatic clues for the luscious poodle bitch about my whereabouts when I spotted a shadowy figure lurking in the trees along the river bank. I recalled one of the chief principles of private detection: where there is one villain, there is likely to be another.

I recognized the smell of the intruder as soon as I got within three feet of him. It was one of the men who had been in the home of Party Girl and Amber. He had a shaved head and a tattoo on his neck. He carried a *pistola* loosely in his left hand and was talking in a low mutter on a cell phone he clutched in his other hand. He was sweating up a storm, terror and adrenaline racing through his system. Also, I detected a faint whiff of pulled pork tacos. How I longed for one myself!

"Yes, boss," he muttered. "They got him! I don't

know how. They're taking him off in an ambulance."
He shifted uneasily. "The girl? She's still here somewhere." Another pause. "But the place is crawling
with cops."

His terror increased by about a hundredfold. "Yes,
I do understand. Yes, you made it perfectly clear.
Yes, next time you see me I'll have the bitch with me."

Somehow I knew he was not talking about the
poodle bitch. He was talking about my partner, Geri.
And I needed to warn her. I took off like a shot of
greased lightning, running, running for the main
building that I had seen her enter with the white-clad
doctor.

Tip

- Sometimes a call of nature—or a diversion—can
  be more productive than a direct interrogation.

Chapter 20

"Don't worry, Doc," said the man, his voice gruff. "I'm going to have a serious conversation with Miss Sullivan."

"Conversation?" Lieberman sounded exasperated. "You better have more than a conversation with her. I've cooperated with you. I expect some cooperation in return."

"Like I said, Doc, no worries."

Lieberman frowned, shook his head, and stalked off.

I studied the man for a moment. Somewhere in his mid-forties, he had salt and pepper hair cut in an old-fashioned crew-cut, and was more than six feet tall, with a stocky build.

"Who are you?" I asked him.

"U. S. Marshall," he told me, opening his coat a bit, to reveal a shiny badge clipped to his belt next to his holstered pistol.

"A Marshall? Why are you—"

"Your sister. Teri Sullivan."

"Teri? Why—"

"Look, here's how it lays out, short and sweet. You need to keep your nose out of this. Your sister's under our protection. She's a material witness in a trial against a crime boss. Trial's coming up in a couple of days. She was safe and secure here until you started meddling."

"What do you mean?"

"We think you were followed here to Forest Glen, Miss Sullivan. There was an attempt to break into the cottage where your sister was staying. We had to move her immediately. These are career criminals who are after her. We've been working to take them down for years. And we finally have a chance. But they'll stop at nothing to keep her from talking. So lay off. Got it?"

"Can I talk to Teri at least?"

"You don't know when to stop, do you? The less you know, the better. If you persist in looking for your sister, I'll put you in protective custody, too, until this is all over. And not a word about this to anyone else."

"OK, OK," I said. "I understand."

"Good." He smiled for the first time. "Bear in mind, you're very likely in danger yourself."

I thought about Amber and knew he was right.

"Speaking of that," I said, "you might want to know about the kidnapping."

"Kidnapping?"

"Yes, my ex-husband's runaway bride, Amber Trout."

"Hold on!" said the Marshall, putting his hand up, palm out. "Tell me the whole story from the beginning."

So I tried to explain. He didn't seem to get the part about the man and the fish and the bicycle but that was OK. He did get the gist of it.

"So you said the Bellevue police have been notified?"

"I think so," I said. "I left to try to find Teri and ended up being admitted and then tranquilized and—"

The Marshall cut me off. "How did they contact you to make the ransom demand?"

'My cell phone," I said.

"I'm going to need that!" he said. "Have they called again?"

"I don't know," I said, horror-stricken. "I had to give up my cell phone when they admitted me here."

Luckily, Lacey who was at the front desk got permission from Dr. Lieberman to return my personal belongings. The cell phone was locked in a drawer in the reception area. Lacey had to send over to Serenity to have them bring the rest of my belongings.

The phone started ringing as soon as I turned it on. It was Felix. In fact, he had called more than twenty times. But there were no calls from unknown numbers.

"I've got to get this," I told the Marshall.

"Geri!" Felix's voice was frantic. "Where are you? What happened to you? I've been calling all night. I was about to report you missing."

I sighed. It was nice to know that someone missed me.

"I'm so sorry," I said. "I ended up getting admitted to a psychiatric clinic and they wouldn't let me use my phone. Will you come and get me?"

Felix's voice was dubious. "They let you go? Already?"

"Hey," I said, trying to keep my voice light, "It's not like I'm crazy or anything."

I saw Lacey's eyebrows go up at that.

"Where are you?" he said.

"Forest Glen." I gave him the address and some general instructions about how to find the place.

"I'll leave right away," he promised. I breathed a sigh of relief. Felix to the rescue! Now all I had to do was get dressed and find my dog.

The Marshall took my phone with a stern warning that I was not to further involve myself in what was turning out to be a Federal case. I tried to follow him out the door so I could look for Pepe, but Lacey stopped me.

"You can't leave until you have your final interview," she said. She sent me upstairs to talk to Dr. Lieberman. He was sorting some papers in a file on his desk when I entered.

He looked up. "You're no longer a patient here, Miss Sullivan, so I shouldn't be giving you advice, but I want to let you know that in my professional opinion, your dog is the focus of your psychological issues. You might want to consider getting rid of him."

"Getting rid of Pepe? That's unthinkable."

Lieberman shook his head. "I don't think you'll ever get better until you lose the dog," he said. "You have an unhealthy attachment to him."

"Well, he's lost now, and I want him back." I said.

Lieberman shrugged. "You're free to go. We can't hold you against your will. Of course, you'll receive a bill for the services we provided while you were here." He went over to the file cabinet and pulled out some papers. "I'm going to fill out your discharge papers. I'll bring them down to the reception desk for you to sign."

I headed back to the reception desk to get my

personal belongings from Lacey. She handed me a plastic bag with my name written across it with a Sharpie. I peeked inside and saw the rumpled, stained wedding dress.

"I can't wear this," I said.

Lacey shrugged. "Our monogrammed bathrobes are available for purchase. We can add the cost to your bill. They're only $99."

"Never mind," I said, thinking I would not want to be caught dead in a bright-blue terrycloth bathrobe that reminded me of my stay at Forest Glen. "I'll put on the wedding dress. Where can I change?"

Lacey pointed down the hall toward the wing that contained the spa. Clutching my purse in one hand and the wedding dress in the other, I scurried down the hall, opening several doors. Sauna. Steam room. Isolation Tank. Where was the bathroom? Although I supposed I could use any of the rooms to change. They were all empty at this early hour of the day.

I ducked inside the room containing the isolation tank, shrugged off the blue bathrobe and wriggled into the soggy, smelly wedding dress. I looked for my black heels, but they weren't in the bag.

Clutching my belongings, I was heading back to the reception desk when I heard a gunshot, the sound of breaking glass, a scream. Then loud voices.

"Where is she?" A deep male voice.

Then Dr. Lieberman's voice. "Who are you and what do you think you are doing?"

"I'm looking for Geri Sullivan," said the first voice.

"How dare you! Get out of here!" said Lieberman. It was nice that he was standing up for me.

But then I heard a grunt and a shriek and a thud.

What was happening now? Had the intruder killed Dr. Lieberman? Knocked him over the head?

"Where is she?" It was the first voice again, the gruff voice.

"I don't know," squeaked Lacey. "Please don't hurt me!"

"Is she in the building?"

"She was here," Lacey squeaked, "but she left." Nice that she was standing up for me too.

"Show me where she went!" commanded the man.

Lacey gave a little shriek that was cut off abruptly.

The next thing I knew I heard footsteps coming in my direction. A heavy tread and a shuffling noise, like maybe a body was being dragged.

I ducked back into the isolation tank room and looked for a place to hide. But the only thing in the room was the isolation tank. It was a long box. It almost reminded me of a coffin, except that it was made of white plastic. A sign above it read: ATTENDANT MUST BE PRESENT AT ALL TIMES. How I wished there was an attendant.

The cover of the tank was angled upward to reveal a slanted opening through which I could see about three feet of water. I jumped in, clutching my two plastic bags. The water was warm, just about skin temperature.

I heard doors being flung open in the hall. I pulled the lid to the isolation tank shut. Darkness. Darkness and warmth. I didn't want to lie down in the water—I felt too vulnerable—but the shape of the thing made it impossible for me to crouch near the back as I wished, just in case the man who was searching for me thought to open the lid of the tank. I put the plastic bag on my stomach and floated.

I felt strangely at peace, even though my dog was missing and someone who wanted to kill me was only a few inches away. I couldn't hear anything. Just a soothing, thumping sound that I eventually realized was the beating of my heart.

Eons went by. Galaxies were born and died and born again. I read the fate of mankind in the labyrinth of lights that danced in front of my closed eyes.

Pepe's Blog: Stranger Danger

My partner, Geri, was in danger! I raced toward the main building, which I had seen her enter with the doctor.

Sometimes it is a disadvantage to be a little dog no taller than five inches. That is especially true when facing doors with handles and knobs that are several feet above your head. Just consider what it would be like trying to enter a door that is five stories tall and you will get a picture of the enormous obstacles I faced.

Usually cuteness helps when height hinders. I can prevail upon others to open doors for me by giving them a soulful look with my big brown eyes or tipping my long pink ears just so. But there was no one around nearby to help me gain entrance so I could warn Geri.

I raced to the front of the building and peered through the glass doors but there was no one seated at the receptionist desk to respond to my scratching. I raced around to the back just in time to see the door slam shut as a man in a suit clutching a gun exited the

building. The gun had not been fired recently. That
was good. The man smelled familiar. One of the men
who had been watching our *casa*. But I could not
smell either Amber or Party Girl in his scent cloud.
Was he friend or foe?

I thought I should follow him and see what he did.
He headed toward the trees where I had been watching the man who was threatening Geri. Perhaps we
could team up to take him down.

But when we returned to the thicket, the man was
gone. Vanished like the slugs whose slimy tracks glistened in the morning sun. The man with the gun was
frustrated. He pulled out a cell phone and conferred
with someone else. But I knew right where the evil
one had gone. I could follow his scent trail as surely
as if he had left a slime trail all the way up to the front
of the main building. Just as I rounded the corner, I
heard shots and shrieks and glass breaking.

Chapter 21

I don't know how much time had passed, but at some point I was roused enough from my peaceful contemplation of the meaning of life to consider that I might want to leave the womb-like shelter of the isolation tank. I reached out my hand, ever so languidly to push the lid open, just a crack, to see if I was ready to be reborn into a chaotic world, and the darn thing wouldn't budge.

I pushed again, harder, and nothing happened. I took both hands and shoved, and nothing. *Nada.*

It began to sink in: the sign that read ATTENDANT MUST BE PRESENT. Apparently, it was not possible to open the isolation tank from the inside. I freaked out. I shrieked. I pounded on the lid. So what if the goon with the gun heard me? At least I would be out of my watery tomb. But even as my cries faded away in the muffled interior I realized that the isolation tank was soundproof. No one could hear me. No one knew that I was trapped inside.

My brain was working feverishly. Was Lacey still alive? Did she know where I was? What would happen when Felix came to pick me up? Would they find me then? And, most of all, where was my dog? My champion, my partner? Never again would I allow myself to be separated from him. Forget Dr. Lieberman.

I curled up in a ball and wept quietly.

And then I heard scrabbling at the edges of the lid. A thump and it flew back. I cowered back. I closed my eyes. The light was so bright. I heard voices, a medley of voices. They grated on my hushed ears. And then I heard the voice I was most longing to hear calling my name: "Geri!"

"Pepe!" I shouted and rose from my lukewarm bath, in my dripping wet wedding gown, to grab my little dog, his pink ears just visible over the edge of the isolation tank.

"Geri!" he said again, licking my face. "You taste like the Dead Sea. Did I ever tell you about my trip to Jerusalem?"

"Don't be ridiculous," I said, and then realized there were several other people in the room.

One was Felix. He was taking in my wet wedding dress with distress in his eyes. Behind him, I saw Lacey and Dr. Lieberman. But no goon with a gun.

"What happened?" I asked.

"Your dog took down the bad guy with the gun," said Lacey. Her eyes were shining. "He was so brave. The guy had me in a headlock and was dragging me down the hall, making me open all the doors with his gun trained on me. Your dog came flying out of nowhere and bit his wrist, so that he dropped the gun. Then the other guy—"

"The Marshall," said Dr. Lieberman.

"Came running in and cuffed him."

"But then we couldn't find you," Dr. Lieberman said.

"I thought maybe you had escaped through the side door," Lacey said.

"But your dog kept coming and scratching on this door, so finally we opened up the door and then your dog scratched at the tank, and so we opened the lid and there you were!"

"I take back everything I said about your dog," said Dr. Lieberman. "Obviously you two deserve each other."

I wasn't sure what he meant by that last sentence, but it didn't matter.

"What did he say about me?" Pepe asked.

"That you are the bravest, smartest best partner any girl could have," I said, kissing him between his ears.

"That's when I arrived," said Felix, clearly wanting to be part of the story. "But why are you wearing a wedding dress?"

"It's a long story," I said, "and I'll tell you in the car. I just want to get out of here." I was shivering.

"I think we should give her a complimentary bathrobe," Lacey said to Dr. Lieberman.

So I signed the discharge papers and got into Felix's car in my bright blue Forest Glen velour bathrobe with Velcro fastenings. The wedding dress went into the plastic bag. Pepe rode cuddled in my arms, and Felix, who usually insists the dogs who travel in his car must travel in crates in the back, did not say a word. I think he was a little miffed that I called out Pepe's name before his.

I only had about thirty minutes to tell Felix everything that had happened as he drove me back to my car, which was still parked in the parking lot at the Bellevue Country Club. It seemed like another day entirely although it had been less than twenty-four hours since the aborted wedding ceremony. I was so glad that the Marshalls were going to take over the search for Amber. Even if it did mean giving up my cell phone.

"But what about you?" I asked Felix, who was shaking his head. "How was your day yesterday?"

Felix laughed. It was actually something between a snort and a laugh. "I thought it was pretty exciting," he said, "until I heard what you were up to . . ."

"The things we were doing," said Pepe. "We were saving lives!"

"So what happened? Did you get the job?" I asked. As a good girlfriend I wanted the answer to be *yes*, because I knew Felix deserved success. As a bad girlfriend, I wanted the answer to be *no*, so he would stay in Seattle.

"We don't know yet," said Felix. "There was a little glitch. The first dog we lined up didn't work out. So they're looking for a new dog to film."

"So you're still filming?"

"Yes. The plan is to shoot today. And look at the rough edit tonight at Rebecca's house. They'll probably announce their decision then. I really want you to be there. I was calling to tell you about that and then . . ."

His voice trailed off.

"I wasn't answering my phone," I said. "They took it away from me at Forest Glen."

"At first, I thought you were just having a good time at the wedding," he said, "but then when you still weren't home at 2 a.m. and then at 3 a.m., well, I started to get worried. . . ."

I could see by the look on his face that he wasn't so much worried about my whereabouts but about who I had been with.

"You did not need to worry," said Pepe. "I can take care of her very well."

"You didn't take care of me when I needed you," I said, thinking of how he had run off.

"I'm sorry, Geri," said Felix. "I felt I had an obligation. Rebecca had set up the whole shoot around my schedule."

"Oh, no, not you," I said. I wouldn't expect him to give up his career just to attend a wedding with me. Would I? That would be so shallow. "I was talking to Pepe."

"Did they cure him of his talking at Forest Glen?" He was trying to bring a note of levity into a serious conversation.

"Actually he started talking again," I said, "and I am so happy about it."

"Did he tell you why he stopped?"

"Yes, he said he was worried because everybody thought I was crazy."

"Oh, so getting admitted to Forest Glen solved that problem," Felix said with a laugh.

"Yes, now everyone knows I am officially crazy!" I said.

I promised to call Felix as soon as I got back to my house. He was on his way back to Rebecca's, but he was clearly worried about me. I don't think he completely believed my story or that I should be wandering around on my own.

I was so happy to get home and get out of the blue bathrobe and into regular clothes. I took a quick shower and put on a pair of black sweat pants, a tank top and my favorite fuzzy sweater. Perfect for lounging at home. I wasn't going anywhere.

Pepe had polished off his bowl of dry food and gone racing into the living room to work on his iPad. I swear that dog is addicted to his technology. Albert the Cat had been furious when Pepe and I walked in the door. He kept up a volley of angry meows.

"If you don't watch it," I told him, while pouring some more kibbles into his bowl, "I'll give you back to Jeff."

That reminded me. I needed to call Jeff and find out if Amber had been returned.

Jeff said that the FBI had taken over and the whole thing was out of their hands. He sounded frantic. "What if they mess it up?" he said. And then, "This is all your fault." I hung up on him.

But I did think I should call Jimmy G and see if he had learned anything new during his stakeout.

"Geri! Thank God you called!" said Jimmy G when I dialed his number.

"What?"

"Jimmy G was worried about you," he said. "Jimmy G was calling your cell phone and this man kept answering and saying Jimmy G should stop calling. Something about an official investigation."

"The Marshalls took my phone away," I said. "They took over the investigation and they told me to stop looking for my sister. Did you learn something?"

"Jimmy G learned that he can bowl better at around four stiff drinks."

"Anything about the kidnapping?" I asked, annoyed.

"No," said Jimmy G. "There was some action last night. A couple of big guys, built like tanks, came in and talked to a little old man in a pork pie hat who was sitting in a booth on the bar side. He gave them some money and they left. I tried to follow them but by the time I paid my bill and got out to the parking lot, they were gone."

"I bet those were the two goons who showed up at Forest Glen!" I said.

"Someone came to the loony bin looking for you?"

"Yeah, but it was OK. Brad saved me at the cottage and Pepe and the Marshall took down the guy who busted into the main building." I paused. "Sounds like the guy in the pork pie hat might know something." Then I frowned as I heard what I was saying. "Who wears a pork pie hat anymore? That's so old school."

"Mobsters," said Jimmy G. "Good guys wear fedoras."

"Whatever." I really didn't think sartorial choices could help you identify criminals. "Are you going back there?"

"Sure. Got to work on my bowling score," said Jimmy G. "But that's not why Jimmy G is glad you called. That old lady has been bugging me. Calling all morning. Every five minutes. She's freaking out."

"Mrs. Snelson?"

"Yes, you've got to call her. ASAP. Get her off Jimmy G's back."

"Will do."

"Thanks, doll."

As soon as Jimmy G hung up, I called Mrs. Snelson.

"Oh, I'm so grateful you called," Mrs. Snelson said. "I've been calling your cell phone since early this morning and I keep getting some gentleman who tells me that it is out of service and I should not call the number again. I was so worried about you, dear."

"I'm OK, Mrs. Snelson," I said. "That's a U.S. Marshall and he's helping me on another case."

"Oh, my!" she said. "Do you think he would be available to help you on my case? It's gotten much more desperate."

"What happened?"

"I woke up this morning to find that someone had entered my apartment while I was asleep and covered my bed with rose petals."

"Oh!" I said. And then added, "I could see how that might be upsetting."

"I want you and Pepe here right away!" she said. "You can help me catch this fiend." And then she added, "I'll make you a lovely hot breakfast. How do you like your eggs, dear?"

Pepe's Blog: Naming
Your Cases

I only have a short time to post an update because
we are off on another important case, the Case of the
Senior Stalker, as I think I shall name it. We have not
yet brought to a satisfactory conclusion our other two
cases: The Case of the Missing Sister and The Case of
the Deadly Decorator. I know Geri does not believe
that her friend Brad is involved in the death of his
client, but I am not convinced. Besides the alliteration in the title is quite nice.

Geri seems to have forgotten all about Amber and
Party Girl, or rather she believes the U.S. Marshalls
and the FBI and the Bellevue police can do a better
job than Sullivan and Sullivan. I beg to differ, but
when I brought this up in the car on the way home,
she told me that since she no longer has her cell
phone, the kidnappers will no longer contact her
and there's nothing we can do about it. I objected to
this as well, and pointed out that we had assigned

Jimmy G to do some surveillance. She muttered something about a pork pie hat, which I don't understand because why would anyone put a nice pork pie into a hat.

I was researching this question when Geri told me that Mrs. Snelson needed us. And she was prepared to make us breakfast. I suppose it does make sense to get fortified before tackling anything too demanding. And some nice crispy bacon would do the trick.

Chapter 22

I called Jay right before we left for Mrs. Snelson's. He was pretty upset when I described my encounter with Brad at Forest Glen. I promised to drive over and give him a more complete update after we were done with Mrs. Snelson. And breakfast. I didn't think it would take longer than an hour.

It had rained during the night and the streets were still wet. But the sun was just poking through the clouds when we arrived at the Gladstone. I parked in almost the same spot I had parked in when we first visited Mrs. Snelson. Bruiser was still chained to the tree in the front yard. He lay in the mud, his massive chin resting on his two front paws, staring rather listlessly at Pepe.

"Don't even think about it," I said to Pepe as we walked by. Pepe has a tendency to bark and growl at bigger dogs. I wasn't sure how Bruiser would react.

"You tell me not to think about the canine prisoner? A poor beast who is confined simply because of his exuberant nature? You ask me not to care about a fellow creature who is—" Pepe was about to launch into a much longer speech when I cut him off

"I thought you didn't like Bruiser," I said.

The big dog lifted his head hopefully at the sound of his name. I could see the bones under the hide of brown and grey. He was definitely a lot skinnier than the last time we had seen him.

"My heart aches for any animal in captivity," Pepe replied. "Have I ever told you about the time that I freed all the animals in the traveling Mexican circus owned by the Amigo Brothers?"

"No, you have not," I said sharply. "And I don't believe for a moment that you did that."

"*Si*," said Pepe. "A mangy lion, two elephants, and a bear who knew how to juggle. I wonder where they are now. The last time I saw them they were heading for the Pacific coast." His voice sounded melancholic. "I wonder if they made it."

"I am sure you were their hero," I said, thinking it never hurts to appreciate good deeds.

"Yes, as I will be for this poor beast," said Pepe. He turned and trotted up the path towards the front door of the run-down house. I shuddered as he passed right under the nose of the big dog, but Bruiser was so dispirited he didn't even snarl or snap. In fact, he staggered to his feet and looked at Pepe with something like admiration as Pepe mounted the sagging front steps of the old wooden house.

"Come back here!" I commanded. Of course, Pepe did not obey me. Instead he scratched on the screen door.

"OK, I'm coming after you," I said, dashing up the front walk and hoping to snatch up my dog before he could cause any more trouble.

But I was too late. Just as I got to the top step, the wooden front door swung open. The smell of marijuana came wafting out. Through the rusted scrim of the screen, I could see a young woman with long dark hair streaked with purple. It was parted in the middle and hanging down, almost obscuring her pale face. She had a nose ring in her nose and her eyes were pink around the rims, as if she had been crying, but perhaps it was just from what she was smoking. She wore a long black dress with a corset bodice that she probably bought at Hot Topic and she had tattoos of snakes and roses coiling up both arms.

"What do you want?" she said, licking her lips, which were cracked.

"Hi, I'm Geri Sullivan," I said. "I was just visiting someone across the street and noticed your dog."

"He's not my dog," she said. She didn't bother to give me her name.

"Whose dog is he?"

"My boyfriend Casey. It's his dog."

"OK," I said, snatching up Pepe, "but will you tell your boyfriend that he shouldn't keep his dog chained up like that?"

"He should be inside," said Pepe. "And he needs more food. Crispy bacon would be good."

"Sure next time I talk to him," she said in a pinched voice. "But I don't expect that will be any time soon. He dumped me to run off with some other chick a month ago and I haven't heard from him since."

"And he left his dog behind?" Pepe asked, shocked.

"Are you having trouble taking care of the dog?" I asked.

She shrugged. "I can't do anything with him. He

pulls too much for me to walk him. And if I let him loose, then those old biddies across the street complain and then the animal control comes and picks him up and puts him in the pound and I have to pay to get him out." She paused. "But come to think of it, that might be a good idea. I can't take care of him."

"No, she cannot send him to *perro* prison!" said Pepe.

"Would you like someone to help you with the dog?" I asked.

"What do you mean?"

"Well, my boyfriend is a dog trainer. He could teach you how to handle him so he doesn't pull when you try to walk him. In fact, he's working on a reality TV show. They're looking for people who are having trouble with their dogs."

"Really, you mean I could be on TV?" Her face brightened for the first time.

"It's possible," I said.

"I bet they pay really well."

"Probably," I agreed.

"Well, that would be awesome," she said. For the first time, I could see how young she was. Maybe nineteen or twenty. "Give him my number," she said. She started rattling off a string of numbers which reminded me I still didn't have my cell phone back. I had to dig around in my purse to find a piece of paper and a pen. Turns out her name was Holly.

"They're looking for someone to film right away," I said.

"Hey, I'm not doing anything else," she said, turning away. I got the impression she was going to run inside and start cleaning up.

"That was a brilliant idea, Geri!" said Pepe, as we were walking down the steps.

"Why, thank you!" I said, with surprise. My dog hardly ever praises me.

Bruiser whined softly as we went by.

"Do not fear," Pepe said to him. "Your time in chains will soon be over." As we headed across the street, he turned to me. "Bruiser says that Mrs Snelson has been feeding him crispy bacon. I hope she saves some for me."

"I smell biscuits!" said Pepe, when Mrs. Snelson pulled open her sliding glass door to admit us. He followed his nose into her kitchen and up to the small, harvest-gold-colored oven.

Mrs. Snelson smiled. "He must smell the biscuits I'm baking," she told me. She patted Pepe on the head. "Just be patient, pup."

"Where fresh-baked biscuits are concerned," Pepe said, "I am patience itself!"

She turned to me. "It's almost like he answered me, isn't it?"

"Sure is," I said, thinking about how Mrs. Snelson hated Pepe when we met her on our first case, but now she thought the world of him. People could change.

She took a can of Pam out of the cupboard. "So, how do you like your eggs?" she asked, picking up a cast iron pan from the stove and spraying Pam into it.

"Don't you want to show me the latest disturbance first?"

Still holding the heavy pan, Mrs. Snelson said, "I'd like to brain whoever did it with this!" She shook it in the air. "I was very upset when I first saw it, but now that you're here, I feel much better." She took a carton of eggs out of her small refrigerator. "You go in and take a look while I get breakfast ready. My father always said that once you're properly fortified, no obstacle is too great. Remind me of how you like your eggs, dear?"

"Over easy," I said. "But my dog likes his scrambled."

"And I like my bacon extra crispy," said Pepe.

"Pepe likes bacon too," I said.

"Great," she replied. "I make mine extra crispy."

"That's the way Pepe likes it," I told her.

"Dog after my own heart," she told me. "Crispy is the best."

Pepe and I headed into the bedroom. The bed was indeed covered with rose petals. They were strewn across it, red and yellow and pink petals, hundreds of them. Must have taken several armfuls of roses. They actually looked very pretty against the green comforter on the bed.

I love roses. If I came home and Felix had done this for me, I think I would have quite liked it, especially if he was lying among them wearing only rose petals.

"And, look, Geri!" Pepe said. "Our trick with the flour worked. Do you see the footprints?"

Indeed, I did. They came into the room and danced all around the bed, overlapping each other so much it was hard to see a distinct print, especially since the carpet was beige and the flour was whole wheat.

We followed the trail back out to the front door. I

opened it and looked out. The footsteps were much more distinct on the dark blue carpet in the hallway. They led away to the right.

"Breakfast's ready!" Mrs. Snelson hollered.

Pepe didn't have to be told twice. He raced toward the kitchen. I brought up the rear.

"Yum!" he said, looking at the small white china plate on the floor. Mrs. Snelson had centered the dish on a floral place mat and provided a matching china teacup full of water. Pepe's plate held a crumbled biscuit, a pile of scrambled eggs, and four strips of crisp bacon cut into small pieces.

Mrs. Snelson was pouring a cup of coffee from her percolator into a mug with her name on it. That is, if her name was Gladys.

Pepe started crunching on the bacon and Mrs. Snelson waved me to a seat.

"I think we should follow the flour footprints first," I said. "We should see where they lead before they disappear!"

"I suppose you're right," she said mournfully, looking at the food on her plate.

"It will only take a minute," I said, hoping that was true.

"A real detective would eat first," said Pepe. It came out a little mumbly because his mouth was full of biscuit.

"I don't know if that's true," I said.

"It could indeed take a good deal longer," said Mrs. Snelson, "but one must strike while the iron is hot. That's what Gumshoe would say."

"Gumshoe?"

"He's the president of our mystery book group,"

said Mrs. Snelson. "He fancies himself a bit of a detective."

"Well, why didn't you call him?" I asked, confused. "If you have a detective right here in the building."

"He's strictly an amateur," said Mrs. Snelson. "Not like you two. Besides," she blushed, "it would be embarrassing to admit the circumstances. And if he figured out who it was, well, he'd have a grudge against that person, and that wouldn't do. We all have to live together. No, I want to take care of this on my own!" She set down her coffee mug and picked up a rolling pin instead.

"Then let's go!" I said.

"Because we are the real detectives," said Pepe, now happy to leave his food, although I noted he had polished off most of his bacon.

Pepe led the way to the front door. I opened it for him and we all tiptoed out into the hall.

"I wish we had some of those booties they wear in the crime shows," said Mrs. Snelson with relish. "Then we could be sure not to contaminate the evidence."

The shoe prints were actually pretty clear out in the hallway. One set, leading away to the right. A rather big shoe size, perhaps a ten or a twelve.

"Looks like a man's ten," said Mrs. Snelson, bending over and inspecting one of the prints.

Pepe sniffed the flour, then sneezed, and said, "It is all-purpose, whole wheat flour, General Mills to be specific."

"How do you know that?" I asked him.

"I know my flour," Pepe said.

"My husband wore a similar size," Mrs. Snelson said.

"Really!" I said.

"Yes, I worked for a baker in Guadalajara," Pepe told me. "He made the best *empanadas* in town. He baked, and I was on rat patrol."

"You're kidding?" Here was yet another of his outrageous stories.

"I do not jest. It was serious business. I was so good at my job, they called me *El Supremo!*"

"Why would I joke about my husband's shoe size?" Mrs. Snelson asked, confused.

"I guess you wouldn't joke about that," I said.

"Certainly not," said Pepe. "The baker, Roberto, he was also a Nacho Libre wrestler. He was known as Doctor *Muerte*. While he wrestled by night, I wrestled the rats. I vanquished untold numbers in my bouts! We had the most rodent free bakery in Guadalajara."

Pepe charged down the hall, keeping to the side of the footprints. Mrs. Snelson followed him, the rolling pin in her hand. I followed behind her. The footprints led to an elevator at the end of the hall.

"That's the service elevator," Mrs. Snelson told me. "Pretty sneaky," she added. "The culprit evidently didn't want to be seen taking the main elevators at the other end of the hall."

We got in and pushed the button for the second floor. Pepe asked me to hold him. He's not a big fan of elevators.

When the doors opened on the next floor, we were lucky—there were a few clear footprints in front of the elevator so we knew we were on the right floor—

but the footprints became fainter and disappeared altogether about halfway down the hall.

"Do you know who lives in this hallway?" I asked Mrs. Snelson.

"Well, yes," she said. "Louise is down at that end, and Edna has the door with the wreath of autumn leaves. She's very crafty." She turned a little pink. "But it's unlikely to be either of them. Not that I have anything against that lifestyle. We all think that Alma and Grace on the third floor are a couple, if you know what I mean."

"What about the men?" I asked, glad to know Mrs. Snelson was so open-minded but eager to get back to my cooling breakfast.

"Three," said Mrs. Snelson with a frown. "Frank down there on the left, and Jim—he must be in 214, and then there's Mort!" Her voice fell when she said his name.

"What's wrong with Mort?" I asked.

"He's a creep," said Mrs. Snelson. "Always lurking around, eavesdropping, and making lascivious comments to all the women."

"That sounds like the sort of person we're looking for," I said. I turned to Pepe, who was zig-zagging back and forth, his nose to the carpet. "Can you tell which apartment the feet entered?" I asked him.

"*Sí!*" he said, with great delight. "This one!" And he stood and scratched on door 217.

"Well, we've found your secret admirer," I said to Mrs. Snelson. I pounded on the apartment door. "We'll just tell him to leave you alone."

"Oh, no!" she said, covering her lips with her hand. "That can't be right!"

"We take a stand against harassment of innocent

old ladies who make excellent biscuits," said Pepe, scratching at the door.

"No, please, it can't be—" said Mrs. Snelson.

"I'm coming, I'm coming. Hold your damned horses," said a voice from behind the door.

And then Door 217 swung open. Behind it was a man sitting in a wheelchair. An older man with a greasy comb-over of dark hair, dark bushy eyebrows, and saggy jowls. His skin was pasty and his lips a rubbery red.

"What's this about?" he asked with a frown.

"Oh, I'm so sorry, Mort," said Mrs. Snelson, hiding her rolling pin behind her back. "There's been a terrible mistake." She turned to me. "You can see that he couldn't possibly have made the footprints!"

"But Geri, the bottoms of his shoes are covered with flour!" said Pepe. He was sniffing as well as he could at the soles of Mort's feet, twisting around to get under the metal footrests of the wheelchair.

Mort kicked out at Pepe with one foot. "Get that dog away from me! Nasty little creatures. My ex-wife had one! Best day in my life when I got rid of both of them!"

"How did you get flour on the soles of your shoes?" I asked. I don't like people who don't like my dog.

"I don't have to explain anything to you," snapped Mort.

"We're tracking down a fiendish criminal," said Pepe.

"Those aren't your shoes, are they?" I asked.

Mort flushed brick red.

"So what if they aren't?"

"We're tracking down someone who committed a crime in those shoes," I said.

"Oh, really?" Mort licked his lips. "What kind of crime? Maybe a little public indecency?" He waggled his eyebrows. "I would like to get publicly indecent with you, Gladys!"

Mrs. Snelson moaned and turned away.

Doors opened down the hall. A woman with henna-dyed hair stuck her head out of one. A man out of another. "What's going on?" the woman asked. "Do you need any help?" the man asked.

"Nothing to worry about, Louise," said Mrs. Snelson. "Thanks for the offer, Frank, but my detectives have everything under control."

"Detectives?" That was Mort. "They don't look like detectives."

"Where did you get those shoes?" I repeated.

Mort crossed his arms across his chest. "Not telling."

"Fine, we'll call the police," I said, turning away.

"OK, OK, not so fast," Mort said, wheeling out into the hall. "I found them in the hall this morning. Looked like my size so I picked 'em up. Nothing wrong with that, is there?"

"Of course not," said Mrs. Snelson to Mort.

"Do you need help?" the man asked, coming out into the hall. "I do a little detecting myself." He looked to be somewhere in his seventies. He had a full head of white hair, was trim for his age, and wore a brown Mr. Rogers-type cardigan sweater.

"It's OK, Frank," she said, turning away and heading down the hall. "Just a misunderstanding."

"Geri," said Pepe. "I smell roses."

"Wait a minute," I called out to her. "I think we need some help from this gentleman."

He gave us a little bow. "Gumshoe Phillips, at your command," he said.

Mrs. Snelson paused. "These are my detectives," she said. "I hired them to find out who was bothering me."

"Bothering you?" The man seemed shocked.

"Yes, someone has been leaving me gnomes, and chocolate, and roses."

"Oh ho!" said Mort. "Someone has a secret admirer!"

"I wish you had come to me," said Gumshoe. "I could have helped you figure it out."

Pepe was sniffing around the bottoms of his pant legs. "¡Mire usted!" he said. "There is flour on the bottoms of his pant legs."

"Are you the secret admirer?" I asked.

Gumshoe's face turned as bright red as the red roses and without saying another word, he went scuttling back into his apartment.

"Gladys and Gumshoe sitting in a tree!" said Mort, chortling.

"Breathe a word of this to anyone," said Mrs Snelson, turning on Mort, her face as pink as the pink roses, "and I'll hit you over the head with this." She took the rolling pin out from behind her back and waved it at him.

He back-pedaled into his apartment and slammed the door.

"Well, that was a nice surprise!" said Mrs. Snelson happily, practically singing as she poured some hot coffee from the percolator into my mug. She had polished off her eggs and biscuits quickly.

"You're not upset?" I asked. "You were ready to brain the person with a frying pan!"

"That was before I realized it was Gumshoe," she said cheerfully.

"Don't you think it's creepy that he sneaked into your apartment while you were sleeping?" I asked.

"It makes sense now that I know it's Gumshoe," she said. "He's so shy. He can barely bring himself to talk to any of the ladies. Not like those other lechers."

"Like Mort."

"Like Mort," she said.

"The Secret of the Sneaky Stalker is solved," said Pepe. "Now on to the Case of the Deadly Decorator."

"Surely you're not talking about Brad?" I asked him.

Mrs. Snelson just looked confused.

"I like the alliteration," Pepe said.

"It sounds like a Nancy Drew novel," I said.

"Those were a little after my time," said Mrs. Snelson. "I liked the Blythe Girl series. They solved mysteries but not ones with dead bodies."

"Well, unfortunately this one does have a dead body," I said, drying my hands on the ruffled dish towel that hung from the sink.

"Well, I appreciate your taking the time for my little problem," said Mrs. Snelson. "Tell your boss to send me an invoice."

Most likely I would be sending the invoice, but I didn't tell her that.

As we went out through the sliding glass door, I paused and looked across the street at the little run-down house and Bruiser who was still lying in the mud.

"I hear you've been feeding bacon to Bruiser," I said.

Mrs. Snelson blushed. "I feel so sorry for him. It's just not right, the way he's neglected."

"Ah, Bruiser has an *amiga*," said Pepe.

"Have you thought of calling the animal control?" I asked.

"No!" said Pepe. "You cannot send him to *perro* prison!"

"It seems like a cruel thing to do," said Mrs. Snelson. "A dog like him. Well, he probably won't be adopted. There are so many of them in the shelters." She was referring to the fact that Bruiser looked like a pit bull and people are reluctant to adopt them because of their reputation for violence.

"I wish I could do more for him," she said, gazing across the street. I told her I had a plan and asked her if I could use her phone to call Felix. He answered right away and said he would pass the information along to Rebecca who was still searching for just the right dog.

Pepe's Blog:
The Linguistic Detective,
C'est Moi!

Obviously I did not like to leave without giving Bruiser some hope, so I promised him that we would be back and bring reinforcements. Geri chided me for barking at him. Despite the fact that I have learned to communicate in Spanish and English and French, she has only a few words of Canine.

I tried to explain this to her as we drove off but she seemed distracted. In fact, she told me to be quiet. She couldn't think with me jabbering away. First of all, I do not jabber. It is gauche. Second, I will be quiet. But I do not think she will like that.

Chapter 23

Jay was a total mess when we arrived at his house on Queen Anne. I've never seen him so agitated. He didn't even invite us in, just stood there in the hallway, flapping his hands, looking like one of his birds with clipped wings.

"Oh, Geri!" he said, "I would offer you something to eat but I can't!" He looked down at the peacock blue vest he was wearing over a pale green shirt. "Do I look all right? I just don't know what's appropriate for a jail visit!" He shuddered.

"Brad's in jail?"

"Well, actually, I don't know where he is. The person I spoke to at Forest Glen told me to call the Bellevue police. And they won't release any information. My lawyer says this is a typical stalling tactic."

"*Si*," said Pepe. "It is a game the *policia* like to play. They isolate the prisoner to obtain a confession."

"It's good you have a lawyer," I said, wishing I had someone I could consult with about this case.

"Well, strictly speaking he's not my lawyer," said Jay. "I called my lawyer and he referred me to his partner—." He saw my look and clarified. "A partner in his firm who can take Brad's case. It wouldn't do for Graham to represent both of us." He faltered to a stop. "Just in case."

"Just in case Brad is guilty," I said. "Surely you don't believe that."

"I don't know what to believe," said Jay, tears appearing in his eyes.

"We'll clear his name!" I said firmly, giving Jay an impulsive hug. He suffered my embrace stiffly, dabbing at his eyes with a silk handkerchief he pulled out of his vest pocket as soon as I let him go.

"I need more information about Mrs. Fairchild," I said. "Did he ever talk to you about her?"

Jay shook his head impatiently as he grabbed his car keys off a silver tray in the hallway.

"The dragon lady?" I followed him out and watched as he locked the front door.

"Oh, the dragon lady! Yes he complained about her all the time. She had no taste. She was totally stubborn. She was always asking for a discount. I totally understood. I have catering clients like that too. I told him not to back down, to use his best judgment, and never offer her a discount." Jay stopped. "I also told him that in some cases it's better to cut your losses than to keep on pursuing a client who's so difficult." He moaned. "If only he had taken my advice."

"Maybe he did," I said, following him to the driveway. His car, a shiny black Lexus, beeped as we approached.

"It seems clear he went over there to ask her for money," Jay said. "At least that's how the police made it sound."

"It also sounded like he was standing in line with

a lot of other contractors," I said. "Do you know who else was working there?"

Jay shook his head. "Brad never mentioned any names." He looked thoughtful for a moment. "I do know he sometimes hired other people to help him with tasks he didn't enjoy."

"Is there any paperwork here?" I asked.

"He kept everything at the shop." Jay pulled open the driver's door.

"The shop!" That reminded me about the rent. "Have you heard from the landlord?"

Jay shook his head. "No. Do you think they've started eviction proceedings?"

"I don't know," I said. "And anyway," I shrugged, "I don't have enough money to catch up on the rent. The landlord told me Brad owes $12,000."

Jay looked troubled. He wedged himself into the driver's seat and put the keys in the ignition, but he didn't turn the car on.

"What is it?"

"Brad asked me for the money," he said in a low voice, "the day before he disappeared. I reminded him that I loaned him the money to set up his business but he was on his own to keep it going. That was our agreement." He looked straight ahead as if the scene was playing out on the other side of the windshield. "We had a terrible fight. He stormed out of the house." Jay gripped the steering wheel so tightly that his knuckles went white. "If only I had given it to him, none of this would have happened."

"He is right," said Pepe.

"You don't know that!" I said.

"Now I will most likely spend that much getting him out of this mess," said Jay grimly, reaching for the key and turning on the car. "But it will be worth it to have my sweet Pooky Bear back home with me."

"Pooky Bear!" said Pepe. "I have never understood pet names."

Pepe and I watched the Lexus back out of the driveway and speed down the street after I made Jay promise to call me and leave a message on my home phone as soon as he knew anything.

"We've got to go to the shop," I said.

"Or canvas the neighborhood," Pepe suggested.

So we did both.

As soon as we entered, it was obvious someone had been in the shop. Nothing was in its right place. The owl was no longer on top of the grandfather clock but was sitting in an armchair near the door. Pepe startled when he saw it and went running under a sofa.

"Scared of a dead owl?" I teased him.

He came out shaking. "I am a victim of my instincts," he said. "An owl like that could carry off a little dog like me in its cruel claws."

"Like the hawk!" I said, pointing up at the bird that soared above us, suspended from the ceiling by white cord.

"Do not remind me," he said. "I once was carried off in the claws of a Mama Hawk who intended to feed me to her babies, but when she sailed out over the ocean, angling toward her nest on a nearby cliff, I managed to escape from her grip. And dropped into the water and was able to swim to safety."

"I don't believe that for a minute, Pepe," I said. I know how much he hates water.

"It is true," he said. "I was lucky enough to land in a school of dolphins and they shepherded me back to shore. Dolphins are very intelligent, you know. I learned a few words in their language. . . ."

"Right," I said. "For instance?"

"'Argerpolowarranfeel,'" said Pepe. It was sort of a watery grumble.

"What does that mean?" I asked.

"It means 'What a brave dog!' in Dolphin," said Pepe with great satisfaction.

I set the owl back up on the grandfather clock, then looked around. The sofas and chairs had all been moved and were cluttering up what was usually a passageway to the front.

"Someone's been here!" I said.

"*Si*, it was *la policia*," said Pepe, sniffing around. "I can smell that unpleasant man who likes to make jokes about me."

"That means they must have gotten a search warrant," I said. I pushed my way through the clutter of furniture towards the front room.

"Most likely," agreed Pepe.

I pushed aside the heavy velvet drapes that shielded the mess in the back room from the front space that Brad uses to entertain clients. He keeps his papers in a file cabinet behind a tall, trifold, Japanese screen, its paper panels painted with graceful bamboo fronds.

The file cabinet itself was gun-metal gray. The four-drawer vertical cabinet had a couple dents in the metal and looked like it had come from the Boeing Surplus store. No wonder Brad hid it behind the screen.

It was clear that the police had also gone through

the file cabinet. The drawers had been left open and most of them were empty except for a few fabric swatches and drapery catalogs.

I did find some envelopes on the floor that had been slipped through the mail slot. Each was addressed to Mrs Fairchild. She had written on them with a red pen "Return to Sender" and "No Longer at this Address." A clever way to avoid payment but not too convincing because the address was the very address where Brad was working. I picked them up and put them on the desk, which had also been cleared of its usual jumble of papers.

I looked around for Pepe who had been unusually silent. I finally found him in the back of the shop, utterly still, his gaze fixed on a tall wooden armoire, his tail absolutely stiff and horizontal, one front paw tucked backwards, his whole body leaning forward. He looked exactly like a bird dog on point.

"What is it, Pepe?" I asked.

"Is it not obvious?" he asked. "I am pointing."

"But you are not a bird dog!"

"I beg to differ. Have you forgotten that I was on that infamous bird hunt on that ranch in Texas with the Vice President of the United States? He may not have pointed his shotgun at the correct target, but I most certainly pointed out the right target to him!"

"Pepe, you know I don't believe that story. You are not old enough to have been alive when Dick Cheney shot his friend in the face."

"Well, believe this!" he said. "There is a clue in that *armario*."

I looked at it nervously. "Is there a dead body in there?"

"*Si, el cadáver*," said Pepe.

I shuddered. "Whose dead body?" I asked.

"Why do you think I am pointing like a bird dog?"

"A dead bird?"

Pepe gave a stiff little nod, never breaking his stance for one minute.

I approached the cupboard cautiously and threw open one of the doors. Inside was a stuffed pheasant. He was sitting on a little piece of wood, with a stuffed mouse at his feet. His yellow eye was staring straight at me.

"How is this a clue, Pepe?" I asked.

He sighed and sat down. "This is the last thing Brad touched. He hid it in this *armario* before he went out the last day he was here."

"Well, I don't see how this helps us," I said.

"It is not accurate," said Pepe, who had relaxed his posture and was studying the tableau critically. "Pheasants do not eat mice."

"Really? I didn't know that."

"*Sí*. They are vegetarians, like you, Geri. Although they will eat insects. I have never seen you do that."

I shuddered again. "No and you never will."

"You might be surprised," said Pepe. "Such a morsel would be most delicious to a hungry Chihuahua crossing the Sonoran desert." He actually licked his lips.

"I guess we have struck out here!" I said. "The police got any evidence that could have helped us."

Pepe's Blog: Birds Are Distracting

I am never happier than when I can illuminate the principles of private detection for my partner, or for you, my faithful readers. When you are looking for clues, there is nothing that is not significant. And I sensed that there was something in the shop that was *muy importante.*

Unfortunately, sometimes it takes my brain a little while to catch up with my intuition. And perhaps I was distracted by all of those birds. The memory of my almost-demise at the claws of a hawk was not pleasant. Nor was the memory of my time crossing the great Sonoran desert, when I had to subsist on locusts.

No, there was something there that I was missing and I could only hope that it would make itself known.

Chapter 24

We headed back to Mrs. Fairchild's house to see if the neighbors had any ideas about who would want to kill Mrs. Fairchild. Unfortunately, it seemed every one did.

Several of the neighbors had witnessed fights between Mrs. Fairchild and her various contractors. A few had noted the names on the trucks: a plumbing company (Toilet Wizards) and a roofing company (Shelter from the Storm). According to one neighbor, a man who was clipping the box hedge along his driveway, he had witnessed a shouting match between Mrs. Fairchild and a guy he described as a "chunky Mexican dude" just days before her death.

"None of us were surprised around here," he said. "It was just a matter of when someone was going to kill her. In fact, we're talking about starting a defense fund for the guy who did it."

"So she was not popular in the neighborhood?" I asked.

He shook his head. "She had fights with the Delcantos about the property line. She actually tore down their fence, claiming it was on her property. And she hired some tree cutters to top off the big evergreen that belonged to the people who live behind her house—don't know their names, but I know there was a lawsuit involved in that."

I wanted to talk to the Delcantos but no one answered the door. I left my card in their mailbox with a note on it. I used one of the Sullivan and Sullivan Agency cards that Pepe had insisted I make back when we worked our first case. No one could tell by looking at it that my partner was a dog.

As we headed back around the block, Pepe stopped to sniff some cypress bushes planted like guardians at the end of a straight sidewalk that led up to a smaller house, unusual for the neighborhood. The mustard yellow paint was fading, and the roof was covered with shaggy moss.

"Hurry up, Pepe," I said.

"I am investigating," he said, just as the front door opened and a skinny old lady came hobbling out, waving her arms and yelling: "Get that dog away from my bushes!"

I scooped up my dog and held him in my arms as she approached. She was wearing a shabby brown cardigan and it looked like her grey, curly hair was uncombed.

"I'm sorry," I said. "He was probably just smelling another dog."

"He was going to pee on my bushes," she declared, "just like all the other idiot dogs in the neighborhood." She pointed to the base of the bushes where the leaves had turned yellow, her hand trembling.

"You have a very nice yard," I said, even though it looked rather boring to me with its straight path lined with shiny white rocks and carefully trimmed box hedges, which enclosed rose bushes—only rose bushes—some still bearing a few limp blossoms.

"Tell her we are investigators," said Pepe. "She is the sort of person who watches everything."

"My dog is actually a working dog," I told her. "We are investigating a crime that happened in your neighborhood."

"Oh, Mrs. Fairchild," she said. "Yes, the police were here asking about her too."

"What did you tell them?"

"I told them about the cars I saw in her driveway that day," she said. "A white van and a red and white MINI Cooper."

Oh dear, Brad drives a red and white MINI Cooper. The very car the police found a day later at Volunteer Park.

"Ask what order they were parked in!" said Pepe.

"What do you mean order?" I asked.

"I didn't say anything about order," she said.

"Which car was in front and which car was in back," said Pepe.

"Which car was in front?" I asked.

"Definitely the van," she said.

This was good. "Great question!" I told Pepe. That meant someone else had been in the house on the day of the murder.

"I didn't ask a question," the woman said.

"Oh, but I have one for you," I said. "Do you know who the cars belonged to?"

"Now how would I know that?"

"Well, maybe there was a sign painted on one of the cars. Or you recognized one of the drivers."

The old woman shook her head. "I never saw the

same people there twice. Except for her decorator. The guy with the little red-and-white car."

"Oh, you know Brad?"

"Was that his name?" Her mouth curved down. "He was in a hurry that day. Stormed up the front steps. Heard yelling as soon as he got inside. If he had any sense, which I don't think he did, he was probably telling her to shove it."

"You know that she was murdered?"

"Couldn't have happened to a better person," she said with a satisfied smack of her gums. "If the decorator did it, then more power to him!"

"Did you hear anything? After the yelling?"

"No, I went back inside. It was time for *Judge Judy*."

"And did you notice the cars later? After your show?"

"They were both gone the next time I looked."

So we adjourned to my house so I could use my computer to do some research. Pepe claimed he was going to help and headed for his iPad on the coffee table, but when I went into the living room to ask him a question, he was gazing dreamily at the photo of a good-looking Australian shepherd.

"A new crush?" I asked. "Don't you have enough girlfriends?'

"Her name is Kiwi," said Pepe, gazing at her image fondly. "She wrote to me because of my blog. She wishes to be a private detective as well. Perhaps she will apply for a position as my assistant."

"What blog?"

"Oh, so you never found it?"

"What do you mean?"

"Well, it is Number 2 in overall usefulness for blogs about private detectives who are dogs. Apparently some dog named Chet has beat me out and there's a bedbug-finding dog named Doodle, who's a close third. Got to keep my eye on him."

"What are you talking about?"

"I have been writing down my thoughts about our cases, hoping you would find them since I could not talk to you."

"Well, it would have helped if you had let me know about it."

Pepe just gave me a look. If he had had eyebrows to raise, he would have raised them. Instead this chiding look was communicated with narrowed eyes and a slightly lowered muzzle.

"I'll try to catch up," I said.

"*Bueno*," said Pepe. "Now tell me, Geri, what have you learned?"

"I have the contact information for five different contractors who worked for Mrs. Fairchild and for the three neighbors who filed lawsuits against her. Oh, and two of the five contractors have lawsuits pending in civil court against her. Two others, a handyman named Toby White and a painter named Eric French, won judgments against her last year and the year before. The old lady has left a trail of enemies behind her.

"So now what, Sherlock?" I asked. "We can't just call these folks and ask them if they murdered Mrs. Fairchild."

"And the weapon is not unique enough to narrow the field," said Pepe. "Almost anyone could have a hammer in their tool box."

"Can we just eliminate the people who won their cases against her?"

"Perhaps the contractors," said Pepe, "because they were probably not foolish enough to work for her again, but the neighbors, no! Who knows what new assaults upon their property she has perpetrated since?"

I plopped down on the sofa beside him.

"And if it was a neighbor, it was most likely to be that old woman who yelled at me!'" said Pepe. "Anyone who dislikes dogs is a person with a black heart."

"I've got the neighbors' names," I said, flipping through my notes.

"On the other hand," said Pepe, "if it was a neighbor, I would have most likely recognized the scent."

"What do you mean? What scent?"

"Oh, I keep forgetting you have not been reading my blog," said Pepe. "Besides Brad's scent on the body—"

"Brad's scent was on the body?"

"Oh, most definitely. How do you think he got all that blood all over him?" Pepe asked.

"I thought maybe he fell into some blackberry bushes while sunbathing at the nude beach."

Pepe frowned at me. "Oh, I see you are making a joke. This is not the appropriate occasion for joking, Geri."

"Sorry!" I said. I sometimes do that when I'm really upset as I was at the thought of Brad being present at the murder scene. "So Brad was in Mrs. Fairchild's house at the time of the murder. Can you tell if it was before or after she was killed?"

"No, but I can tell you that someone else was

present. Someone who smelled like Budweiser and Camel cigarettes."

"Oh, well that should make it easy to find them!" I said.

As usual, Pepe did not respond to my sarcasm. "Let us consider the circumstances," he said.

"It happened in the kitchen," I said. "Do you suppose that's significant?"

"*Si,* a kitchen with no aromas of food."

"She was renovating the kitchen," I said. "So it could have been someone she called in to hang cabinets or install the flooring or hook up one of the appliances."

"It smelled like fresh paint," Pepe pointed out.

"Yes, so perhaps a painter." I looked down at the list, discouraged. We still had a huge list of suspects.

"Someone who knew that Brad would be arriving at the house shortly after it happened," said Pepe.

"Yes, but who would know that?"

"A neighbor might see him come in."

"What if Brad hired someone to help him?" I asked. "Like how I work for him!" I frequently reupholstered furniture under Brad's direction. Less recently since I had been so wrapped up in the private eye business.

"I can imagine how it went down," said Pepe. "Mrs. Fairchild on the telephone with Brad, complaining about the shoddy work done by the man he hired. The man standing there, shuddering under the assault of her cruel words."

Pepe does have a tendency to purple prose. I blame it on all the *telenovelas* he watches.

"Brad rushes to meet with her and calm her down. He wants to inspect the work, which she disparages, to see for himself it is the travesty she claims. But as he is racing to the scene, the man pulls out a hammer and bashes her in the head. Brad arrives too late. She dies in his arms."

'That would explain the blood all over him when he was found later that day," I said. "But then, what happened to the murderer?"

"Two possibilities, my dear Sullivan," said Pepe. "Either the fellow had run off before Brad arrived. Or Brad took the weapon out of his shaking hand and sent him off to clean up."

"In either version," I said thoughtfully, "Brad knows who the killer is."

"*Bien hecho*!" said Pepe.

"Why wouldn't he say something?" I asked.

"Because he is not speaking," said Pepe.

"Perhaps he feels guilty," I speculated.

"Perhaps he is afraid others will think he is crazy," said Pepe.

"But they already do," I said. "Oh! You're being ironic."

"*Si*," said Pepe.

"So the next step is to talk to Brad," I said.

"If he is talking," muttered Pepe.

"We'll just have to convince him it's in his best interest to talk."

"Maybe it is not," said Pepe.

Just then the phone rang.

"Oh my God! I forgot to call Felix!" I said, rushing to pick it up. I had promised to call him as soon as I got home.

"You've got to give them what they want! Otherwise, they're going to kill me!" It was a woman's voice. She spoke in a breathy whisper.

Pepe's Blog: How to Keep Your Blog Au Courant!

You may have wondered, dear reader, how it is that I am able to keep so up to the minute on my blog posts when in the middle of such exciting events and dire circumstances. I must admit that it would be much easier if I had a smart phone, but, alas! I do not have pockets in which to carry it. Although do not mention that to Geri, who keeps trying to put me into clothes. Those are for girl dogs, not for a macho Chihuahua like me.

Instead I must type these reflections after the fact, but with the intention of convincing you that I am speaking to you poised on the very cusp of an incident. It is a technique I have learned from watching reality TV shows where the contestants always appear to be speaking about what is currently happening although they cannot possibly be stopping their frantic cupcake making or dress designing to convey their thoughts.

In this case, my careful grooming of my partner, my slow and insidious leading her to the insights necessary to solve the case of the Deadly Decorator, my training, as it were, was interrupted by a new crisis, but one in which I knew I could shine.

Chapter 25

I looked at the caller ID. It read "Amber Trout."

"Amber?"

"Yes. Who do you think it is?" She sounded irritated.

"Where are you? Is it safe to talk?"

"I'm in the bathroom. I told them I had to go. They don't know I still have my cell phone. I tucked it into my bra."

"Why me?"

"Why not?" She sounded even more irritated.

"You don't have to be so snappy!" I said. Pepe had rushed over to listen and I switched the phone so it was on speaker so he could hear.

"You would be too if you had spent the last night tied to a chair in a basement."

"What does it smell like?" asked Pepe.

I heard a little dog barking. The sharp outraged barking had an echo.

"Is that your dog?" I asked.

"Yes, Party Girl's in here with me! Thank God!"

"Did you call Jeff?"

"Yes, but he just handed his phone to the FBI. I don't want to talk to them. These guys said they'll kill me if the FBI shows up. They want your sister."

"Ask her how it smells," Pepe said again.

"What does it smell like?" I asked.

More barking on the other end

"What?"

"What does it smell like? Where you are?"

I could practically see Amber shaking her head.

"Pizza! It smells like pizza."

"Hey! Who are you talking to?" I heard a gruff male voice, muffled somewhat.

"Tell him you're talking to your dog," I said. "I do it all the time."

"I'm talking to my dog!" Amber shouted out. "She has more intelligent things to say than you!"

I had to admire her moxie. "Does she really talk to you?" I asked.

"What?"

"Ask her what sounds she hears?" said Pepe.

"Sounds?" I asked. "Anything that would help identify the place?"

"Yeah, it sounds like a bowling alley. You know the thud, the crash of the pins, some shouting."

"I think I know where you are," I said. "I think my boss is staking out the place."

"Let me talk to Party Girl!" said Pepe.

"What?"

"Hold the phone down by me!" he said.

"But—"

"Geri, it will only take a minute. I have a plan."

"Pepe has something he wants to say to your dog," I told Amber.

"What?"

"Just make sure your dog can hear him," I said.

"Geri, are you crazy? I'm holed up in a bathroom in a basement and they're going to kill me and you want your dog to talk to my dog?"

"Hey! You're taking too long in there!" I heard pounding on the door. "I'm busting down this door in ten seconds."

"Trust me!" I said.

She laughed bitterly.

I held the phone down by Pepe and he barked into the receiver. I heard some frantic barking on the other end.

"I'm coming in!" said the male voice and I heard a thud and the crack of wood. There was a thunk as the cell phone fell to the floor. I could hear a volley of fierce growling. Then silence, then a male voice shouting, "Ow! Ow! Ow! Ow! Ow!"

"Well done, Party Girl," murmured Pepe, listening intently. "Now she should go for the chair to finish him off."

I heard light footsteps, then a thunk, then a thud and a grunt. Then silence.

A few minutes later, Amber was back, picking up the cell phone.

"Oh my God!" she said. "That was amazing."

"You took down the bad guy?" I asked.

"No, Party Girl talked! I heard her talking! She told me to pick up the chair and hit the guy over the head with it." There was a moment of silence and the scrape of nails on the floor. "You are Mommy's good, good girl," said Amber, making kissing noises.

"What's up with the bad guy?" I asked, not wanting to break up the celebration but knowing every moment counted.

"It looks like he's out cold. Or maybe I killed him! Oh my God, what if I killed him?"

"You've got to get out of there," I said. "Look for an escape route."

There was some scuffling and some scraping. "Nothing here," said Amber. "No it's locked," she muttered. She got back on the phone. "All the windows are boarded up and the door to the outside is padlocked."

"Where did the guy come from?"

"Down the stairs?"

"Did you try that?"

"Umm, wouldn't there just be other guys like him up there?"

"Maybe. But if it's a bowling alley, there should be customers. You could listen at the door."

"I'll check."

I heard the creak of steps. Silence for a minute. Pepe listened intently.

"Tell her it's safe!" Pepe said.

"But how do I know?"

"I know," he said. "Tell her it's safe."

"If the door is unlocked," I said.

But it was. I told her to go ahead and the next thing I heard was a blast of sound. Jan and Dean singing about Dead Man's Curve. The clash of bowling pins being knocked down. A shout of triumph.

"Jimmy G is there somewhere," said Pepe. "I heard his voice."

"Is there a bar?' I asked.

"Yeah, looks like back in one corner. The signs say MUST BE 21 TO ENTER."

"Poke your head in. Look for a guy wearing a fedora and a really loud tie. If you see him, that's my boss, Jimmy G."

"Uh, OK." I heard more laughter, snippets of conversation, a hollered order for food, the thunk of a bowling ball rolling down a lane. Then all the sounds got quiet, except for the clink of glasses and Frank Sinatra singing about what a good year it was.

"I see him!" said Amber. "He's sitting at a booth with an old man with a pork pie hat."

"Is there anyone else with them?"

"No, just the two of them."

"Go up and tell him you're a friend of mine," I said. "Give him a fake name. Just ask him if he can give you a ride home."

Pepe's Blog: Looking
for Operatives

I am in the process of developing a new business plan. Geri has been a remarkable partner thus far. But I believe we need a new concept, something that will set us aside from your ordinary detective agency.

This is essential if you hope to open your own agency. Humans use words like brand and platform. But those are vague concepts. The trick is to look bigger than you are, bark louder than the other dogs, and make yourself memorable. Chihuahuas know this.

I'm thinking of something along the lines of Charlie's Angels. Perhaps Pepe's Pets? A cadre of good-looking operatives who can fan out across the city, sniffing for clues and marking our territory.

And if you, my good reader, happen to be an attractive female dog looking for a chance to use your talents to solve crimes and make the world a safer place, free from cats and cockroaches, then leave me a comment below.

Chapter 26

"So you talked to Party Girl and she understood you?" I asked Pepe.

"*Sí.* Why would she not?"

"It sounded like you were just barking to me," I said.

"Because you do not speak Dog. Just like most dogs do not speak English. To most dogs, your language sounds like gibberish."

"How come Amber could suddenly understand Party Girl?" I asked.

"Because I told Party Girl how to say what needed to be done in English, of course," said Pepe. "Now we must turn our attention back to the matter at hand. The murder of Mrs. Fairchild."

"What if that guy in the pork pie hat recognizes Amber?" I asked. "Jimmy G thought he might be a mobster."

"Call Jimmy G," suggested Pepe.

"Yes, if only he will answer his cell phone," I said. Jimmy G hates the cell phone. He prefers the old-fashioned, rotary dial phone in his office. And, sure

enough, there was no answer on Jimmy G's cell
phone. So I called Amber's.

She answered on the first ring. "Oh, Geri!" she
said. Her voice was light and breathless. "Your boss is
such a hero."

"What happened?" I asked.

"Well, your boss said it looked like Amber needed
a drink. And so he ordered a Cosmo. And Amber was
drinking it and talking to him and the nice old man
with the pork pie hat, and the next thing you know,
that huge goon who Amber smashed over the head
with the chair came wandering in, all dazed-looking."

"Have you picked up Jimmy G's annoying habit of
talking about himself in third person?" I asked.

"Amber doesn't think it's annoying. Amber thinks
it's cute."

"Oh, please!" I said. "What happened next?"

"The goon said to the old man, 'Hey boss, this
chick just hit me over the head and her dog bit me on
the ankle.' And the guy in the pork pie hat said, 'Why
am I surrounded by idiots?' And he asked Jimmy G,
he said, 'Would you consider working for me?' And
your boss said as cool as could be, 'I only work for the
good guys.' And the guy with the pork pie hat just
shook his head and said, 'Well, if you ever reconsider, let me know.' And then they shook hands and
Jimmy G scooped Amber up and whisked Amber
away in his shiny red convertible."

"That's very touching," I said. "Are you sure you
weren't followed?"

Amber laughed again. "Not the way Jimmy G is
driving. No one could follow us. Whoa!" I could hear
tires screeching. She giggled again.

"So is he taking you home?"

"Where are you taking Amber?" I heard her ask him.

"Where ever you want, princess!" I heard Jimmy G say.

"Look, call me again when you get someplace safe," I told her. "And be sure to call Jeff and your parents and let them know you're free."

"Free! Free as a fish on a bicycle!" said Amber.

I hung up the phone and gave Pepe the gist of the conversation. "She sounds like she's high or drunk," I said.

"Freedom can do that to you," Pepe observed solemnly.

"Right. Well, it sounds like she's safe. At least as safe as anyone can be with Jimmy G."

"It is better than having her come here," said Pepe. "Especially since we must leave."

"We must leave?"

"*Si*, we must go find Brad and get him to tell us what he knows about the murder."

It was turning out to be a pretty busy Sunday considering that I had planned to stay home all day and recover from my stint at Forest Glen.

I didn't have any luck finding Brad by calling Forest Glen. The receptionist there (who was not Lacey) simply said she couldn't give out any information on their "guests." When I asked for Dr. Lieberman, I got his voice mail. The county sheriff who had jurisdiction over the rural area where Forest Glen was situated told me they didn't have anyone in their system by the name of Bradley Best. The Seattle police told me the same thing. I even called my friends, homicide detectives Sanders and Larson. To my surprise, Sanders did answer his phone.

"Funny you should call at this moment," he said. He didn't sound amused.

"Why do you say that?"

"We just got done questioning your friend, Brad."

"What did he tell you?"

"That's just it. Nothing. He's all lawyered up. Thanks to you alerting his partner. But I don't think he would talk even if he didn't have a lawyer."

"I need to talk to him," I said.

"Well, good luck with that." He hesitated for a moment. Then he said, "Hold on." I could hear a muffled conversation.

"You know that just might be something we could work out. Can you come downtown to talk to us?"

"Yes! Anything to help Brad!"

Pepe had plenty of advice for me on the trip downtown. "You know that they record all of these conversations, Geri," he said. "You cannot say anything that would implicate Brad."

"Of course I know that!" I said. "But how do you know that?"

"*The First 48*," he said. "One of my favorite shows."

"I've never heard of it."

"It is a reality TV show which follows homicide detectives as they try to solve murders. I find it instructive in my study of police procedures, but it would also be a great benefit to criminals if they watched it."

"What would they learn?"

"Never talk to the police. Ask for a lawyer right away."

"Well, apparently Brad isn't talking," I said.

"Maybe he also watches *The First 48*," said Pepe.

The Seattle Police Department headquarters were downtown in an imposing building in the area that houses all the government offices including the jail, the courthouse, and City Hall.

Unfortunately, they were adamant about not letting a dog into the building.

"But he's just a little Chihuahua," I said. I didn't dare try to claim, as I have in the past, that he's a therapy dog because I assumed the police would have some way of checking on that.

"Chihuahuas are the worst!" said the rather humorless black woman at the front desk. "You're safer around a German Shepherd or a Rottweiler."

"You can say that again!" said Pepe who was indignant. And then he growled.

"See what I mean," she said, narrowing her eyes and pointing to the sidewalk.

I didn't know what to do, but luckily as I stood there, I saw Jay exiting the building.

"Jay!" I shouted.

He seemed surprised to see me. "How did you know Brad was here?" he asked.

I told him about my phone call with Sanders. "Did you get a chance to talk to him?"

"Briefly. I just dropped off some street clothes for him. He was wearing only a bathrobe." Ah, the famous Forest Glen complimentary bathrobe. "They're holding him for questioning. But I got him a lawyer and hopefully he's not saying anything."

"You don't think he did it?"

"How would I know?" said Jay. "I don't know where he's been for the past week. And he won't tell me."

"He's not talking?"

Jay shook his head sadly. "He barely seemed to know me."

I remembered Brad's dazed look at Forest Glen.

"Probably for the best," said Pepe. "The police listen to everything you say when you are in jail."

"Do you think he would talk to me?" I asked.

Jay shrugged. "I don't know. You are his best friend." He said it grudgingly. Jay and I have never been close.

"Here!" I said, thrusting Pepe into his arms. "I can't take him inside, but I'm going to go try to talk to Brad."

"I need a drink. I'll be in there," said Jay, pointing at a bar across the street.

"Great!" said Pepe. "I am a big fan of bar food."

I went back into the police headquarters and passed through the security system without a problem. The uniformed officer at the Information Desk called the homicide unit and soon my friend Detective Sanders appeared. He was all dressed up in a black shirt with a pearlescent tie and pressed black pants that fell perfectly to the floor to reveal the pointed toes of some fancy cowboy boots. Ostrich, perhaps.

"Going some place special?" I asked, wondering why he looked so fancy on a Sunday afternoon.

"I take pride in my appearance is all," he said with a brief once over for me. OK, so I was still wearing my sweatpants and a t-shirt. That's my normal Sunday attire.

"I'm here to see my friend, Brad," I said.

"He's in a world of trouble," Sanders said. "And he's not talking to anyone."

"Perhaps that's smart," I said.

"Only if he's guilty," said Sanders. "We want to clear his name and send him home. But we can't until he tells us what he knows."

"Maybe he would talk to me," I said.

Sanders shook his head. "I doubt it, but it's worth a try. That's why I invited you to come down." He set off down a long hall and I followed. Couldn't help but admire his fine form as he loped ahead of me. But I reminded myself that I have a boyfriend. Which reminded me that I still had not called him.

Sanders turned left at another corridor and we passed a kitchen area containing a refrigerator, a table, and a vending machine. A man in a suit was on his cell phone, pacing back and forth. Just beyond that was a conference room with one glass wall, and I saw Brad sitting at a table, looking down at the table, his whole posture drooping. He was wearing a pair of tight red corduroy pants and a black t-shirt with a mesh inset. He looked like he was ready to go clubbing. It told me something about how Jay viewed Brad. Maybe that was how Brad was dressed when they first met. Which was probably back in the eighties.

I was so overjoyed to see Brad that when Sanders opened the door to the room, I rushed in and hugged him.

Brad seemed happy to see me too. Tears sprang into his eyes and he smiled at me wistfully. But he didn't say a word when I asked, "How are you?" I sat down next to him and grabbed his hand. He seemed so frail. His hand was shaking.

"Hey!" said a man at the door. It was the man in the suit I had seen pacing in the kitchen area. "Who are you?"

"Geri Sullivan," I said. "I'm Brad's friend."

"Chuck Caster," he said. "Brad's attorney. I've advised him to say nothing."

Sanders rolled his eyes. "Not that it matters since he's not saying anything anyway."

"My client is suffering from traumatic amnesia. We're going straight from here to a hospital to have him evaluated. He doesn't remember a thing about the events of the past few days," said Caster.

"But you do know who did it," I said to Brad. "You saw it happen, didn't you?"

Brad shook his head no. But I could see the fear in his eyes.

"Please stop talking to him," said the lawyer. "He's in no shape to answer questions."

"Was it someone you hired?" I asked again. "If you could give us a name, the police would go after him instead of focusing on you."

Brad opened his mouth.

"Don't say a word!" said the lawyer. He turned to Sanders. "Is he free to leave? You don't have any grounds for holding him."

"Not at the moment," admitted Sanders. "But we still need to check his alibi."

"What alibi? He's not talking."

"That's precisely my point," said Sanders. "We can't clear him until we know where he was on Tuesday afternoon when Mrs. Fairchild was killed."

"I'm so sorry," said Brad. It came out as a mumble.

We all turned around and looked at him. He looked frightened. "I am so sorry."

"Be quiet!" said the lawyer.

"Sorry about what?" said the detective.

"You were totally right," Brad said to me.

"Right about what?" I asked.

"I told you to be quiet," said the lawyer.

"About the color," he said. "It was the wrong color."

"What's he talking about?" asked Sanders.

"I don't know," I said. But then a memory stirred. "The color of the kitchen at Mrs. Fairchild's house?"

Brad nodded. "Very unflattering!" he said. "She hated it!"

"He's talking about a paint color?" asked Sanders.

"Apparently so," said the lawyer.

Pepe's Blog: Seahawks or Chihuahuas?

I had never before realized the intricacies of this game called football until the fans of our local team kindly instructed me in the strategies employed by the players during our sojourn at the Sportz Bar. The team is ineptly named the Seahawks. Since I do not believe such a creature exists, I propose to nominate myself as the team mascot. Can you imagine a team named the Seattle Chihuahuas? I can. And I think a bobblehead of me would bring in much revenue. Who would not like to have a Chihuahua guarding their car? Perhaps, if I can say this without blasphemy, more effective as a theft deterrent than a plastic statue of the Virgin Mary.

But I digress. Geri and I were on the home stretch, or should I say "in the red zone" when it came to solving the murder of Mrs. Fairchild.

Chapter 27

The police agreed to transport Brad to Harborview for evaluation and Chuck went with them to make sure the transfer was handled properly. I told Sanders I had some additional information and he ushered me into an interrogation room where I told him about the white van and my theory that the killer was someone Brad had hired to work for him.

"So all you have to do is figure out who Brad had hired to help him," I said eagerly.

"Well, thanks for that tip," said Sanders, setting down his pen. "I'm sure we'll hop right on that." He looked tired.

"Oh," I said, recognizing the sarcasm. "You've already done that."

He nodded. "And came up with a big fat zero. Brad doesn't keep very good records. We couldn't find any indication that he was working with anyone else."

I winced.

"We're still combing through the records," he said. "We haven't found his cell phone, but we can get those records. And bank statements. Those might help. We can see who he was paying." He shook his head. "Meanwhile, I suggest you stop poking your nose into this. If Brad isn't the killer, and you find the person who is, you could become a victim. And we don't want that happening, do we?"

I agreed that we didn't want that.

After talking with Sanders, I headed across the street to get my dog. The bar was noisy and crowded, filled with big screen TVs and people wearing blue-and-green Seahawks jerseys. Pepe was roaming up and down the bar begging for snacks—and getting them too. Jay sat on a bar stool with one empty seat beside him, practically right under one TV where men in blue jerseys and helmets scrambled around in the rain, clashing with and running away from men in white jerseys and white helmets.

Jay saw me coming. He looked around for Brad, then realized I was alone, and cast his eyes back down on the glass of amber liquid in front of him. Pepe came trotting down the bar dodging glasses and schooners, carrying a French fry in his mouth. He laid it down in front of Jay. I thought that was a sweet gesture, until I saw that he had placed it there so he could gnaw on it, breaking it down into small bites.

Jay asked if I wanted anything to drink and I thought that sounded like a good idea. I ordered a Cosmo in honor of Amber and her liberation. We drank silently for a while. Then the whole room erupted in screams. I startled, then saw they were all on their feet looking at the screens where I saw a lone man in a blue uniform, dodging and twisting and heading down the field, all alone, the ball grasped in his hands.

"That's a one hundred and one yard kickoff return for Leon Washington!" shouted the announcer and the whole room cheered. People were pounding each other on the back and clinking glasses. Pepe did a victory lap along the bar.

"Let's get out of here," whispered Jay. "I can't stand all this happiness when Brad is suffering." He tossed back his drink and I did the same.

After gathering up Pepe, we threaded our way through the crowd, almost as gracefully as Leon Washington. Pepe was disappointed at leaving his new friends, but I just wanted to get home.

Rain was falling as I drove home with Pepe curled on the seat beside me.

"How are we going to prove that Brad is innocent?" I asked Pepe.

"Have you considered that he might be guilty?" Pepe asked.

"How can you say that?"

"A detective must be willing to look at all the facts, even if they do not please him," said Pepe.

"Well let us assume it was not Brad, for a moment," I said.

"Then it must be the man who smells like Budweiser and Camel cigarettes," said Pepe.

"What are you talking about?"

"So you have still not read my blog? Which I wrote only for your edification?"

"Pepe, we've been busy avoiding thugs and getting out of loony bins and rescuing runaway brides. Poor Teri!" My mind went to my sister. "I hope she is safe. Anyway, what's this about Budweiser and Camels?"

"Those are the scents I smelled on the corpse of Mrs. Fairchild," said Pepe.

"So we just need to find a contractor who smells like Budweiser and Camel cigarettes," I said. "That shouldn't be too difficult."

As usual, Pepe missed my sarcasm. "Indeed!" said Pepe. "We will do a scent lineup."

"Pepe, there's no way I can get all the suspects to come in and stand in front of you. And, anyway, even if you could identify the murderer—"

"Your lack of confidence is most disturbing to me," said Pepe. "It is not if but when."

"Even when you identified the murderer," I continued, "the police could not take your word for it. Because you don't talk!"

"Rather, it is they who do not listen," declared Pepe

Back at home, I turned on my computer to do some research while Pepe went scrambling for his iPad, doubtless to write another blog entry. I decided to search for his blog and found it pretty quickly. I was shocked to find his latest entry, recruiting attractive female dogs to work with him. It sounded like he was planning to go off on his own. I couldn't believe my own dog was plotting to eliminate me.

It was a dark moment. Was it possible my best friend had killed a woman simply because she didn't like the paint color he had chosen to paint her kitchen? Was it possible that my dog was planning to replace me? Was it possible my boyfriend was falling in love with an attractive pet therapist from Laguna Beach? And was my sister about to be killed by the Gang who Couldn't Shoot Straight?

That reminded me that I had never done any searching to see if I could verify the Marshall's assertion that my sister was a key witness in a murder trial. I entered a few key words and quickly found what I was searching for. Phil Pugnetti, the ostensible head of the Pugnetti gang, was going to appear in Federal court on Tuesday (only two days away) to face conspiracy charges for a murder that happened in 1992 in one of the strip clubs he owned. The suspected trigger man who had allegedly committed the murder had been killed the following year and his murder was still unsolved. I was shocked when I read his name: Ted Lister. He was supposedly a smalltime drug dealer who worked for Pugnetti and whose girlfriend danced in one of Pugnetti's clubs. I knew that name because I knew his girlfriend. Teri had been living with Lister when she disappeared. She must have either been present when Pugnetti was instructing Lister to commit the murder or she had learned about it later from her boyfriend. Either way, she was obviously the key to putting Pugnetti away, because, as the article made clear, law enforcement had tried for years to indict him on many charges—extortion, money-laundering, and prostitution—but they had never been able to assemble enough evidence to press charges against him.

As I was heading out to the living room to share what I had learned with Pepe, and confront him about his treachery, my phone rang.

"Geri, where are you?" It was Felix.

"Where are you?" I asked, suddenly thinking I had totally missed a promised dinner or a date.

"At Rebecca's for the wrap party. We're about to watch the rushes. Are you coming?"

"Oh, sure. I can be there in fifteen minutes." All I had to do was change my clothes, rush out the door, and drive up the hill to Rebecca's grand mansion.

I found a place to park about a block away and walked back through a misting rain with Pepe, who found it necessary to leave his mark on several stone walls and tree trunks and rhododendron bushes. A huge van with the name of a lighting company on it was parked in Rebecca's driveway, along with a trailer that I assumed was used for costumes and make-up. We passed through the wrought-iron gate and between the stone lions and mounted the steps to the front door. I remembered the first time we came to Rebecca's house when the door had been open and Pepe had scampered inside to find the corpse of Rebecca's husband lying in the living room.

Now the living room was full of glamorous people in glamorous clothes: women wearing tight, sparkly dresses and high heels, men in designer suits. I was really underdressed in a simple black cocktail dress from the fifties and black tights. I wished Felix had told me it was a fancy affair. I stood on the threshold, afraid to enter, while Pepe went running off as soon as he saw the precious Pomeranian, Siren Song, who was basking on an orange velvet pillow under the baby grand piano.

Then Rebecca spotted me and came hurrying over.

"I'm so glad you're here, Geri," she said, giving me the quick air kisses she had adopted after many months in Hollywood. "Just wait until you see how well Felix did in his segment." She paused and looked

around, then spotted him in the corner, talking to
Caro. She was wearing a short magenta satin dress
which showed off her long legs. They were laughing
together. I felt a little pang in my heart. Had I lost
Felix to the glamour of the life he had left and the
beautiful women in it?

Rebecca grabbed me by the elbow and hurried me
over there.

"Felix, just look who I found!" she declared. "Caro,
this is Geri Sullivan. She's a private detective!"

"Oh, really!" said Caro. She looked surprised. "I
had no idea that's what you did. That must be so interesting."

"She's being modest," said Felix. I thought for a
moment he was referring to me and would brag
about all of the murders I had solved. But instead he
said, "Caro has had some success, as well, solving
crimes that involve animals."

I tried to smile. "I'd love to hear all about it," I said.
And so she proceeded to tell me about some woman
who had been shot in her car, leaving her famous
Siamese cats as orphans, and another client who had
been murdered in his house and it was his dogs who
alerted everyone to the identity of the murderer. I
tried to look impressed.

Where was my dog who was supposed to be helping me figure out who murdered Mrs. Fairchild? He
seemed to getting busy with Siren Song under the
piano. Maybe I should ask Miranda Skarbos to help
me figure out who killed the dragon lady. I saw the
famous pet psychic on the other side of the room,
this time dressed in a long black dress with volumi-
nous chiffon sleeves that fluttered as she waved her

arms about. Her brightly hennaed hair was gathered up in a messy bun on top of her head.

"So when you come down to visit Felix, you can always stay with me in Laguna Beach," Caro was saying, when I tuned back in. "I think you'll love it."

"What?" I looked at Felix.

"Oh!" That was Caro when she saw the expression on my face. "I didn't realize you hadn't told her yet."

"There's nothing to tell," said Felix with a dismissive wave of his hand.

"Can I have your attention?" That was Rebecca, clapping her hands in the doorway. "The media room is ready. Follow me!"

I grabbed Felix as the crowd surged towards the door. "What was Caro talking about?" I asked.

"Don't worry," said Felix. "Caro thinks I'm going to get the lead in the show, but I know the film business. There's nothing certain until you've signed the contract."

Just the thought of Felix leaving for California sent a chill through my body.

The basement had been set up like a theater. One wall was completely covered by a screen, which must have been concealed behind the red velvet curtains, which were parted and held back with gold ropes, like stage curtains. The settees and couches and armchairs had been shifted away from the wall so people could lounge on them, facing the screen. There was even a popcorn machine on the bar, and the scent of freshly popped and buttered popcorn filled the room. On a sideboard stood an array of champagne flutes full of sparkling, golden liquid. I helped myself to one of them, as did most of the guests, although several headed for the bar for more potent concoctions.

Rebecca took up a position in front of the screen and called out the names of several people she wanted to thank, including the director, and her production assistants. I took a seat on one of the settees with Felix in the middle and Caro on the other side. I looked around for my dog but couldn't see him anywhere.

As Rebecca was talking, a server came around and refilled our champagne glasses. I was surprised to see mine was already empty. I really wanted some of the buttered popcorn. I realized I hadn't eaten since breakfast at Mrs. Snelson's. I wondered if Pepe had found something to eat.

"And now, the moment we've all been waiting for!" declared Rebecca. "You'll get a chance to see all of our pet experts at work and then we'll announce who won the lead role in the show."

I felt Felix tense beside me. He grabbed my hand and squeezed it. The lights went dim. The first person to appear was Caro and to my surprise, the dog she was working with was Bruiser. I recognized the tattooed young woman who owned him. She told a sad tale of how her beloved dog had been taken away from her and put in a shelter, and all because of an interfering old lady across the street and an annoying little Chihuahua.

"Hey, that's me!" said Pepe. He jumped up onto the sofa and settled down in my lap, turning around several times before finding just the right spot.

"So you did use Bruiser!" I whispered to Felix.

"Yes, thanks to your suggestion," he said. "I knew you were worried about him when you found him chained up."

Wow! I was impressed by his thoughtfulness. He really did listen to me.

Caro patiently explained to Bruiser's owner, Holly, that no dog should be kept chained up in a yard. The inability to move and respond to perceived threats or explore interesting smells would cause any animal to go stir crazy, becoming either depressed or aggressive. Bruiser quickly responded to Caro's gentle manner and was soon lying down and sitting on command with an eagerness and aptitude that was surprising. Holly seemed to be amazed too and just kept repeating, "Wow!" over and over again.

Then it was Felix's turn. We watched as he greeted Bruiser who was once again chained to the tree. The dog clearly responded immediately to Felix's touch as Felix stroked his back and rubbed behind his ears.

I could totally relate. Holly was impressed by Felix too. She was almost as eager to please him as Bruiser was. They went out for a walk together and the dog who strained and lunged at the leash when Holly was at the other end trotted alongside Felix, matching him step for step and watching his every move.

And who wouldn't be looking at Felix? He was wearing a white t-shirt and a pair of soft jeans that fit very nicely indeed. Holly was grateful and threw her arms around Felix when he left her with instructions to take Bruiser for a walk every day, three times a day, to give him the companionship and exercise he needed.

The final episode featured Miranda Skarbos. She sat down in the mud and stared at Bruiser, who stared back at her with his big golden eyes. Miranda scratched her head, then scratched Bruiser's head.

He whined and rolled over on his back, exposing his belly.

While idly stroking him, Miranda began to speak. "The dog, he says that he is neglected. He loves his person, but she is too busy to give him the attention he needs. He seeks it from people as they walk by, but they misinterpret his barking as aggression and complain about him to the police, which makes his person mad at him. He only wants to be loved. And he says there is a woman who lives across the street who loves him. Her name starts with an *S*. She is an old lady, but she makes excellent snickerdoodles. He wants to live with her instead of with Holly."

The camera now panned to Holly who had been standing on the porch during this conversation between Miranda and Bruiser.

"Fine!" she said. "If he wants to go live with someone else, let him!" She stomped into the house and slammed the door.

The film stopped there.

"Unfortunately," said the director. "We weren't able to identify the old lady in question. The building across the street is senior housing. It's full of old ladies."

"I know who it is!" I said. "Bruiser is talking about Mrs. Snelson!"

Everyone turned around to look at me.

"You know this old lady?" Felix asked.

"Yes, she's my client," I said, sort of proud to be able to say I had a client.

"Do you think she's interested in adopting a dog?" Rebecca asked.

"I don't know," I said. "I can ask her."

"That would be great," Caro said. "We were stumped

about what to do next. Given the lack of enthusiasm shown by the owner, we were nervous about leaving the dog with her."

"It would be great if we could film her with the dog," said the director. "Then we'll have a happy ending for this episode."

"So what does this mean for the show?" I asked.

"Well, that's the wonderful news!" said Rebecca. "I wanted to have you all together when I announced it." She paused a moment to be sure all eyes were on her. "We had a hard time deciding which pet expert to feature, since all three of you were so good. So we've changed the concept."

I sensed more than saw Felix slouch in dejection. He seemed upset. It looked like maybe he wasn't going back to L.A. after all.

"We're going to call it *Pet Interventions* and set up the show so viewers can vote at the end as to which solution to the pet's problem they think is best. Audience interaction is such a key element of a successful show."

There was a buzz of excitement in the room. Felix turned to grin at me, then reached over and bumped fists with Caro, who was also smiling.

I tried to look pleased, but I was annoyed. I hated that idea. I never trust the audience to vote correctly. They always get all their friends to vote. Of course, they should all be voting for Felix. I would probably never watch the stupid show.

"Assuming we get a green light from the studio, we'll start filming in January in L.A."

"Ah! Los Angeles in January!" said Pepe, lifting

his head. "It will be paradise compared to Seattle in January."

"I happen to like Seattle in January," I told my dog. "Grey skies, lots of rain, staying inside, drinking lattes, reading books. . . ."

Caro looked confused. So did Felix. "What are you talking about, Geri?"

"Just responding to something Pepe said," I said.

"So your dog is talking to you again?" Caro asked, her eyes bright.

"Yes!" I said.

"Was that because of our advice?" Felix wanted to know.

Pepe just rolled his eyes. "I am talking because Geri no longer needs me to be silent."

"I needed you to be silent?" I asked him.

"*Sí*," he said "You had to learn to trust your own instincts the way a dog does. I believe you have finally achieved enough self-confidence to be my partner."

"You needed him to be silent?" Caro asked.

"Apparently, yes," I said. "So I could become more confident."

"You no longer need a bicycle," Pepe said.

"Or a man," I said. Felix looked at me, puzzled. But I told myself it was better for both of us. He didn't need me. He was moving on.

Pepe's Blog: The Value of Sidekicks

Geri seems to have forgotten that we have not yet solved the case of the Disappearing Decorator. That is, we did find the missing decorator, but we still do not know who killed the old lady. And despite the bewitching aroma of the luscious Siren Song, I knew there was a clue to be found in the Tyler mansion. I had caught a faint whiff several times of a familiar scent.

Everyone was busy celebrating the announcement of a new reality TV show, which, I might add, was something worth celebrating as it meant the bothersome Felix would soon be leaving our vicinity, allowing Geri to spend more time with me. But I enlisted the help of Siren Song and Fuzzy, testing out my new theory that a detective dog could be more effective with sidekicks, and we prowled through the mansion, sniffing for clues. I instructed them to snuffle out the scents of Budweiser and Camel cigarettes, but Siren Song claimed to have never smelled Budweiser. Try to describe the scent of human pores off-gassing Budweiser. I will give a reward to the reader who comes up with the best description.

I tried my best and we did finally locate the scent— it was Fuzzy who found it—in a closet off the main hallway. I asked Geri to get Rebecca to open it so I could examine it more closely. She was reluctant to do so, claiming that Rebecca would think she was crazy if she said her dog found a clue there. I said that she could take credit for my discovery. Generous of me, no?

Chapter 28

Rebecca called for another round of champagne and everyone (except Felix who asked for a glass of Perrier) toasted the success of *Pet Interventions*. Among that happy crowd of people who were looking forward to fame and fortune, I was perhaps the only person who wasn't elated.

Felix was making the rounds, thanking the cameramen for their work, chatting with the director. His eyes were shining and he seemed happy.

I drifted around the room, feeling about as useless as a bicycle in a school of fishes. Pepe had disappeared, probably off chasing Siren Song. When he finally reappeared, Siren Song was at his heels, along with Felix's little dog, Fuzzy.

"Geri! Geri!" Pepe was practically squeaking with excitement. "I found a clue!"

"Great!" I mumbled. "What is it?"

Fuzzy gave a series of sharp barks. I could almost imagine she was scolding Pepe.

"OK, OK, Fuzzy was the one who found the clue!"

said Pepe."But it is *muy importante*. You must get Rebecca to open up a hall closet."

"Why would I do that?" I asked.

"Because there is a clue as to the perpetrator in there," said Pepe.

"Perpetrator of what?"

"Of the murder of Mrs. Fairchild."

"Why would that be here?" I asked. And then remembered that Brad had worked for Rebecca. "Brad?" I asked with a gasp.

"Not Brad!" said Pepe. I could swear he sounded cross. "Although his scent is in the closet as well, but so is the faint scent of Budweiser and Camel cigarettes."

The dogs accompanied me as I set down my glass and went in search of Rebecca. She was deep in conversation with one of the production assistants, but I waited patiently, offering my congratulations to both of them, until the P.A. drifted off and Rebecca turned to me.

"I suppose you'll be coming down to L.A. with Felix!" she said gaily. "That will be great. Siren Song and Pepe can have play dates."

"I don't know," I said, glancing over at Felix. I always knew where he was in a room, just like Pepe always knows where I am. "I'm pretty happy with my life in Seattle."

Rebecca glanced at Felix too. "I wouldn't leave a man that good-looking alone in L.A., but it's up to you."

"Maybe he'll commute," I said.

"We'll be shooting for six weeks straight, twelve hours a day," Rebecca said. "That's how it's done with these shows. And, you know, once he's down there, I'm sure he'll get other offers. He's very talented."

I had to agree, but I had another agenda. "Rebecca, I need to ask you to open your hall closet for me."

"What? Did you leave a coat there? I can get Luis to fetch it for you."

"No, it's just that Pepe found a clue there."

Rebecca looked at me like I was completely crazy.

"I mean, yes, I did put my coat there," I stammered, "and I need to leave to go pursue a clue in a case I'm working on."

"What about Felix?" Rebecca asked, glancing over at him. But he was totally absorbed in the conversation he was having with the director. Caro had joined them.

"I'll catch up with him later," I said.

"Which closet?" Rebecca asked.

"Oh, yes, which closet?" I asked Pepe.

"The one closest to the back door on this level," Pepe said. He trotted ahead of us and stood in front of the door. Siren Song and Fuzzy flanked his sides.

"Well, it's not locked," said Rebecca, looking even more puzzled. She pulled the door open to reveal a utility closet filled with several brooms and a mop in a bucket. A paint can sat on the top shelf.

"Up there!" said Pepe. "That paint can on the left!"

"Can I see one of the paint cans?" I asked.

Rebecca practically rolled her eyes, but she took hold of the paint can I pointed out and held it up by its wire handle.

"That's it! That's it!" said Pepe, jumping up and down with excitement. "It smells like Budweiser and Camel cigarettes."

I looked at the paint can. It had clearly been

opened. A faint splash of lemon yellow paint showed on the edges of the lid and had dripped down over the label. But it did not obscure the name of the paint: "Citrus Circus."

"Is this yours?" I asked. It didn't seem like a color that Rebecca would want in her home.

"No, Brad left it the last time he was here," she said.

"But Brad doesn't drink Budweiser or smoke Camel cigarettes!" I said.

"What are you talking about?"

Good question. What was I talking about? I was trusting my dog with his preposterous theories of scent detection.

"Maybe Brad got it from someone else," Pepe suggested.

"Did Brad get this from someone else?" I asked.

"How would I know that?" Rebecca asked. "Do you want it?" She thrust the paint can at me. "I thought you were looking for your coat."

"I guess I put it in another closet," I said, holding the paint can. The handle cut into my fingers. I felt like an idiot.

"Take it, Geri! It is evidence!" declared Pepe.

"In that case, I should not move it from the scene," I told him.

"I think Brad meant to take it with him," Rebecca said, shutting the door. "But he was distracted by that phone call and left it behind. So I put it away in the closet."

"What phone call?"

"I don't know who it was, but the guy was furious with Brad. I could tell it was a man because his voice was so loud."

Rebecca was on her way back to the media room. I followed, with the dogs trotting behind me.

"Could you hear what they were talking about?"

"Well, yes, the other guy said that he wanted to get paid and if Brad wasn't going to pay him for his work, he was damn well going to get it from the old lady."

"And what did Brad say?"

"Brad just tried to calm him down. You know, I had just paid him and he had a lot of cash in his pocket so he told the guy not to bother Mrs. Whatever—and he would be right over and make sure the guy got paid. Then he just ran off and left the paint can in the hall so I put it away."

"Could it have been Mrs. Fairchild?"

"Who was calling him?" Rebecca paused at the entrance to the media room.

"No, the name of Mrs. Whatever. Could it have been Mrs. Fairchild?"

"I suppose," said Rebecca. "It really wasn't memorable."

"I think you just helped us solve a murder!" I said, giving her a quick hug.

"Aren't you going to come in?" she asked, looking puzzled. "Isn't Felix going with you?"

"I'm sure I'll catch up with him later," I said. "Right now, Pepe and I have some urgent detective business to take care of."

Pepe's Blog: Advice
from the Love Dog

I may not be a Love Dog, but I knew that Geri was making a big mistake by walking away from Felix like that. I whispered my farewells to Siren Song with a promise we would be together soon and a suggestion of what we might do then. Judging by the gleam in her sparkling dark eyes and the delicious scent she emanated, she was already anticipating that moment eagerly.

With Fuzzy, who I view as my Girl Friday, I was more business-like, simply thanking her for her assistance in the case. She's a cute little mutt but there is no chemistry between us. That is good for it is a bad idea for a detective to develop an affection for his assistant. Romance and business do not mix.

Meanwhile, thanks to my clever detective work, with a little help from my sidekick, Fuzzy, we were finally going to solve the mystery of the Disappearing Decorator. Although I wasn't entirely sure what Geri had in mind.

Chapter 29

"What do you have in mind?" Pepe asked as soon as we were in my little green Toyota and heading down the hill toward home.

"Well, obviously we have to figure out the name of the guy who was arguing with Brad."

"And how are you going to figure that out?" asked Pepe.

"I want to check the shop again," I said. "Maybe I can find something the police missed."

"Excellent!" said Pepe. "Exactly what I was going to suggest. My strategy to improve your skills is working nicely."

He couldn't even let me take credit for an original thought, but had to insist that it was his idea first. That's my dog!

"You know, Geri," he said, in a softer voice. "I am not a Love Dog, but I can tell you sent the wrong message to Felix when you left the party without saying good-bye to him. "

"What is a Love Dog?" I asked, not really wanting to talk about Felix.

"Apparently there is a reality TV show called *Love Dog* where a dog matches up single people by sniffing out their compatibility. Right now they have some big goofy golden retriever playing the part, but I think I would make a very nice Cupid. What do you think?"

"Yes, Pepe," I agreed. "You would certainly make a good Love Dog." I was a little distracted as it was raining heavily and I was at the bottom of the hill, trying to make a left turn.

"So what is your strategy with Felix?" he asked.

"I don't have a strategy," I said, making my left turn.

"There are two ways to interpret your behavior," said Pepe. "You are either being passive-aggressive and asking him to chase after you to find out what is wrong. Which might work, but it could backfire. Or you are ceding your property to the other women at the party. Neither is a good idea."

"So says my dog," I said bitterly. Brad's business was on the right. I pulled around the corner and drove into the narrow parking lot in back of the row of shops.

"Hey, I am a detective dog and a dog with many loves."

"Yes, what's the story with Siren Song and Fuzzy? They are both females. Why aren't they jealous of each other?"

"Fuzzy is my sidekick rather than my amour and Siren Song is secure in my affections."

The parking lot was empty. I was able to pull into the spot directly in back of Brad's shop. I turned off the car. "Until she finds out about Phoebe." Phoebe was the lovely farm dog Pepe had been courting during our last case.

"Ah, yes, we should take a little trip to Sequim once this case is finished," said Pepe in a dreamy voice.

It was raining when we got out of the car. I fumbled around in my purse for the key to the back of the shop. It creaked open and we both stepped in, out of the rain. I reached for the light switch and flipped it up. Nothing. I had forgotten the electricity was turned off.

"How am I going to find anything," I asked Pepe, "without any light?"

"If we get to the front office, you will be able to see by the light of the streetlights," said Pepe.

I looked at the dark cavernous space in front of me. "But I'm not sure I can make it that far."

"I will lead you!" said Pepe. "Did I ever tell you about the time I was trained to be a sight dog?"

"That's pretty ridiculous, Pepe." I said. "You're too small to be a sight dog."

"I was a sight dog for a dwarf," Pepe said

"If you mean a real person, and not a fairy tale creature," I said, "you're not using the politically correct term."

"That was his billing in the circus," said Pepe. "Enrique the Blind Dwarf."

"This is the same Mexican circus where you liberated the animals?" I asked.

"*Si.* That was after they fired me because Enrique tripped over me and broke his nose. The secret was that he was not blind. He just pretended to be so he could feel up the women in the audience, but he was drunk a lot and that was why he tripped over me. The circus owner didn't see it that way and I was dismissed."

"Poor Pepe," I said.

"Just hold onto my tail," he said.

I bent down and put my hand on his tail. I was almost doubled over as we started out. Everything looked different from this perspective. A little light filtered in from the front room. Dark shapes loomed over me. Pepe was not a good guide dog. He seemed to think I was as slim and as tiny as he was. He kept zigging and zagging and knocking me into things off which other things tumbled and then shattered. Of course, it didn't help that everything had been moved around by the police.

As we got closer to the front of the shop, I straightened up. I pushed aside the heavy velvet curtain that hid the back room from the front showroom space. Suddenly my eyes were dazzled by the harsh light of the streetlights that flooded the room through the big front window. And Pepe squeaked in fear.

I jumped back, then saw he was reacting to another of the taxidermy animals Brad loves. This was a stuffed lynx sitting on top of a cabinet against the wall by the door.

"I will take the back of the shop," Pepe told me, "while you reconnoiter this area. Between us, we can make short work of this." He dashed under the curtain without waiting for my reply. One of the only things Pepe had ever been afraid of were cats, so I didn't even tease him about being scared of a stuffed one.

I opened the shoulder-high wooden cabinet that the lynx was sitting on. The lynx, too, appeared about ready to catch a meal—it was crouched down as if to spring, its pointy ears laid back, and was snarling, its long fangs exposed. I must admit, it gave me a little pause as I opened the cabinet door.

There was nothing on the three shelves inside

except a very old can of walnut wood stain, a small and stiff natural bristle paintbrush that Brad must have forgotten to clean, and lots of dust.

Against another wall, behind the graceful French provincial table that Brad used as a desk, was an antique apothecary. More than six feet tall, with zillions of small drawers in it. I opened drawer after drawer until a very large (and thank God) very dead wolf spider fell out of it and bounced off my foot. Dead or not, I let out a yelp.

"What is it?" Pepe called out from the back. "Find something?"

"No," I told him, not wanting to explain my fear of big, hairy spiders.

I checked the file cabinet again but it was still bereft of any paperwork. Not a single thing that indicated that Brad ever kept track of his clients on paper. Which really didn't surprise me.

"Have you seen a computer?" I called out to Pepe.

"No, Geri," he said, "but I am hearing something I don't like."

I stopped and listened, but all I heard was the rain beating on the window of the shop.

As I listened, I saw the unopened envelopes that had been addressed to Mrs Fairchild, still sitting on the desk where I had put them. I realized these must have been delivered on Saturday after the police had searched. That would explain why they had missed them.

"I think I found it!" I shouted, tearing open one of the envelopes. Sure enough, it contained a bill made out to Mrs Fairchild, written on fancy stationary in Brad's delicate handwriting, listing several items of furniture, a consultation fee, and painting services provided by Harry Richards. "The guy's name is Harry Richards!"

"This is not a good time to say anything," said Pepe, and then he started growling.

I heard footsteps, then a loud thunk and a yelp. Followed by silence.

"Pepe, what happened? Are you OK?"

"No, he's not OK!" A figure appeared in the doorway, shoving the curtain aside. He was standing in the shadow so I couldn't see his face clearly, but I could tell by his silhouette that he was a big man with broad shoulders. He was wearing a leather jacket and heavy motorcycle boots.

"What did you do to my dog?"

"He got in my way," he said. "I tripped over him. What are you doing here?"

"I just came by to pick up some paperwork," I said. I waved the envelopes at him.

"Well, thank you," he said, stepping forward into the light. The curtain swung shut behind him. I could see him better now. He was probably in his fifties. He was overweight and not terribly well-groomed. A musty smell came from him. He had long dark hair pushed back behind his ears, wet from the rain, and a thick beard in which rain drops glistened. His eyes were a startling shade of blue. "I've been looking for those too. Been watching the shop for days, hoping someone would show up."

"I can't give them to you," I said gaily. "Brad asked me to deliver these to him."

"Brad?" He looked shaken at that. He even staggered back a little.

"Yes, Brad."

"I thought he was dead," he said, shaking his head.

"Why would you think that, Harry?" I asked.

"Because . . ." He faltered to a stop. "It doesn't matter. I need to get paid. And I need that invoice to prove what's owed me."

"So you can collect it from Brad's estate?" I asked, trying to ascertain what he knew about Brad.

"Well, that's what I was thinking," he said.

"What made you think Brad was dead?"

"Well, I saw him, didn't I? Lying in a pool of blood next to the old lady he killed. He probably tried to commit suicide after he killed her."

"With a hammer?" I asked. "I've never heard of anyone killing themselves with a hammer."

Then I heard Pepe's voice, a whisper coming from behind the curtain. "Do not dispute his version of events, Geri."

"Are you OK?" I asked.

"I will be when you give me those papers," said Harry, taking a step forward.

"I will be once we trap this murderer," said Pepe. "Tell him there are more papers in the back room"

"But there aren't any more papers in the back room."

"I have a plan," said Pepe.

"What about the back room?" Harry asked.

"There are more papers back there," I said. "Follow me!"

"I'm glad you are turning out to be obedient," Harry said. He still had not taken his hand out of his pocket. "That's the way I like my women."

I pushed aside the curtain and peered into the darkness of the back room. I still couldn't see anything except what the streetlights illuminated—a narrow path along the wall. I fumbled for the fancy gold ropes that Brad uses to tie back the curtains so there would be a little bit of light. Harry bumped into me. That's when I felt the gun at my back.

"You're going to do exactly what I say," he said.

"Geri, you must do exactly what I say," said Pepe.

"Yes, of course," I said.

"I'm going to tie you up and then you're going to tell me where to find the rest of the papers," Harry said.

"That is perfect!" Pepe said. "Tell him to use the cord by the door."

"You've got to be kidding?"

"No, I'm not kidding," Harry said, waving the gun at me. "If you're a good girl, I won't kill you."

"It's part of my plan," said Pepe. "Trust me!"

"Right!" I said to Pepe. "I suppose you're going to use that cord over there," I said to Harry.

"Don't mind if I do," he said happily.

I sat down in an arm chair near the doorway and Harry put the gun down on a cabinet behind him. Maybe Pepe was right. It was smart to separate the man from his gun. But Pepe couldn't reach it. And even if he could, he couldn't fire it. I really hoped he knew what he was doing. Especially as Harry picked up the length of white cord (it looked like drapery cord) and began twining it around my legs and the legs of the chair.

During previous encounters with malefactors, Pepe had usually made a run straight for their ankles. He could inflict some damage on an Achilles tendon with his tiny teeth. But this guy was wearing thick motorcycle boots.

"You know, I really didn't want to do it," Harry said as he started twisting the cord around my arms and looping it around the back of the chair. "I'm really not a bad guy. That old lady just made me so angry. Calling me those names. Saying I was worthless. I had the hammer in my hand because I was trying to tamp down the cover of the paint can that was the cause of all the problems. The old lady insisted the color was all wrong and wanted me to do the whole job over. She made me so mad I got up and lunged at her and Brad got in the way. I didn't mean to hit him. In fact, I didn't hit him. He just ran into the hammer which was on its way down. But then he went down, and laid there, with all that blood gushing down his face."

I could see tears running down Harry's face by the faint light that was filtering through the doorway, thanks to the looped-back curtain. When he went on, his voice was shaky. "Then the old lady started shrieking and saying she was going to call the police."

His hands were shaking too. He was having a hard time tying off the knots. Remembering what I had read in detective novels, I had tried to puff myself up so the ropes would be loose when he was done, but he was doing a good job. I could feel them cutting into my flesh. I really hoped Pepe knew what he was doing.

"I knew I had to get rid of her because she was a witness. I didn't want to do it. And boy was she tough. She fought like a wildcat. Really, I know you're judging me but that was the hardest thing I've ever done—killing that old lady."

He stopped and sat back on his heels. "They say it gets easier." He shook his head. "I hope that's true."

I didn't like the way that sounded. I had to think of something fast. "Brad's not dead you know."

"What?"

"Brad's not dead. He got a concussion or something like that, but he's alive. So the police know everything. I'm surprised they're not here already. In fact, the only reason I'm cooperating is to give them time to get here. They're listening to our conversation right now." I was making things up, but it sounded pretty good. I thought Pepe would be proud of me.

"What do you mean?"

"It was all a trap. To lure you out of hiding and get you to confess."

He stood up abruptly. He reached behind him to get his gun. And at that moment, Pepe shouted, "Geri, duck!" And the next thing I knew there was a weird whistling sound and then the huge redtail hawk that soared above the workspace came flying down. Harry started screaming as it struck him claws first. He toppled backward against the cabinet with the lynx on top of it and the lynx fell down, tangling its claws in his hair before the whole cabinet went down, pinning him to the ground. He seemed to be out cold.

"Ha!" said Pepe. He jumped up on my lap. I could see a tiny bit of blood on the corners of his mouth.

"Pepe, are you hurt?" I asked.

"The cord, it was tougher to chew through than I thought," he said, "but it helped that he used it to tie you up. That made the tension tighter so I could get a better grip on it."

"That was your plan? To make the hawk fall on him?" I asked.

"*Si* and it worked, did it not?"

"What about me? How am I supposed to get out of this chair?" I asked.

"Oh, I had not thought of that," said Pepe.

Just then I heard barking outside the back door. The door opened and Fuzzy the dog burst into the room, heading straight for me.

"Geri?" I heard a familiar voice. "Geri, are you in there?" It was Felix.

"I'm right here!" I shouted. "Pepe just saved me. But I need help getting out of this chair."

"Humph!" said Pepe. "Felix and Fuzzy to the rescue. Showing up when the danger is past! Figures!"

"How did you find me?" I asked Felix much later, after the police had been called and taken Harry Richards away and we had gone back to my house, where Pepe was sulking in front of his iPad because the police gave Felix credit for saving me no matter how many times I tried to tell them about Pepe's clever plan.

We were in bed together and had just made love. There is nothing like making love after you think you might die. You treasure every sweet moment, every touch, every kiss, every sensation. So we were both rather exhausted, mentally and physically and emotionally, lying in each other's arms in the darkness.

"You're not going to believe this," said Felix, nibbling on my shoulder.

"What?"

"Fuzzy told me."

"What?"

"Yes. At first I was hurt when you disappeared. I thought you were trying to ditch me. But then Fuzzy told me all about how she found the paint can and how you were going to figure out the name of the painter. And I knew you. I knew you would run off and take action. So I figured you would go to the shop and I was right."

I rolled over to face him. "You're saying your dog talked to you? And you heard her?"

Felix looked back at me with his eyes shining. "Just don't tell anyone else, OK? I don't want them to think I'm crazy."

Pepe's Blog: Overlooking
Your Chihuahua

As usual, I get no credit. Apparently no one will believe that a Chihuahua is capable of capturing a vicious murderer. Instead they gave all the credit to Felix.

It is true that I had not thought through my entire scheme. But that is the way I roll. Fast on my feet. Flexible and ready to adjust to any change of plans. Fearless in the face of danger. That is the Chihuahua way.

Geri did pretty well considering she is not a Chihuahua. She was brave. And she was quick to respond to my direction. All in all, I am very happy with the way her training is proceeding. She will make an excellent partner some day.

Chapter 30

Felix had to leave early the next morning, but before he left he made us both coffee and brought it to me in bed.

"You deserve special consideration," he said, ruffling my hair, "after catching a murderer."

"Oh, it's nothing," I said. "You tame wild beasts!"

"I know another wild beast I would like to tame," said Felix, leaning over to give me a kiss.

"Say what about me?" asked Pepe, who was standing in the door. He was obviously still in a bad mood from being overlooked the previous night.

"I'll get you some nice crispy bacon," I said. "Later."

Felix gave me a strange look, then turned around and saw Pepe in the doorway.

"Oh, you're just talking to your dog," he said.

"Just like you talk to yours!" I said.

I swear Felix turned pink. "But it's our secret," he said, leaning down to give me another kiss.

"Of course!" I murmured.

* * *

Pepe's request for bacon reminded me that I wanted to call Mrs. Snelson and tell her about the plan to have her adopt Bruiser. After Felix left and I finally got out of bed, I dialed her number.

"Oh, hello, Geri!" she said when she heard my voice. "I was going to call you and thank you, but I've been so busy. Right now I'm in the middle of making breakfast."

I remembered Mrs. Snelson's breakfast with pleasure. Those fluffy eggs. The real butter on the toast. But not the coffee. Her coffee was always dreadful.

"What's that, darling?" she asked someone in the room with her. Then she whispered into the receiver, "I've got company."

"A certain gentleman?" I asked.

"We've been spending a lot of time together," said Mrs. Snelson. Then I heard barking in the background.

"What's that?"

"Oh, Prince wants another piece of bacon."

" Prince?"

"Yes, well, we rescued that dog that was chained up across the street."

"Bruiser?"

"Was that his name? We changed it to Prince. Because he really is a prince, aren't you, love?" A sharp bark seemed to confirm that.

"How did you get him loose?"

"Gumshoe used a bolt cutter. He's quite a handy man!" And she gave a girlish giggle.

I told her about the film crew and how they would like to film her with the dog. She was happy to cooperate and told me to pass along her number to the director.

"Well, I guess the Case of the Romantic Marauder is solved," I said.

"Yes, I'm very happy with your work. Tell your boss to send me an invoice. "

I promised to do so and hung up, rather bemused. "Bruiser and Gumshoe are getting your crispy bacon," I told Pepe.

He did not reply.

I thought I would call Jimmy G while he was on my mind. I hadn't heard from him since he had rescued Amber the previous day. But when I called the office, Amber answered the phone.

"What are you doing there?" I asked.

"Your job, apparently. Jimmy G says you don't cut it as a girl Friday."

"How many times do I have to tell him I am not his girl Friday!"

"Isn't that the truth," said Amber. "Because now Amber is Jimmy G's girl Friday."

"No! What? That can't be true."

You don't think Amber is capable of doing your job?"

"It's not my job!" I said again. "Never mind, let me speak to Jimmy G."

"Jimmy G is unavailable right now," said Amber. Something in the tone of her voice made me think that he was sitting right there, probably leaning back in his chair with his fedora tipped over his eye and winking at her.

"Well, tell him I want to get paid for the Mrs. Snelson case," I said.

"Snelling?"

"No. Snelson."

"Nelson?"

"No, Snelson. Just like Nelson but it starts with an S."

"What a weird name," said Amber. "You'll have to spell that for me. And slowly."

"Just tell Jimmy G the old lady with the pooping dog problem. He'll know who I'm talking about. And remind him that we're splitting the fee sixty-forty. That's what we agreed on."

"Amber will make sure Jimmy G gets the message," said Amber primly.

No sooner had I hung up the phone than it rang again. It was Dr. Mallard's office calling to say they had a last minute cancellation and the doctor could see me and my Chihuahua.

"But he's talking again," I said. I looked at Pepe who was sitting in the kitchen doorway with his back to me, clearly giving me the silent treatment. "Actually, I would like to see the vet as soon as possible," I said.

"No, absolutely not, there is no need for me to see a doctor. I promise I will never stop talking to you again," said Pepe, turning around quickly.

"Dr. Mallard can see you at one," said the receptionist.

"Is that a threat?" I asked Pepe.

"Is the vet a threat?" he asked me.

"OK, you win," I said.

"I'm not sure I understand," said the receptionist.

"Never mind," I said. "My dog has just promised he will never stop talking to me again."

"That's lovely!" said the receptionist in a falsely cheerful voice. "We wish you the best of luck."

I had just taken a shower and was getting dressed so I could head to the store to get a treat for Pepe when the phone rang again.

"What now?" I said, snatching it up. Pepe was dancing at my feet, eager for his promised reward.

"Geri? It's Colleen Carpenter. Do you remember me?"

"Yes, of course I remember you," I said. Colleen owned a lavender farm in Sequim. She was also the owner of a lovely black and white dog named Phoebe, who had captured Pepe's fancy.

"How are you? And Phoebe?" I asked.

That got Pepe's attention. "Tell her Pepe is thinking of her every day," he said.

"Pepe is still head over heels for Phoebe," I said.

"Well, funny you should say that," said Colleen. "Because Phoebe just had puppies."

"What?"

"What is it, Geri? Did something happen to Phoebe?"

"Yes, and the puppies bear a striking resemblance to your dog."

"Really?" I stared at Pepe. It must have scared him.

"Tell me she is all right," he moaned. "My love. The moon around which I revolve."

"How many?" I said.

"Five and they are all healthy."

"Did you have to call a vet?" I asked.

"I must speak to her," said Pepe. "She is the only

one for me. I will eschew all other loves now that I realize what I have lost." He was pacing in circles around my feet.

"Yes, but we didn't call Hugh Williams. We used the old vet in town."

"That's good," I said. "We never trusted Dr. Williams."

"Is it terminal?" asked Pepe. "Is she dying? How much time do we have to be together before the end approaches?"

"No, no, no," I said. "She's not sick. She's not dying."

"What?"

"My dog—he's worried about Phoebe," I told Colleen. I spoke to Pepe. "Phoebe just had puppies. Five of them. And apparently they look just like you! How can that be?"

A look came over Pepe's face that I had never seen there before. It was almost like he had seen a ghost. He shivered and then a big smile spread across his face. If you don't think a dog can smile, then you have never seen a happy Chihuahua.

"I suppose it happened in the usual way," he said smugly. "When can I see them?'

"Pepe wants to meet his progeny," I told Colleen.

"We'd love to see you again," she said. "Any time."

After picking up some beef jerky for Pepe at the local grocery store, I decided I should go over to Jimmy G's office and find out what was happening with Amber. I wanted my phone back. And it would give me a good chance to make sure Jimmy G sent out the invoice to Mrs. Snelson.

Jimmy G's office is in an old brick building on the edge of downtown, just about a block from the

Greyhound bus terminal. The elevator wasn't working so Pepe and I headed up the echoing concrete stairwell to the third floor. As usual, the building seemed to be deserted, although there were signs on the frosted glass doors that lined the hallway, indicating the occupants were engaged in various enterprises including an import-export business, a bookkeeping service, and whatever Center Stage Productions produced. Jimmy G's office was at the end of the hall and I could hear Amber's voice prattling away even before we opened the door.

As we walked in, she scrambled off Jimmy G's lap where she was poised with a steno notebook in one hand and a pen in the other, and stood by his side. Jimmy G looked abashed. His fedora was sitting on the desk so I could see the bald spot on the top of his head and a big lipstick imprint on his cheek.

Otherwise, he was dressed like normal, if you consider it normal to dress up like a detective from the forties in a striped shirt, a wide tie, and red suspenders. It was Amber's outfit that surprised me. She was all dolled up in a form-fitting navy blue dress that looked like it came straight out of an old-fashioned pin-up magazine and her hair was twisted back into a French bun.

"I'll just type that up right away, Mr Gerrard," she said, and pranced over to my desk in the corner. She sat down at the old typewriter and started batting at the keys.

"What's going on here?" I asked.

"Got a new girl Friday," said Jimmy G.

"But I'm your girl Friday!" I said.

"You told Jimmy G not to call you that," he said.

"Well . . ."

"Plus you told Jimmy G you wanted to be a full partner in the firm."

"Well, that's true," I said. "It's just a little hard to come in and find out I've been replaced."

I glanced over at Amber bent over her task, poking at the keys with two fingers. A tiny and fluffy black-and-brown Chihuahua was sitting in a basket beside the desk. She was wearing a little crocheted pink top. Pepe scurried over there and murmured something into her ear. She growled and nipped at Pepe, who jerked back from her.

"Party Girl!" Amber admonished her dog.

"What were you doing, Pepe?" I asked my dog.

"I was merely whispering sweet-nothings in her ear," he said innocently. "Perhaps she has no appreciation for the Bard of Avon."

"So what can we do for you?" asked Jimmy G, clapping his fedora back on top of his head. He leaned back in his chair and put his feet up on his desk, which contained the usual clutter of paper bags and newspapers, not to mention a full ashtray.

"I came to pick up the invoice for Mrs. Snelson," I said. "I think I'll deliver it to her myself. So I can make sure I get my cut."

"I'll get right on that as soon as I finish typing up this dictation," said Amber.

"And I wanted to know if you ever called the Marshalls and told them you were safe," I asked Amber. "I need my cell phone back!"

"Sure, I told them," she said. "They gave me a number to give to you. Now where did I put that?"

She began poking around in the desk drawer.

Just then the phone rang. Amber jumped up to get it, tottering a little on the high heels she wore.

"Gerrard Agency," she said in a sing-song voice. She definitely had the secretarial role down pat. Her forehead crinkled as she listened to the caller. "No, this is not Geri. This is Amber." She looked distressed. "Hold on, I can't understand you. No, don't hang up! Geri's right here!"

She motioned to me to come over and grab the receiver of the black rotary phone.

"Geri! Thank God, I found you!" It was my sister, Teri. I recognized her voice immediately, although it sounded like she was hyperventilating. "I called your home phone and you weren't there. So I thought I'd try your work."

"Teri! What's going on? Are you OK?"

"No, I'm not OK! There was a shoot-out at the hotel. A couple of big guys shot the Marshalls who were supposed to be protecting me. I just barely got away. Can you come and get me?"

"Where are you?" Jimmy G and Amber were both staring at me. They could hear the panic in my voice. So could Pepe who was right at my feet.

"I just ran up the street and I ended up at some little coffee shop on Capitol Hill." She turned away from the phone and asked someone, "What's the name of this place?"

I heard a mumbled response in the background.

"Café Argento," she said. "It's a little coffee shop on the corner of Olive and Twelfth."

"I know where it is," I said. Brad had sold some fancy mirrors to the owner and I helped him deliver them. After that I used to stop by for a coffee whenever

I was in the vicinity, because I loved the friendly atmosphere. "Did you call the cops?"

"I don't trust them. If the Marshalls couldn't protect me, then—"

"I'll come and get you," I told my sister. "Just stay safe. I can be there in ten minutes, maybe less."

"What's going on?" Amber asked.

"Hurry!" Teri told me, then hung up.

"What is it, Geri?" asked Pepe.

"I've got to go rescue my sister!" I said. "She's just escaped from some guys who tried to kill her."

"Your sister Teri? She's the reason they kidnapped me," said Amber. "They kept asking me about her, even though I told them I didn't know her. What did she do, anyway?"

"Long story," I said, whirling around and heading for the door. "She's scheduled to be an eyewitness in a murder trial. I'll tell you more about it later; I've got to go."

"Do you need help?" That was Amber, asking with a gleam in her eye. "I would like to meet her!" Party Girl jumped to her feet, apparently eager for action. I thought I heard her say. "Oh, goodie, another rumble!"

My boss rose to his feet and adjusted his fedora so it slanted down over one eye. "Jimmy G will drive. My bird's way faster than your old Toyota," he added, referring to his old, red Thunderbird convertible.

"*Andale*!" said Pepe, beating all of us to the front door.

Pepe's Blog: How to Handle a Car Chase

There is nothing I like more than a good car chase. Unfortunately, they are better on television than in reality, especially if you are a little dog. The force with which the driver brakes and swerves around corners can throw a little dog all over the interior of the vehicle and that is not pleasant.

The safest way for a dog to travel in a car is inside a nice soft pet carrier that is securely fastened with a seat belt. (Not, I might point out in a smelly plastic crate in the back of a stinky dogmobile like the one Felix drives.) But such a device was not available in this situation.

So the second best thing, the thing that I did, was to jump into Geri's arms and have her hold me close while Jimmy G drove like a maniac. I even closed my eyes for a little bit. I do not like the way Jimmy G drives. Also I was storing up my courage for the upcoming confrontation.

Chapter 31

We all piled into the Thunderbird, Amber with Party Girl in the front seat, me with Pepe curled up in my arms in the back, and drove up the hill to Café Argento in no time flat. I filled Amber in about my sister and the gangsters along the way.

Café Argento is on the ground floor of a brand-new condominium complex. A wine store occupied the other retail space and both flanked a small fountain in a courtyard that led to the main entrance of the building.

It is hard to find parking in the Capitol Hill neighborhood, even more difficult because it's near Seattle Central Community College, so students attending classes take up most of the parking not being used by people patronizing the many nearby restaurants, bars, and coffee shops. As Jimmy G circled the block for the second time, I finally convinced him to let me and Pepe out and we dashed across Twelfth Street and into Café Argento.

But Teri was nowhere in sight. A guy with glasses was sitting working on a laptop at one of the narrow tables against the wall. Two women had their heads bent over some papers in front of them on one of the square tables near the windows. They looked up in surprise when I skidded to a stop in the middle of the restaurant.

"Where is she?" I asked out loud.

"Hey!" That was Pepe coming up behind me. "You could have been hurt running into traffic that way. Did you not hear me tell you to *heel*?"

The owner, Faizel, a handsome guy with dark hair and dark eyes, waved me over to the counter. "Can I help you?" he asked.

"I'm looking for my sister," I said.

He raised his eyebrows.

"Teri!" I added.

"You two look alike," he whispered. "Follow me!"

He came out from behind the counter and used a key to open the door to a storage room that was lined with silver shelves full of restaurant items: bags of coffee beans, stacks of napkins. And in the middle, sitting hunched up on a stepstool, was my sister Teri. She was wearing black sweatpants, a pink t-shirt, a black hoodie, and a pair of grey sneakers.

"Geri!" she jumped up and flew into my arms.

I held her tight. "I've been so scared," Teri told me, her head buried into the crook of my neck. I could feel her trembling.

Faizel left us and went back into the shop as Jimmy G and Amber entered. I saw Terri shrink back. "It's OK," I said. "They're with me."

I waved them over to the storage closet and introduced everyone. Teri still seemed reluctant to come out of the closet. Amber was lingering by the door.

Suddenly, Party Girl started growling.

"Did you try to woo her again?" I asked Pepe.

I was interrupted by Amber shouting out, "Oh my God! It's him!"

"Who?"

"Him!" She was pointing out the window. "Isn't that the gangster you were telling me about?"

I looked to see where she was pointing and saw an older man with a pork pie hat across the street from the café. He seemed agitated. He was pacing up and down, and seemed to be muttering to himself.

"Hey, that's Phil!" said Jimmy G.

"You mean Phil Pugnetti?" I asked. "The guy Teri is supposed to be testifying against?"

"Oh my God, he's going to kill me!" Teri said.

"Quick!" I said to Jimmy G. "Go distract him!"

"Sure!" Jimmy G headed out the door.

"I'm coming with you!" said Amber. That was brave of her. Party Girl followed. Meanwhile, I waved Faizel over. "Is there a back way out of here?"

"Yes, follow me," he said. He grabbed his keys and led us around the corner and into the foyer to the building, through a hallway lined with elevators that would take tenants to their condos above. We went out a back door marked EXIT, which took us into a narrow walkway behind the building.

It was hard to decide which way to go. One way would lead us out to Twelfth Street, the other to Olive Street. Since Pugnetti had been on the corner, I didn't know which was better, but I took a chance and pointed us toward Olive.

Turned out I guessed wrong.

We had no sooner opened the gate which clanged shut behind us, than Pugnetti, who was arguing with Jimmy G on the corner, turned and spotted us.

"Hey, you! Stop!" he shouted, whirling around and heading straight for us.

Teri took off running down the street toward the park with me and Pepe following close behind. As we sprinted across Eleventh Avenue, I glanced back and saw Pugnetti following us, waving something in his right hand. *A gun!*

"Go right, Teri!" I shouted. That would take her by the playground. I didn't think Pugnetti would dare to shoot around the little kids scrambling all over the play structure and swinging on the swing set. But what did I know about gangsters?

Teri swerved to the right and into the park, heading toward the playground. Pugnetti stopped to catch his breath at the curb. He was an older man and heavyset. I doubt he did a lot of running.

Jimmy G and Amber caught up with him.

"Go get that broad!" Pugnetti yelled at Jimmy G waving his gun toward Teri. "A couple thousand for you, if you do."

"Sure," said Jimmy G.

I scrambled to catch up with Teri. Would Jimmy G really sell out my sister for money?

Teri was galloping past the playground, her long hair flying. The moms and kids watched us go by, their eyes big, their mouths open.

Teri was approaching the water feature built into the park and designed to cover one of the city's many reservoirs. On one end was an old stone building and a long reflecting pool. At the far end, the pool flowed from a strange cone-shaped fountain. Benches were set on either side so people could look out at the water and on one side, long lawns swooped down to the sidewalk. Those lawns were usually dotted with

dogs playing with their owners and that was true,
especially today with its unexpected sunshine.

I turned at the corner and looked back. Jimmy G
was fumbling in his jacket and pulled out a gun as
well. Was he actually going to carry out Pugnetti's
bidding? I knew my boss wasn't trustworthy after the
way he double-crossed me during our last case, but I
didn't think he would be willing to kill someone.

Teri was far out in front, heading alongside the
long, narrow reflecting pool with Pepe at her side. I
stopped, thinking I could maybe distract Jimmy G,
talk some sense into him. Amber was limping behind
him, having lost one of her high heels. And Pugnetti
brought up the rear, moving slowly. As he reached the
start of the reflecting pool where water flowed through
a grate and underground, he stopped and tried to
steady his gun with his other hand, taking a bead on
Teri.

I stepped into the path of the bullet. Not a smart
thing to do. Jimmy G lifted his gun, spun around
and aimed at Pugnetti. He missed—I saw the bullet
ricochet off the building—but he startled Pugnetti
enough so Pugnetti's bullet went astray, actually hit-
ting Jimmy G's fedora and knocking it off his head.
Jimmy G was so shaken up he dropped his pistol into
the reflecting pool.

Amber screamed.

As Jimmy G bent to retrieve his gun, Pugnetti fired
again, missing again. The ducks who had been floating in the pool took off with a big whir of wings.
Amber, who was right behind Pugnetti, took off her
other shoe and flung it at him. Pugnetti spun around
and fired at her.

"Hit the ground" shouted Jimmy G and she did.

But I couldn't tell if she had been hit or had taken cover. As Jimmy G went flying toward Amber, Pugnetti resumed his hunt of Teri who was almost at the fountain at the far end. She was screaming, "Help! Help!"

That's when I became aware of all the other screaming that was going on. I'd been so intent on getting away from Pugnetti, that I hadn't noticed all the screeching people who'd heard the shots. The soccer players in the sports field were looking our way. The moms were huddling with their kids in the playground area. People playing Frisbee with their dogs on the lawns were running for the sidewalk. And dogs, all the dogs, were barking furiously.

Pepe, who had been trailing Teri, turned around and yelled. "Calling all *perros*! Come to the rescue of the humans! Attack this evil dog-hater!"

And suddenly all the dogs in the park were running toward Phil Pugnetti. Big dogs, little dogs, fuzzy dogs, smooth-haired dogs, dogs trailing leashes, and dogs running free. I heard their owners calling their names.

"Dixie, come back!" said a woman chasing after a small black poodle.

"Sweet Pea, no!" One of three women who were sitting on a bench together with their dogs jumped up as her fuzzy little dog jumped off her lap.

"Orchid, come!" said her companion, whose dog, a small Chihuahua, hit the ground running.

"Andy! Get back here!" shouted the third woman, whose black cocker spaniel jerked his leash free from her hold.

"Buster, stop it!" said a long-haired woman who was being towed towards the melee by her big brown curly-haired dog who was straining at the end of his leash.

Just as Teri darted behind the fountain and Pugnetti raised his hand again to shoot at her, the dogs got to him. Pepe and Party Girl were leading the pack. The dogs jumped on him from behind, and his gun went flying. He fell to his knees and one of the bigger dogs pushed him over. All of them were barking.

Pugnetti curled up in a ball on the gravel walkway, his arms over his face. "Get them off of me!" he screamed. The dogs were swarming him like angry bees.

"Help! Help!" screamed Pugnetti. "I'm afraid of dogs."

The dogs milled around him, barking and snarling and snapping.

"They're going to kill me!" moaned Pugnetti.

"That would be justice!" said Teri, coming out from behind the fountain. She grabbed Pugnetti's gun and aimed it at him.

Jimmy G and Amber came loping up. Jimmy G was carrying his pistol, which he must have retrieved from the pool.

"You're OK?" I asked Amber.

"Yes," said Amber. "Amber just dove for cover, like Jimmy G suggested."

"Your job is done. *Gracias* brave comrades!" said Pepe to the other dogs. They began to disperse, returning to their owners gathered in a circle around us.

The police arrived on bicycles, guns drawn, and quickly took Pugnetti into custody as soon as the other park-goers verified our story that he had been firing a gun. Jimmy G had slipped his pistol into his shoulder harness and, luckily, no one mentioned that he had been shooting as well, or he would have been in jail too.

As we waited to be interviewed, I picked up Pepe and kissed him. "You are my hero," I said.

"And you are Amber's hero," said Amber, throwing her arms around Jimmy G and giving him a big kiss right on the lips.

"And both of you are my heroes," said Teri, throwing her arms around me and Pepe. She patted him on the head. "He promised he would rescue me that first day he sneaked into Serenity."

"You can hear him talking?" I asked Teri.

"Well, sure," she said. "Didn't you hear him just now? He was telling all the other dogs to jump Pugnetti."

"So you don't think I'm crazy?" I asked her.

"If you are, then I am too!" she said with a laugh. "Maybe we should check ourselves into Forest Glen. I never had a chance to try out the float tank."

Epilogue

The Chinese Room on the top floor of the Smith Tower was the most elegant venue for a wedding and reception that I'd ever seen. The way it was decorated was fantastic: ornate coffered ceilings, intricately-carved pieces of furniture and a carpet with an Oriental pattern of cherry branches. One wall was painted a deep Chinese red and the others were covered with wallpaper displaying vivid wild flowers. And the view was astounding. Floor to ceiling windows on three sides provided a view of Seattle from the docks to the Space Needle. An observation deck ran around the outside.

Since it was Halloween, Brad and Jay had decided all the guests should come to their wedding in costume. After much deliberation, Pepe decided to dress as Cupid because he was still attached to the idea of being a Love Dog. So he wore a pair of small, shiny, gold wings with a little gold bow and arrow hanging at his side.

"Adorable, am I not?" he asked me, appraising himself in the mirror just before we left for the wedding.

"Very," I told him.

Then he turned to me and said, "But I do not approve of your costume, partner."

"Too bad," I said, studying myself in the mirror on the closet door in my bedroom. I had decided to go as a lion to match Felix's costume as an animal trainer. I was wearing a body-hugging caramel-colored fleece jumpsuit with a big net ruff around my neck and two felt ears attached to a headband nestled in among my curls. A tail with a pouf at the end of it attached to my rear end completed the look, along with some fuzzy boots.

"You just don't like cats," I said.

"They are evil creatures," said Pepe, glaring at Albert the Cat who sat on the bed watching us and pretending to be disinterested. "At least, you will have Felix to keep you in line."

Felix was waiting for us in the living room and he looked magnificent in a shiny red coat with yellow epaulets, tight white pants tucked into shiny black boots and a top hat. Of course, he carried a small whip in his hand and pretended to flick it at me as I came into the room.

"Down, girl!" he said as I pretended to pounce on him.

We arrived at the Smith Tower thirty minutes before the wedding was to begin. Almost forty stories tall, it had been the highest building west of the Mississippi when it was built in 1914. Now it is dwarfed by some of the larger skyscrapers in the Seattle downtown, but it's still impressive. I particularly liked the copper and brass elevator, which was operated by an old-fashioned elevator operator wearing a uniform with gold braid on the collar and sleeves.

He seemed to find our costumes hysterical, especially me and Fuzzy, because we were both dressed as lions, although Fuzzy's costume was minimal, just a beige ruff around her neck. "A little one and a big one," he said, shaking his head and looking at Felix. "You're going to have a hard time taming those two."

About half the guests had arrived when we went inside. Everyone was in costume, even Jimmy G, who had eschewed the private eye look to dress more like a forties gangster with a shiny grey double-breasted suit and a plastic Tommy gun slung over his shoulder. Also on his shoulder was Amber, playing the role of gun moll, at least I think that's what she was supposed to be, in a skin-tight red dress and a fur wrap and a long black cigarette holder.

She came hobbling across to greet us, a bit hampered by her tight skirt. "Don't you two look cute," she said, giving me a pouty little air kiss. "What do you think of Amber and Jimmy?" She waved at herself and Jimmy G who came up behind her, an unlit cigar clenched in his teeth.

"You guys look great together," I said. I still wasn't sure if they were dating or if Amber just enjoyed playing girl Friday to Jimmy G's private dick persona. What I did know for sure was that she wasn't marrying Jeff. My sister Cheryl still wasn't speaking to me. For some reason, she blamed it all on me.

"Going for the gangster look," said Jimmy G, resting his arm on Amber's shoulder. "Seeing as how we put away a notorious gangster."

Well that wasn't really true. Phil Pugnetti had been convicted of conspiracy to commit murder based on

Teri's testimony, and it didn't help that he was facing additional charges for discharging his weapon in a public park, endangering the lives of many.

"Hey, I was the one who put down Pugnetti!" said Pepe indignantly.

"You and the other dogs," I said. "Where's Party Girl?" I asked Amber.

"She's partying, of course," said Amber. "That was a joke. She's here somewhere."

"Did you get a costume for her to wear?" I asked.

"Yes, she's a princess," said Amber.

"I must find her!" said Pepe. "And shoot her with my arrows of love. I will sweep her off her four feet." With that, he dashed across the room, his wings flapping, and disappeared into the crowd.

Brad and Jay came up to us, both dressed in powder-gray tuxes with tails and matching top hats and sporting lilac bowties.

"That was Pepe as Cupid who came flying by, wasn't it?" Brad asked me.

"He's got romance on his mind," I told him.

"So do we," said Jay. He and Brad smiled at each other. They had been inseparable ever since Brad was released from the hospital. He still had not completely recovered his memory of that traumatic day when Harry had hit him over the head with a hammer and he woke up next to Mrs. Fairchild's corpse, but with Jay's help and some counseling, he was getting back to work and had managed to pay the landlord the back rent.

"I hope you haven't forgotten the rings," Brad told me.

"No way," I said. I showed them the gold chain I wore around my wrist. Two gold rings dangled from it. "I put them both on this gold chain for Pepe to wear as your ring bearer."

"Wonderful," said Brad. "I love having Cupid as our ring bearer."

"Me too," said Jay.

"Say," said Amber. "You're both out here together. Isn't it bad luck for the groom to see the bride before the wedding?"

"Honey," said Jay, "since both of us are grooms, it doesn't matter."

"Oh . . ." said Amber, giggling. "I guess that's true."

I noticed a middle-aged man in black, wearing a clerical collar. He was standing by the south-facing window, talking to Mickey and Minnie Mouse. "Is that the minister?" I asked Brad.

"No, that's just Fred. He always dresses like a priest on Halloween. He gets a kick out of giving benedictions to everybody."

"Geri!" I turned around and saw my sister, Teri. She must have just arrived. She was dressed as a hippie, wearing a pale green long skirt, an embroidered blouse, and a garland of flowers in her hair. A tiny purple velvet purse hung from a cord looped around her waist.

"Peace!" she said, flashing me the peace symbol.

"I'm so glad you made it," I said, giving her a hug. She had been staying with me ever since the trial, but she had left over the weekend on a mysterious errand. I wasn't quite sure where she was going and I was a little bit worried. Would I lose her again?

"I've got great news," she said. "I've been hired as a woof."

"What's a woof?" Felix asked.

"A worker on an organic farm," said Teri. "And you'll never guess where I'm working?"

"No, I can't guess," I said. "Where?"

"Sequim!" she said with a squeal. "I'm working for your friend Colleen Carpenter on her lavender farm. She's paying me a stipend and giving me free room and board."

"That's awesome!" I said. I liked Colleen and thought she would probably be a great boss. "How did you manage to hook up with Colleen?"

"She called one day when you were out," said Teri, "and I told her about how I was looking for a job and she invited me to come check out her farm. Things are quiet right now but that's OK because she needs help doing the craft projects with all the lavender she harvested."

"Congratulations," I said. I wasn't sure whether to be sad because my sister was moving on or happy because I would get my couch back. Pepe had been quite put out because he couldn't watch as much TV as he liked with Teri sleeping in the living room.

"And look!" said Teri, with excitement. She pulled a photo out of the tiny velvet purse. "I'm adopting one of Phoebe's puppies! Pretty soon, I'll have my own dog to talk to."

I studied the photo which showed a tiny funny-looking fuzzy dog with big ears, big brown eyes, and a body dappled with black and white. She didn't look like Pepe and yet she looked a lot like Pepe. "I'm calling her Pepita!" said Teri happily.

Brad, who had been listening to our conversation, looked over my shoulder. "Oh my God! That is the most adorable thing I have ever seen," he said. "Are there more where she came from? Jay finally agreed we could adopt a dog because he knows how much I've always wanted one."

"I'm told there are four more," I said.

"Yes, but they're going like hotcakes," said Teri. "I think the people next door with the cocker spaniels are going to adopt one as well."

Just then, somebody rang a gong. I hadn't noticed it before, but it hung on a black-lacquered stand in the corner. The woman who rang it was quite striking. She was heavyset, almost as wide as she was tall, and she had long flowing grey hair. She wore a long black dress with dramatic sleeves that fluttered around her hands.

"Oh, I guess she's dressed as a witch," I said, noticing her black fingernail polish.

"She is a witch!" said Brad. "That's Luna Llewellyn and she's going to marry us."

"Yes, you should get your dog," said Jay. "That's the signal that the wedding's about to begin. We need our ring bearer."

Brad and Jay encouraged everyone to take a seat as Felix and I went in search of Pepe.

"Boy," he told me. "You sure know some of the strangest people."

He was right, I thought as we picked our way through the tide of costumed folks, which included zombies, cowboys, a Klingon, and Big Bird.

We finally found Pepe in a corner with Fuzzy and Party Girl. The two girl dogs seemed very cozy, curled up next to each other, while Pepe stood to the side, his little tail down.

"What is it Pepe?" I asked.

"My arrow of love went in the wrong direction," he

said, staring gloomily at Fuzzy and Party Girl. "They prefer their own company to me."

"That's OK," I said. "I've got something that will cheer you up! But it will have to wait until after the ceremony."

We found seats behind Jimmy G and Amber. The wedding was dramatic, to say the least. Luna got our attention by waving around a large knife, which she used to inscribe a magic circle around the assembled company, muttering to herself as she drew it. She called upon the Spirits of the East and South, West and North in a ringing voice. She called upon the god Pan and asked him to stir up some mischief and she called upon the Goddess of Love, Aphrodite, and asked her to shower us with pleasure. She lit candles and burned sage and poured water and sprinkled salt around, all to create a sacred space.

Then she asked Brad and Jay to stand in front of her. They held each other's hands and recited their vows to each other, promising to live together in harmony for the rest of their lives.

"And now for the rings!" said Luna, in a voice that seemed like it was so commanding it was echoing back from the distant mountains.

I slipped the gold chain over Pepe's neck and he went running up to the front, as everyone oohed and ahhed at the sight of the little Cupid. Not to be outdone, Fuzzy and Party Girl ran up there too and sat to either side of Jay and Brad, like attendants. Lots of cameras clicked and flashed, trying to capture that tableau.

Luna wrapped colored cords around the hands of Jay and Brad, saying that she was "handfasting" them. I shuddered a little at that. It reminded me too much of the cords that Harry had wrapped around me. Once taken into custody, he had quickly confessed and was now serving a sentence of fifty years in the state prison.

More cameras clicked and flashed as Luna pronounced Brad and Jay "man and man" and told them they could kiss.

It was a long heartfelt kiss and I felt my heart flutter as Felix took my hand in his. Then Luna dismissed the spirits and thanked the god and goddess and enlarged the magic circle so we could all stay within it as we celebrated their union.

"That was really beautiful," Felix told me as we got in line for the bar.

"Geri, have I told you that I have been to many weddings conducted by a witch?" Pepe asked me. He always likes to insert himself into my conversations, especially my conversations with Felix.

"You have?" I asked.

"*Si*, I worked with a witch in the Yucatan," he said. "Her name was Gisella Sanchez."

"Have what?" asked Felix, turning to me puzzled.

"Pepe's just telling me another one of his stories," I said.

"Oh really, what's this one about?" asked Felix lightly.

"She used me for love spells," Pepe went on. "She said that Chihuahuas were the best dogs for that sort of thing. She assisted many villagers to find their true loves."

"You wouldn't believe me if I told you," I said, smiling. I had finally given up on convincing other people that Pepe talked. I certainly wasn't going to share his ridiculous stories. I wasn't even sure they were real.

"Have you heard anything from Fuzzy lately?" I asked as we got near the front of the line and ordered our drinks, champagne for me, a Perrier for Felix.

"Not a word," said Felix, looking over at his dog, who was chasing Party Girl around the tables that were being set up in the ceremony space. "I have to admit I'm relieved."

After the toasts and the first dance, after the cake cutting and the hysterical bouquet tossing (Big Bird caught the bouquet), after the fabulous meal served by Jay's employees—who outdid themselves putting together a buffet so their boss could enjoy his wedding day—and after Brad presented Jay with the magnificent stuffed pheasant he had prepared for him as a wedding present, Felix and I slipped out onto the observation deck. The rain had stopped and we stood there looking out over the lights of the city. The red and white lights of tiny cars moved along the shining streets below us. Inside, all of our friends were celebrating and feasting and dancing and drinking.

Except for Jimmy G and Amber. They were a little farther down on the deck. Jimmy G was smoking one of his stinky cigars and Amber was smoking a cigarette in her long black holder.

"Geri, I have something important to ask you," said Felix, taking my hand in his.

Oh, no! I could feel myself start to shiver. I wasn't ready for this. Whatever it was. Or maybe I was. Wasn't he the best thing that ever happened to me?

"Except me, of course," said Pepe, who was suddenly at my feet.

"Can you read my thoughts now?" I asked.

"I don't know," said Felix. "Are you thinking that you should move to L.A. with me?" he asked. "Because that's what I was thinking. I love you, Geri."

"I love you too," I said to Felix. It was the first time we had exchanged those momentous words. "But—"

"Aha! Cupid strikes again," said Pepe. "All over the place, people are coupling up and it is all because of my magic arrows of love!"

I looked through the window into the Chinese Room. It was true. The Klingon was dancing with a woman in a Star Trek uniform. Big Bird was swaying back and forth in the arms of a man dressed in a pink tutu and tights. Even Teri was caught up in a conversation with Fred, the minister. Her eyes sparkled as he made the sign of the cross over her head.

"Oh, I forgot to show Pepe the photo!" I said. "Can you excuse me for a moment, Felix?"

He looked sad but followed me back inside. As we went through the door, Jimmy G called out. "Don't forget to come by the office tomorrow to sign the partnership agreement."

Felix looked puzzled.

"Jimmy G has promised to make me a partner in the Gerrard Agency," I said.

"The Gerrard and Sullivan and Sullivan Agency," said Pepe.

Teri looked up as we came in.

"Father Fred is blessing my new endeavor," she said. "Oh, speaking of fathers, did you want me to show Pepe the photo?"

I nodded. Meanwhile Fred addressed Felix. "I do

blessings of the animals too," he said, "if you want your lions blessed."

"It might be a good idea," said Felix. "They are misbehaving."

"Only the big one," said Fuzzy who had appeared at his feet.

I looked down at her. Did I just hear her speak?

Felix looked horrified. He saw me looking at his dog. "Did you hear that?" he asked me.

Meanwhile Teri had knelt down and showed Pepe the photo of Pepita. Pepe studied it, his mouth hanging open.

"Geri, it is a miracle!" he said. "We cannot move to L.A. I have parental duties now, and we must get Sullivan and Sullivan off the ground!"

"Yes, and I don't want to leave Party Girl," said Fuzzy.

"What if we move in together but stay in Seattle?" I asked Felix.

"We might have to," he said. "I think I might need to check myself into Forest Glen."

Acknowledgments

What a pleasure it is to be able to thank all the people who made this book come alive.

First of all, of course, *muchas gracias* to Pepe Fitzgerald, the Chihuahua who inspired the series, for allowing us to flaunt him at readings and conferences, and *muchos* smoochos to Shaw Fitzgerald, who found him and thus brought him to our attention. Curt's wife, Stephanie, aka the Saint, has put up with Curt's mumbled excuses about how he is too busy writing to do X, Y, and Z, even though it looks like he is only watching TV or smoking cigarettes out on the back porch. And our writing group has listened faithfully and suggested revisions to whatever small snippets of the story they heard as we went flying through this particular book.

Faizel Khan (whose wonderful coffee shop, Cafe Argento, we finally worked into our story) has provided a supportive place for us to meet and argue about who to kill next. Another special thanks to Sparkle Abbey. We first met Marylee and Anita (another writing team) on our first panel at Bouchercon, and we have been mutual fans for each other's work ever since—they even let us steal one of their characters for this book. Our friends, the Sisters in Crime of Seattle, have contributed wisdom and enthusiasm, attending our book launches and partnering with us at bookish events. Writers cannot thrive without the support of other writers and Waverly is happy to be part of two amazing groups: the Seattle 7 Writers and the Shipping Group. And writers cannot survive without readers—we have been humbled and touched by the notes and fan letters, comments, and reviews we receive from our fans.

Finally, we are indebted to Team Pepe for making these books a reality. Michaela Hamilton, our editor at Kensington Books, and her staff are geniuses at making our books look and sound appealing and getting them into the hands of our readers. And our agent, Stephany Evans, was our first fan and tireless supporter in our quest to make Pepe Sullivan as famous as Lassie.

Bonus content!
Keep reading to enjoy
a special holiday treat . . .

A Chihuahua in Every Stocking

A delightful Barking Detective story,
previously available only as an e-book.
First time in print!

Chapter 1

For the first time since my divorce, I was looking forward to Christmas. Instead of being a fifth wheel at my sister's house, watching her kids open their presents and enduring an awkward holiday dinner during which my sister and her husband would grill me about my lack of employment, I was going to celebrate Christmas at my house and toast to all the good things that had happened during the past year. My new job, working at a private detective agency. My new boyfriend, Felix Navarro. And my new pet, my Chihuahua, Pepe. I was determined to create the total Christmas experience: a wreath on the door, bayberry-scented candles, cookies baking in the oven, eggnog in a crystal punch bowl, and a pile of presents under a fat Christmas tree glittering with ornaments and sparkling with lights.

Unfortunately, I had waited until the last minute to get the tree. Felix kept promising he would go with me, but he was too busy working as a dog trainer. Apparently pets frequently misbehave around the holidays, just like people. So by the time I arrived at the Christmas tree lot on December 24, the trees had been thoroughly picked over. Most of those left were either too big or too expensive or both. My Chihuahua, Pepe, tried to help.

"This one! This one, Geri!" he said, rushing back and forth between me and a Noble fir leaning against the chain-link fence that defined the tree lot. But as soon as I pulled the tree out and twirled it around to see if it was the right one, he dashed off down the next aisle to the Grand firs.

I put the Noble fir back and followed him. He was standing in front of a huge tree with bushy branches that towered over my head.

"That's too big, Pepe!" I said. "Where would we put that?"

The woman next to me looked puzzled. I saw her glance around, but there was no one in the aisle but me and my little white Chihuahua.

"I'm talking to my dog," I said.

She smiled weakly and went scuttling away.

I was a bit disappointed. It isn't that unusual. Most people talk to their dogs. It's just that very few dogs talk back. Mine does. He's been talking since I adopted him from the Humane Society. He was a rescue, one of a group of Chihuahuas, flown up from Los Angeles where they were being abandoned in record numbers.

"Over here, Geri!" I heard him say. He had vanished, crawling through the fragrant branches of the evergreens and into the next aisle. I went around the corner and found him sniffing around the trunk of a Douglas fir. It was a beautiful tree, about six feet tall, with thick branches, stiff green needles, and plenty of room for ornaments.

"Good work, Pepe," I said as he danced around the trunk with glee. "This tree is perfect!" He scurried ahead of me toward the cashier at the front of the lot, while I followed a bit more slowly, dragging the tree along the path.

As we approached the counter—a piece of plywood on top of two sawhorses—I almost stumbled over Pepe. He had stopped in front of a spindly little tree that was propped up against a trash can. Maybe someone had planned to buy it and changed their mind or maybe the owner of the lot had decided it would never sell and was going to toss it out.

"What is it, Pepe?" I asked.

"This tree," he said. "It is so sad."

"Yes, it is sad," I said, thinking he was referring to the spindly branches, the big gap on one side, the long bare stem on the top.

"It reminds me of me when I was in dog prison," Pepe said.

I was surprised. "You mean because it looks abandoned?"

"*Sí*. It is hopeless, in despair, afraid no one will take it home as I felt before you came to my rescue."

"Oh, Pepe, that is so touching," I said. I wanted to scoop him up and kiss his little white furry head, but I couldn't let go of the big Douglas fir. It would have squished him.

"Can we take it home, Geri?" he asked.

"What? You mean instead of this tree?" I asked, shaking the one he had picked out. A few needles drifted down. Perhaps it was too old. Perhaps it was too big. I didn't have any ornaments yet. My sister had inherited the Christmas decorations from our childhood. I was planning to ask her to share them with me, but maybe I should start my own tradition, beginning with this scrawny tree.

"*Por favor*, Geri," Pepe said.

"Sure, Pepe," I said. "If you really want that tree, we'll get it."

"*Muy bien*," said Pepe. "We will call the tree Arturo."

"Arturo?" I asked as I set the big tree aside and picked up the tiny tree. It was about three feet tall and weighed about the same as Pepe, probably about seven pounds. "You name trees?"

"*Sí*," said Pepe. "Do you think animals are the only beings with souls?"

Back at home, Pepe seemed content to let me set up Arturo in the tree stand I had purchased along with a single strand of small white lights. I put the tree on my dining room table. The top just barely cleared the dangling crystals of my chandelier. I heard Pepe go into the living room and turn on the TV. Yes, he does know how to turn on the TV. He can work the remote control with his tiny paws.

"Geri, come quick!" he said. He sounded upset.

I tightened the screws that would hold Arturo upright—I was already feeling nervous about putting the screws on a tree with a name—and hurried into the living room. Pepe was watching the news, which was odd, as he usually prefers the telenovellas on the Spanish language station.

"What is it?" I asked.

"Look!" said Pepe. On the screen was a photo of a white Chihuahua wearing a pink collar. She looked a lot like Pepe, except she had a brown splotch on her chest.

Her name was Chiquita. According to the announcer, she belonged to a little girl named Sophie. Sophie also wore pink: a pink puffy jacket and pink snow boots decorated with white snowflakes. The camera zoomed in on her face. She had big, dark brown eyes that were filled with tears.

"Please help me find my dog," said Sophie. "She is my best friend in the whole world."

The camera panned up to show a distraught middle-aged man behind her, his hand on her shoulder. He was wearing horn-rimmed glasses and a gray sweatshirt with a college emblem on it. I couldn't read the name of the school. "We don't have a lot, but we are willing to offer a reward to anyone with any information." His voice vibrated with emotion; his face was gaunt.

The camera cut to a young female reporter who was bundled up in a heavy blue parka, wearing brightly patterned knit gloves on her hands. She stood on a snow-covered street, with various Bavarian-styled buildings trimmed with hundreds of twinkling white lights in the background.

"This is Sharon Jacobson, reporting from Leavenworth, Washington," the woman said. "This is where Tim Rohrbach and his five-year-old daughter Sophie stopped this morning during their trip from Colorado Springs to Seattle. Sophie wanted to talk to Santa, and her father was inclined to indulge her. Sophie's mother died just two months ago from breast cancer. Tim and Sophie are moving to Seattle so they can be closer to Sophie's grandparents. They left their car briefly, but when they returned, the car was missing, along with the trailer containing all of their household possessions. Even worse for Sophie, her dog, Chiquita, is also missing. The Chihuahua was napping in the backseat when the car was stolen and hasn't been seen since.

"A few hours later," the reporter continued, "the trailer was found abandoned eighty miles west of Leavenworth, outside of Monroe. However, it was completely stripped. And the car is still missing. Even worse, so is Chiquita the Chihuahua.

"Hey," said the reporter, holding up one gloved hand for emphasis, "it's Christmas, folks. This sort of thing shouldn't happen. Please keep your eyes out for a blue Volvo station wagon with this license plate WTW712. If you have any information, please contact the authorities. Tim and his daughter are still in Leavenworth. The owners of the Black Forest Inn have generously put them up, as Sophie refuses to leave without her Chihuahua. We're hoping to get her reunited with her dog so she can have a happy Christmas."

"That poor little girl," I said.

"Geri, we can help her!" said Pepe.

"How?"

"We will go there and track down her Chihuahua. Are we not private detectives?"

Well, yes, my dog thinks we are private detectives. He even insisted I make cards reading *Sullivan and Sullivan Detective Agency*. They are decorated with clip art images of a red magnifying glass and a paw print. I actually work for an eccentric PI named Jimmy G, who owns the Gerrard Detective Agency, and I'm only a trainee. But Jimmy G was spending the holidays gambling in Reno, and the office was officially closed until the new year.

Pepe clicked off the TV. "How far away is this Leavenworth?"

"About a two-hour drive over Stevens Pass," I said.

"*Vamanos!*" he said, jumping off the sofa.

"But what about the snow?" I asked.

"No *problemo*," said Pepe. "I can track through the snow. Did I not find the famous Olympic skier Hans Duckworth when he was buried by an avalanche in the Alps?"

"Don't be ridiculous," I said. "I don't believe that at all." Pepe was always telling me these preposterous stories. According to him, he had fought bulls in Mexico City, wrestled an alligator in an Alabama swamp, and raced in the Iditarod.

"It is true, Geri!" He seemed hurt. "I burrowed into the snow and brought him a hot toddy, which kept him warm until the search-and-rescue team was able to dig him out. If you Google his name, you will find the story. Of course, they left out the role I played, but people often overlook us little dogs. That is why we must go find Chiquita."

"But Felix is coming over . . ." I said. I was already anticipating the delicious dinner I would cook, the eggnog we would drink, and the sweet lovemaking that would follow—

Pepe interrupted my thoughts. "We will restore the Chihuahua to the little girl and be home before dinner," he said. "But we must make haste. *Andale!*" he added, running to the door.

There was nothing to do but follow in his tiny

footsteps. If your dog is loyal to you, you have to be loyal to him. I grabbed my warmest clothes—my winter parka and mittens and my snow boots—and a sweater for Pepe (he steadfastly refuses to wear clothes, but I had a feeling he might change his mind once we got to Leavenworth) and off we went.

Chapter 2

It was snowing as we drove into Leavenworth, a tourist destination high in the Cascade Range. It did look like a magical place. I could see why Sophie thought she might find Santa there. The main street was lined with picturesque Bavarian-style buildings: two and three stories tall, the eaves decorated with scalloped trim and crisscrosses of half-timber on the walls, and all of them festooned with hundreds of tiny white lights. A giant Christmas tree, dotted with red ornaments and looped with swags of red ribbons, towered over a gazebo.

The Black Forest Inn stood just off the highway. It was one of those old-fashioned motels with all the doors facing onto outdoor walkways that ran the length of the building facing the parking lot. The doors were painted green, the eaves were embellished with scalloped gingerbread trim, and the wooden railings of the balconies were festooned with garlands. I parked my green Toyota and went into the lobby, carrying Pepe in with me. I wasn't going to leave him in the car, certainly not in a town where there were dognappers.

The middle-aged woman at the front desk directed me to #205, which was where Sophie and her dad were staying. Apparently people had been dropping by ever since the broadcast, bringing food and clothing and stuffed animals.

We headed up the wooden stairs and down the balcony, Pepe running ahead of me. In his eagerness, he scratched on the door with his tiny paws. I don't know how she heard the tiny sound, but the door flew open. I saw a little girl, wearing corduroy pants, a pink turtleneck, and pink snow boots. She fell upon Pepe, covering him with kisses.

"Chiquita!" she cried.

"Oh no!" said Pepe, looking at me with his big brown eyes.

"You found Chiquita!" That was Tim Rohrbach, appearing behind his daughter. He was still wearing the same sweatshirt.

"Um, no," I said. "This is *my* dog, Pepe."

Sophie had gathered Pepe up and was clutching him to her chest. Now she held him out in front of her face and examined him with her eyes narrowed. As she took in the facts—that he was a male dog and that he was missing the brown splotch, her face crumpled and she burst into noisy, snotty tears.

"I'm so sorry," I said, reaching out to take Pepe away from her gently. "We didn't mean to raise your hopes." I introduced myself to Tim and Sophie. "We want to help you find Chiquita."

I explained that Pepe and I were private investigators. Sophie cheered up.

I set Pepe down and he trotted around the hotel room, sniffing and snuffling.

"Do you have anything that has Chiquita's smell on it?" I asked.

Sophie shook her head. Tim said helplessly, "We left everything in the car."

"*Halto!*" Pepe said excitedly. "I believe I have found the scent of Chiquita the Chihuahua!"

"Where?" I asked.

"The car?" Tim asked, thinking I'd directed my question to him. "Well, we left it in—"

"I think my dog found something," I said.

"What? Where?" Tim asked.

Pepe was standing up on his hind legs under the coats that were hanging from hooks by the door. He put his front paws on the wall for better balance, looked up at the coats, and sniffed with enthusiasm. "The scent is coming from the little girl's coat up there. Take it down for me, *por favor.*"

I took the puffy pink coat off the hook and held it close to Pepe.

"Aha!" he said after a few sniffs. "It is just as I thought. It bears a most pleasant, *perro* scent that must surely belong to the *bonita* Chiquita."

"What is he doing with my coat?" asked Sophie.

"Pepe has picked up the scent of Chiquita," I said.

"That makes sense," said Tim. "The coat was in the backseat with Sophie and Chiquita."

"I let her use it for a pillow," Sophie said. Her mouth drooped.

"A *muy* thoughtful thing to do," said Pepe, looking at me. I always complain when he curls up on my clothes—his favorite place to sleep.

"What now?" I asked.

"We must take the coat and go outside," Pepe told

me. "I will see if I can pick up Chiquita's scent and follow it."

"We have to take the coat?" I asked Pepe.

Tim thought I was talking to him. "It's OK with me. If it will help, you should take it."

"Pepe will use it to find Chiquita," I told Sophie.

"I want to go, too!" shouted Sophie.

Tim knelt down beside his daughter and put an arm around her. "You can't go out without your coat, sweetie. It's too cold. They will bring it back." He stood up. "You will bring it back?"

"Of course," I said. I could see where he would be a little nervous after losing everything. "Can you tell me more about where you last saw your car?"

"Sure!" Tim went out on the balcony and pointed to the gas station on the other side of the highway. "I pulled over because Sophie needed to use the restroom. That's why we left Chiquita in the car. We were only going to be gone a few minutes. But then Sophie saw Santa."

"You saw Santa?"

"He was smoking a cigarette!" said Sophie indignantly.

"Sophie marched right over there and told him it was bad for his health. He was so"—he rolled his eyes a little—"grateful for the advice that he invited her over to the store to find out what she wanted for Christmas." He pointed to a purple building with a big sign that read YE OLDE GIFT SHOPPE.

Sophie nodded, her eyes big and brown. "I asked him to bring my mommy home."

"Um, sweetie," said Tim, "you know that Mommy isn't coming home again. And you know there is no such thing as Santa Claus."

I was surprised that he would discourage her from believing in Santa Claus. Surely that was a harmless belief at her age.

Pepe spoke up. "Geri, what is he talking about?"

"You're wrong, Daddy!" Sophie said firmly. "Everyone knows there is a Santa Claus. And Santa Claus can do anything."

"Ah, wisdom from the mouth of a child," said Pepe, seemingly relieved.

"You believe in Santa Claus?" I asked him.

"Of course. Only a fool would not," said Pepe.

"I don't believe in confusing children with the idea that mythical creatures are real," said Tim.

"Of course I believe in Santa," said Sophie. "And Santa promised me he would bring Mommy home. He wanted to know where we lived. I told him we were moving to Seattle and I didn't know our address yet." Her face got sad. "I hope he figures it out." She bit her lip.

Tim looked at me and shrugged. "We were only gone about fifteen minutes. When we got back to the gas station, the car was gone."

"Poor Chiquita!" said Sophie. "She will be so worried about me!"

"*Andale*, Geri!" said Pepe. "We have work to do!"

Chapter 3

"Brrrr!" said Pepe as we walked along the highway toward the crosswalk. "It is cold enough to stop jumping beans from jumping," he added, dodging the patches of snow that still remained here and there.

"Do you want to wear your doggy sweater?" I asked him. "I've got it in my purse."

"*Gracias*, but no," he told me. "The chill keeps me alert."

"With all the snow, do you think there will any smells left for you to find?"

"Fret not, my dear Sullivan," he said, going into his Sherlock Pepe mode. "Where there is a scent, there is a way."

At the gas station where Tim had left the car and trailer, I could still see the imprint of tire tracks in the slushy snow. The police had marked off the spot with orange cones, but there was no other evidence of the crime.

Pepe sniffed around the edges of the melting snow and evidently picked up Chiquita's scent.

"*Sí*, she was here at this very spot," he said, looking

up at me. A few flecks of snow stuck to his nose. "Follow me. The scent leads this way."

He headed across the street, toward the main part of town. The sidewalks were thronged with people, all bundled up in coats and hats.

Pepe led us straight to the front door of Ye Old Gift Shoppe. The name of the store was painted in Gothic letters on a shield-shaped signboard hanging from a metal bar over the front door. The two windows were framed with tiny white lights.

"Chiquita must have been following Sophie," Pepe said.

A sign in the window said TALK TO SANTA, and there were photographs of a jolly red-and-white Santa flanked by two elves. But the store seemed to be closed, which seemed odd on such a busy day. The lights were off. A sign hanging on the door said BACK IN FIFTEEN MINUTES.

Pepe snuffled along the edges of the building. "Then something happened, something that caused her much distress." He looked up at me. "She went this way." He darted off down one of the side streets, then doubled back up an alley, toward what might have been the back door of Ye Old Gift Shoppe. "Yes, something happened here. Chiquita was quite angry."

"Is she inside?" I asked, trying to peer in the window, but I couldn't see much. Just a back room that seemed to be empty except for a few cardboard boxes.

"No, someone picked her up and carried her off. Her scent is faint, but I can still follow it! This way!" Pepe kept going down the alley. It ended at the

entrance to a little park. I could hear a river flowing but couldn't see it.

Pepe trotted down a concrete path that descended
in meandering curves toward the river. Posters of
Chiquita the Chihuahua were already taped to the
posts of the street lamps that lit the path. There was
no one else around.

"Do you really believe in Santa?" I asked Pepe. I
had been wondering since our earlier conversation.

"Of course," he said. He stopped in the middle of
the path. "Why do you ask? Do you not believe in
him?" He looked disturbed.

"He's an imaginary being," I said, "a combination
of old myths and modern advertising."

"I suppose you think I am imaginary," said Pepe.

"Well, no, I don't," I said.

"Case closed," said Pepe.

I really didn't see how that settled the Santa issue,
but it was clear he didn't want to talk about it.

Pepe kept his nose down to the path, zigzagging
back and forth. Suddenly he froze. "¡*Ay caramba!*" he
said. He was looking at what appeared to be a log
lying in a snowbank under the boughs of an evergreen tree.

"What? Have you found Chiquita?" I asked, dashing forward. "Is she OK?"

"No, it is not Chiquita," said Pepe. "I found an elf!
And he is not OK."

"What?" But he was right. As I got closer, I could
see that Pepe was standing beside the body of a
young man. He wore a forest-green elf suit, light
green tights, and pointy-toed velvet shoes. He lay on
his back with his eyes staring up at the sky above,

unseeing. His face and hands were as white as the snow. The snow around him was stained pink.

"A *muy muerte* elf."

"Oh my God!" We had seen dead bodies before on previous cases, but we had never seen a dead elf. I pulled my cell phone out of my purse and dialed 911.

"What should we do now?" I asked Pepe as we waited near the tree for the police. "And where's Chiquita?"

"I do not know," said Pepe. He sniffed all around the body and under the nearby bushes. Snow fell off the branches. He shook it off.

"This elf was holding Chiquita. I smell her scent on him. But then she ran off. She hid in the bushes. Someone picked her up. A woman who smells like many other dogs. I smell a miniature collie. Some kind of poodle. Maybe a corgi. Perhaps a dogcatcher?"

He began to shiver. Pepe had been picked up off the street in Los Angeles and put into a shelter for many months. He was terrified of dogcatchers, who he called the dog police. They are one of the only things he fears. Besides cats.

"Do you think the person who took Chiquita was the murderer?" I was horrified at the thought.

"I do not know," said Pepe. "It is possible."

Just then a silver car bearing the logo of the Chelan County Sheriff's Department pulled up at the edge of the park. A tall, lean man in a tan uniform emerged from the car and headed toward us. He had olive skin, a sheaf of dark hair, and a bushy mustache.

"Drew Baker," he said, flashing a badge. "And you are?"

"Geri Sullivan," I said. "And this is my dog, Pepe. He's the one who found the body."

The deputy bent over the body, shaking his head as he peered at the boy's face. "I warned him," he said. "I told him this is how he would end up."

"You know him?" I asked.

Drew straightened up. "Yeah." He shook his head again. "Local kid. Repeat offender. Dropped out of high school. Started hanging out with the wrong crowd. Got into drugs."

He went back to his car and we followed him. He picked up the microphone attached to his radio and spoke into it. "Got a 187. The victim is Trevor Edwards. Get the coroner here and the CSI techs. And someone's got to notify his mother."

He hung up and shook his head again. "Tough for a mom to learn her boy is dead the day before Christmas," he said.

"Very sad," I agreed, thinking of Sophie and her dual losses: her mother and her dog.

"Especially since she's a single mom and he's her only child," Drew said. "Now tell me what you and your dog were doing here."

I explained that we were helping Tim and his daughter, Sophie.

"You mean you are investigating the theft of the car and trailer?" the deputy asked with a frown.

"Not really," I said. "We're looking for the Chihuahua."

Drew gave me a stern look. "We've identified a person of interest and have him under surveillance.

No need for civilians to get involved. In fact, it's dangerous. You could ruin our investigation."

I wanted to tell him about what Pepe had learned, but that's one of the problems of having a talking dog. You can't really explain how you know what he told you.

Meanwhile, two other official vehicles arrived: an ambulance, though it was too late to render aid to Trevor, and a shiny black Cadillac. A few people had wandered over from the shops and were gathered at the edge of the park, pointing and whispering. Drew took my contact information and let us go as more deputies rolled out crime scene tape and someone threw a gray tarp over the body of the unfortunate elf.

Chapter 4

"Are you sure you don't want to wear your sweater?" I asked Pepe as we headed back into the little town. The trail had gone cold, literally and figuratively. Pepe was shivering. He shook his head impatiently. His long ears actually flapped a bit at the ends.

He put his nose to the ground and led me back to Ye Olde Gift Shoppe. It was still closed. In one window, a toy train chugged through a lighted village of porcelain English cottages. The other window was filled with a white Christmas tree covered with silver glitter-crusted globes and candy canes.

I studied the photo of Santa in the window, this time looking at the two elves in the background. One was a young woman with long dark hair and a pointed chin. The other was a young man with a long, pale face.

"Look, Pepe!" I said, scooping him up so he was on the same level as the photo. "Trevor was one of the elves!"

"Good work, Geri!" said Pepe. "We must find the

other elf. And Santa. They may know the connection between Trevor and Chiquita."

He headed down the sidewalk and stopped at the door to the neighboring restaurant, which bore the name The Bratwurst Factory. Looking through the leaded windows, I could see that most of the tables were full. A red-faced man in lederhosen was wandering along the aisles, playing the accordion.

"We are in need of refreshments," Pepe said firmly. "Let us go in."

"They won't let you in," I told him.

"Barbarians!" said Pepe. "In France—"

"Yes, I know." We had been through this before. According to Pepe, in France dogs were allowed in all the best restaurants. "I'll put you in my purse." He hated this, but it had served as a good way to hide his presence in the past, so I always carried a big leather purse, about as tall as Pepe. I plunked him in, then gripped the handles firmly. I could hear him muttering inside, but the noise was covered up by the sound of the accordion playing "I'll Be Home for Christmas."

The hostess seated us at a tiny table for two in the dim recesses of the restaurant, right by the kitchen door. I peered at the huge menu, which was full of food I considered barbaric: sausages and goulash, schnitzel and sauerbraten. There was only one vegetarian option for me: egg noodles tossed with cheese and peas. But Pepe was excited as I read him the options. "This is truly a feast for a beast," he said proudly.

I pulled out my cell phone and called Felix. He said he had just finished up with his last client and would see me in an hour.

"I wish that was true," I said with a sigh. "But I'm not home."

"Where are you?" he asked. "I hear accordions."

I quickly filled him in about my impulsive trip to Leavenworth with Pepe and how we had just stumbled upon a body in the snow. He was a little bit shocked, I could tell, by the fact that we had gone directly from finding a dead elf to eating in a German restaurant. I blamed it all on Pepe.

But the truth was, I was hungry, too. I hadn't eaten anything since my breakfast oatmeal and coffee. I was just promising Felix that I would be home soon when the waitress showed up at our table.

She wore a short dirndl skirt, an embroidered vest that cinched in her waist, and a frilly white blouse that showed off her cleavage. She had a pale face and a pointed chin. She looked familiar.

"You're one of the elves!" I said suddenly.

She seemed startled.

"You work next door at the Gift Shoppe," I said. "With Trevor." I hesitated.

"Yeah, in the mornings," she said. "Then I come over here and work the lunch and dinner shifts."

"What's your name?" I asked.

"Sarah," she said. She pointed to her name tag. "Can I take your order?"

"Why is the store closed?" I asked.

She shrugged. "Who knows?" She pulled a notebook out of her apron. "So what can I get you?"

"Really, I want to buy one of those cute little lighted houses for my niece," I said. "Do you know when Ye Olde Gift Shoppe will reopen?"

"You can get those little houses anywhere in town," she said in a bored voice. "They have them for a dollar cheaper over at the Quainte Parlor at the other end of town." She tapped her pen on her little notebook.

"You should ask her when she last saw Trevor the elf," Pepe said.

"Speaking of Trevor," I asked Sarah, "when did you see him last?"

She looked startled but recovered quickly. "Santa sent him off on an errand. I haven't seen him since."

She looked around the crowded restaurant. The accordion player had moved on to "Silent Night." "If you're not ready to order, I'll come back."

"Order the food, Geri," said Pepe. "She is obviously too busy to talk right now. We should question her when she is more at ease."

"You're right," I told my dog.

"I am?" asked Sarah, thinking I was talking to her. "So does that mean you want me to come back?"

"No," I said. "I'm ready to order."

She put her pen to the order pad, asking, "What would you like?"

I ordered the egg noodles and a side of bratwurst for Pepe.

When Sarah left, Pepe said, "I suspect she knows more than she is telling us about Trevor the elf."

"We'll have to find out," I said.

"*Sí*," he said, then sniffed at the air, happily enjoying the aromas that filled the restaurant. "But on full stomachs."

The place was still packed when we finished our meal. Another waitress brought us our check. I didn't see Sarah. Perhaps she was on a break. Perhaps she had taken off.

By the time we left the restaurant, it was getting dark outside. Night comes early in the Pacific Northwest in winter, especially in the mountains. Carolers dressed in costumes—forest-green coats and shiny black boots for the men, long green dresses and mantles for the women—sang in the gazebo.

We needed to report back to Tim and his daughter and return Sophie's coat. And I wanted to see if any rooms were available for the night at the Black Forest Inn. It didn't seem likely we would find Chiquita tonight. The good news was that she was probably inside, rather than lost in the snow.

On our way back to the motel, with Pepe snuggled inside my coat, we passed Ye Olde Gift Shoppe again. I stopped to study the photo of Santa and the elves.

"Geri," said Pepe. "There is a light on by the cash register."

He was right! One rather dim recessed lamp over the main counter illuminated that area. The sign on the door still read CLOSED.

"And the door is ajar," Pepe told me. "Is that not strange?"

It *was* ajar—open about three or four inches.

"I smell danger," said Pepe. "Look! There is a red pant leg and black boot on the floor. See it? It is sticking out just past the counter."

My heart sank as I saw what my dog saw.

"Santa!" yelled Pepe, squirming out of my grasp and falling into a snowbank outside the front door. He scrambled to his feet, dashed through the door, and disappeared into the shop. "We must help Santa!"

"Pepe!"

I hurried into the store and found him standing over a very dead Santa Claus.

"*Mein Gott!*" said Pepe, adding German to his retinue of foreign languages. "Santa *ist tot.*"

He sure was. If *tot* meant "dead." Someone had draped his Santa hat over his face, but there was no mistaking the pool of blood in which he lay. His white beard was splattered with red. His round-as-a-bowl-of-jelly stomach pointed up at the sky, as did the toes of his coal-black boots.

Pepe shook his head. "Think of all the little children who will not get—"

"This isn't the real Santa," I interrupted. "Children will—"

"—who will not get to sit in his lap here in the store, I was going to say," Pepe finished. "Hey! What is that?" He ran over to the man's left boot.

"What is what?" I asked.

"This!" he told me, nudging something narrow and shiny black that was sticking up a few inches out of the boot.

I pulled it out and looked at it. It was a switchblade knife about six inches long.

"What is Santa doing with a switchblade in his boot?" asked Pepe.

"I don't know." I looked at it more closely. There appeared to be dried blood on the tip.

"Geri," said Pepe, taking a step back. "This is one bad Santa."

Chapter 5

Of course, I called 911 again. I looked around the shop while we waited. I could see why Sarah referred me to the store down the street. Many of the shelves were half empty. The items that were in stock were made of cheap materials. In one corner, behind the artificial white Christmas tree, a white-painted wooden armchair, presumably Santa's throne, sat on top of a white drop cloth sprinkled with gold glitter.

Pepe was busy sniffing the floor around the body. "I smell the same woman here that I smelled around the dead elf."

"So a woman murdered both Trevor and Santa?" I asked.

"It is possible," said Pepe. "But you are jumping to conclusions, my good Sullivan. All we know is that the same woman was in both places."

"Did she have Chiquita with her?" I asked.

Pepe shook his head. "Chiquita's trail is cold."

It was only minutes before the whole crew arrived: Drew Baker, the EMTs, the deputies, the coroner, and two new additions—two homicide detectives. They asked me and Pepe to come down to the sheriff's station for questioning.

We agreed to meet them there, which gave me enough time to reserve a room at the Black Forest Inn and call Felix again to tell him the bad news: I wasn't going to be home for Christmas Eve.

We also paid a visit to Tim and Sophie to return the coat. They were happy to hear that Pepe had been able to follow Chiquita's trail but not so happy to hear we hadn't found her.

"What if she is lost in the snow?" Sophie asked her father, burying her head in his shoulder.

"It seems likely someone picked her up," I said. "We just have to find that person." I didn't mention that the person might be a murderer. Surely even a murderer of elves and Santas would not harm an innocent Chihuahua.

Then we got in the car and drove to Wenatchee where the sheriff's station was located. Wenatchee is on the eastern side of the Cascades, a small town on the Columbia River that is the center of the apple industry in Washington State.

The sheriff's office was small. There was only one interview room and we had to wait as it was already in use. As we sat in the lobby, a door slammed. I looked up and saw Drew escorting Sarah down the hall toward us. She was still wearing her dirndl skirt and white blouse with a puffy orange down jacket draped around her shoulders. Her eyes were red and puffy; she had obviously been crying.

"You!" she said, stopping to look at me. "What are you doing here?"

"What are *you* doing here?" I asked.

"And the dog?" she said, looking at Pepe. "You found my dog!"

"What do you mean your dog?" I clutched Pepe closer to me.

"Trevor was going to give her to me for Christmas," she said, reaching out for Pepe.

"You're talking about Chiquita?" I asked, swiveling away from her so she couldn't grab Pepe.

Sarah stiffened. "No, I'm not!" She turned to Drew, who still held her by the elbow. "Can I go now?"

He nodded and she whirled out the door.

"So you know she knows Trevor?" I asked him as he ushered me and Pepe into the interview room. A box of Kleenex sat in the middle of the table.

"Of course she does. They dated all through high school," Drew said. "But how do you know that?"

"We met her at the Bratwurst Factory," I said. "I recognized her from the photo in the window of Ye Olde Gift Shoppe."

"I thought I told you to stop investigating," he said.

"We didn't do it on purpose," I said.

"Why do you keep saying *we*?" he asked.

"My dog is my partner," I said.

His eyebrows shot up.

"Have you figured out who killed Santa?" I asked.

Drew shook his head. "His name is Jack Stringer. He and his wife, Barbara, own Ye Old Gift Shoppe. He's a total misanthrope. Hates people. Pretty ironic that he was playing Santa. But I guess that's when they make most of their income for the year. According to Barbara, the store wasn't doing too well."

"Then why was the store closed on the busiest day of the year?"

"What do you mean?"

"When we went by around three-thirty, there was sign up saying 'Back in fifteen minutes.' But when we went back there after eating, the store was still closed. Except the door was ajar." I explained again what we had seen.

Drew frowned. "It must have happened when Jack was closing up," he said. "Barbara was at home preparing Christmas Eve dinner. They were expecting their kids and grandkids. Someone must have tried to rob him."

"And the switchblade, with the blood on it?" I asked.

"I guess Jack tried to defend himself. We could be looking for a perpetrator with a knife wound."

"How did Trevor die?" I asked.

"We're still waiting for the autopsy results. No one's available because of the holiday. But it does appear to be a knife wound."

"So maybe Trevor tried to rob Santa, but Santa stabbed him during the struggle and Trevor wandered off, mortally wounded, only to die in the snow," I proposed.

"Nice theory, Sullivan," said Pepe, "but the facts do not support that."

But Drew looked impressed. "We'll have to investigate that angle," he said, standing up. Evidently we were dismissed.

To my surprise, Sarah was waiting for us in the parking lot. She was shivering, hunched over in her bright orange down jacket.

"Give me my dog!" she said, making a grab for Pepe, who I was holding in my arms.

"This is my dog!" I said, tightening my grip on him.

Sarah shook her head. "Trevor promised her to me."

"I can prove this is not the same dog," I said. "For one thing, this is a male dog. His name is Pepe." I flipped Pepe upside down to display the proof.

"Geri!" squeaked Pepe, struggling to right himself. "Though I am proud of my manliness, this posture is *más indigno*." I turned him back over.

Sarah's face fell. "Now I have nothing left to remember Trevor by." Tears started to trickle from her eyes. I felt sorry for her.

"Come on," I said, "let's get something warm to drink." All of the restaurants and coffee shops were closed, but we finally found a bar that was open and ordered two coffees to go. The coffee was strong and bitter. It suited my mood. Sarah needed a ride back to Leavenworth, so I offered to take her.

"So when did Trevor promise to give you the dog?" I asked as I pointed the car back up the hill. It was still snowing. Sarah wept quietly in the passenger seat. It was so dark I couldn't see her, so I could only tell she was crying because she kept swiping at her eyes and sniffling.

"When the dog showed up at the shop," she said.

"Were you working then?"

"Well, yeah. Jack had just taken a smoke break and he came back with this little girl, who he jumped to the head of the line in front of all the waiting kids, which didn't make the moms happy. So we were trying to calm them down. He said something about the little girl's mom being dead so she needed special treatment."

Obviously Sarah had not been watching the news,

but it was odd that she hadn't seen any of the posters that Tim and Sophie had posted all around town.

"Then he saw maybe one or two more kids. And then the little white dog came in. Headed right for Jack. Barking furiously. It spooked him. He told Trevor to get rid of it."

"I find it puzzling that Santa would not use the gendered pronoun," said Pepe.

"People who don't appreciate dogs treat them like objects," I said.

"Right," said Sarah. "And Santa hated animals."

"How well did you know him?" I asked.

Sarah shrugged. "Everyone in town knows him. But we all think he's a jerk. So is Barbara. They were made for each other. I just took the job because I wanted to make some extra money for Christmas while I was home on break."

"On break?"

"Yeah, I'm in my second year at Western Washington," she said, naming the state university in Bellingham.

There were no other cars on the road. Everyone was home with their families, probably enjoying a big dinner, maybe opening presents and singing carols and decorating trees. I thought about all the wonderful plans I'd made for this holiday and felt sorry for myself.

"So tell me about your relationship with Trevor," I said.

It took her a moment to respond. "He was my first boyfriend. We dated through most of high school. But we broke up when I left for college." She paused. "Still, every time I came back to town, we ended up hanging out together. It's just so comfortable being with him."

"You knew he was doing drugs?" I asked cautiously.

Sarah shrugged. "There's nothing else to do in Leavenworth, except wait on the tourists. I told him he needed to get out and make something out of himself. But he felt like he couldn't leave his mom, she really needed him, yadda, yadda, blah, blah, blah."

"What's the story with his mom?"

"She's sort of eccentric. Some people call her crazy. She lives in a cabin out in the woods and has about a dozen little dogs."

"A miniature collie? A poodle? A corgi?" Pepe asked.

"A miniature collie? A poodle? A corgi?" I asked.

Sarah swiveled around to face me. "How do you know that?"

"I'm a private detective!" I said. It seemed OK to brag a little. After all, it was Christmas Eve and I was working.

"Wow!" she said. "That's so cool!"

"So Trevor's mom has several dogs?" I asked.

"Yeah, so Trevor asked her to hide the Chihuahua so Santa would think he had disposed of it. But he promised I could take her when I left to go back to school."

"Santa wanted Trevor to kill the dog?" That was Pepe.

I was equally shocked. "Santa wanted Trevor to kill the dog?"

"I told you, he's a jerk!" said Sarah.

"Geri, we now know where Chiquita is!" said Pepe.

"Oh, that's true!" I said. Wow! We were going to be able to do what we had promised: give Sophie back her dog. And just in time for Christmas.

"Can you tell me where Trevor's mom lives?" I asked Sarah. We had reached the outskirts of Leavenworth. All the parking lots were empty. The white lights sparkled on empty streets. Everyone had gone home.

"Sure. She lives at the end of Snowflake Lane," said Sarah. "Just take a right here." She pointed at a dark road that veered off just in front of the Black Forest Inn.

I thought about Tim and Sophie sitting in their motel room. I imagined their happiness when we showed up with their precious dog.

Chapter 6

The road wandered among the tall trees for a little while. It had been plowed at some point, but the surface was now covered with a few inches of fresh white snow. I steered the Toyota cautiously. It was silent. Sarah had stopped sniffling. She peered out the windshield.

"There," she said, pointing at another road, which was half hidden behind a bank of snow-covered bushes. I made an abrupt right turn, tires sliding, and hit a snowbank with a big chuff. The car stopped. This road had not been plowed.

"How are we supposed to get there?" I asked, trying to see what lay ahead. It was all black. I didn't see any lights.

"It's not far," said Sarah, jumping out. "We can walk!" She was definitely in a hurry now. Maybe she still thought she would get to keep Chiquita.

"Do you want to wear your sweater?" I asked Pepe.

To my surprise, he said yes. I rummaged through my purse and pulled out the rumpled sweater. It was one of several items we'd won during the *Dancing with*

Dogs competition. I had chosen the most wintery design: pink felt with white snowflakes appliquéd on it. I wrestled it over Pepe's head quickly, hoping he wouldn't object, but of course he looked around at the snowflakes dancing across his flanks.

"Geri, this sweater is for a bitch," he said.

I just can never get used to him using the B-word, even though I know he means a female dog. "Yes, but it looks really cute on you," I said.

Pepe just shook his head, as he does when annoyed, and trotted off, following in Sarah's slushy footsteps. Already far ahead of us, she was just a dark silhouette in a veil of falling snow.

"Wait up!" I shouted, but she kept going.

I scooped Pepe up (he protested) and clomped after her. Sarah went around a bend in the road and we lost sight of her. I struggled to get through the snow, slipping and sliding.

By the time I reached the curve, I couldn't see Sarah. But I could see her footprints leading across a cleared area and toward a dark A-frame cabin set back among the trees. The only visible light was an orange flicker in one of the front windows.

"Are we going the right way?" I asked Pepe.

"*Sí*, but hurry please. I am freezing to death out here," he said, shivering in my arms. I tucked him inside my jacket.

I couldn't help thinking it was Christmas Eve and I was wandering around in the woods in the dark. Snow was falling and the air was scented with pine, but I was shivering, and not just with cold. What was Sarah doing? Was she luring us into a trap? Perhaps this was the thieves' hideout!

Pepe must have had the same idea. "Go around

to the back," he whispered. "Let us reconnoiter. If we can find Chiquita, I will convince her to leave with us!"

But stealth wasn't going to be possible. I had angled off, thinking I would go around the side of the house, but as I got within a few yards of it, we were assaulted by a volley of barks and yips, squeals and growls.

"Ah, I believe we have found the collie, the poodle, and the corgi," said Pepe.

The front door flew open and we saw a woman silhouetted against the dim glow from the indoor lights. She was surrounded by a swirling, leaping pack of little dogs.

"Come in! Come in!" she called. "It's so cold out there."

Pepe and I approached cautiously but were somewhat reassured when we saw Sarah at her side.

"This is Carol," Sarah said. "She's Trevor's mother."

"Oh!" I reached out my hand to her. "I'm so sorry for your loss."

I couldn't read the expression on her face, but her body stiffened. "It's been hard," she said, her voice a bit raspy as if she had been crying for hours, "but I'm trying to make the best of it." She turned and went back inside, a pack of little dogs following at her heels. "My little darlings are a comfort."

We were in a large room with a sharply pitched ceiling that soared to a peak overhead. In the center of the room, a small cast-iron stove provided the only warmth. Candles flickered on the windowsills.

Carol offered to take my coat and Pepe's sweater, which she hung up on pegs near the door. She was wearing a pair of scuffed moccasins, black sweatpants, and a gray flannel shirt. Her hair was dyed a bright red. Cut short, it stood out on the top of her head, a bit like a rooster's crest.

"Would you like a cup of hot chocolate?" she asked.

I nodded. "And Pepe might need some water." Carol headed into the kitchen and Pepe followed her, along with all the other dogs.

"What's going on here?" I asked Sarah as I looked around. There was no indication that it was Christmas in the house: no tree, no holiday lights, no presents, no garlands. But there was evidence that a lot of dogs lived there. A doggy odor permeated the air and the carpet was stained. The sofa was covered with fur and lumpy pillows.

"I told Carol you were here for the Chihuahua," Sarah said. "She got really upset."

Pepe came running out of the kitchen. "I found her!" he said. "I found Chiquita!" Following him was a white Chihuahua with big brown eyes. She looked almost like Pepe except she had a pale brown splotch on her chest.

"Chiquita!" I said. I bent down to pet her.

Carol came back into the room with three mugs of steaming liquid in her hand. She frowned. "That's Lolita!" she said. "Trevor gave her to me!"

"He did not!" said Sarah hotly. "He gave her to me and I named her Chloe like the dog in *Beverly Hills Chihuahua*. You were just supposed to be holding her for me until I went back to school."

Carol slammed down the mugs on the sideboard. Some hot liquid splashed out and hit a beagle, who yelped. Carol snatched up Chiquita and held her close.

"Sarah told me you want to take away this dog!" she said, looking at me defiantly.

"Yes, I want to return her to her rightful owner. A little girl is missing her dog desperately and it's Christmas Eve."

"What's she talking about?" Sarah asked, looking from me to Carol and back again.

"The dog was stolen," I said, "along with a car and a trailer full of stuff."

"I told Trevor not to get involved with Jack and Barbara," Carol said. "They had this scheme. Jack was getting information from the kids who talked to Santa and then using it to make a list of houses they were going to rob on Christmas Eve. But when he saw the chance to rip off that family that was moving, he couldn't resist. He sent Barbara to get the car and Trevor was supposed to get rid of the dog." Carol whirled around, facing Sarah. "Everything would have been fine if it wasn't for you opening your big mouth. It's your fault Trevor's dead!"

"What are you talking about?" Sarah asked.

"After you told Jack that Trevor was going to give me the dog, Jack followed Trevor to the park where I was supposed to pick her up. He was angry that Trevor was jeopardizing their scheme. He wanted the dog dead because otherwise someone might recognize her and figure out what happened. I guess they fought over the dog and Jack killed Trevor. I got there just as he was dying."

"That is true," said Chiquita. "I was there when it happened."

I looked at the little dog, confused. Had I just heard her talking?

Carol choked back tears. "I held my boy in my

arms as he took his last breaths. Then I went looking for the dog. I found her shivering under a bush. Poor little Lolita. She was so traumatized!"

"My name is not Lolita," said Chiquita. "Or Chloe."

"Geri," said Pepe. "There is something important you should know."

"So you were the one who confronted Santa," I said to Carol.

"You bet I did!" said Carol. "I put Lolita in my car and then I headed straight for the Gift Shoppe. Jack was just closing up. He didn't know I knew. He was all Ho! Ho! Ho! What do you want for Christmas, little lady? I said, 'I want you dead.' And then I shot him."

She pulled a gun out of her jacket pocket and pointed it, trembling, at me and Sarah. "Unfortunately, I'm going to have to do the same thing to you."

Sarah and I took a reflexive step back.

Chiquita put a paw on Carol's arm. "Oh no," she said, looking up at Carol. "You cannot shoot them. Somebody who loves dogs so much could never kill innocent people."

"What?" Carol stared at the little dog she held, her eyes widening with disbelief. "Are you talking to me?"

"Yes, I am," Chiquita told her.

"She *is* talking," I said.

"Yes, she is. I can hear her, too," said Sarah, as dumbfounded as Carol.

"Of course she is talking," said Pepe.

"We all talk," said a beagle who stood and put his forepaws on Carol's knee.

"Yes," said the Shih Tzu who also stood and put her forepaws on Carol's other knee.

"Yes, yes, and yes," said all the other dogs, running up and dancing around the stunned Carol.

"We love you," said the corgi.

"Yes, we do," the toy poodle told her.

"I can't . . . believe it . . . ," said Carol.

"I can't believe it," said Sarah.

"I can't believe it," I said.

"Why not?" Pepe asked me. "I talk to you all the time, do I not?"

"You can't kill them," said a miniature collie. "If you do, you will have to kill all of us because we are witnesses."

"I must be losing my mind!" Carol backed up and almost fell onto the sofa, her gun hand wobbling. "What's happening?" she asked, sagging into the cushions.

"It's Christmas Eve," said a silky Yorkie, jumping up onto the sofa. The other dogs followed, climbing all over Carol, nuzzling her and licking her face and hands, and echoing the Yorkie's sentiments. "We can tell you how we feel about you."

"We know you're really good at heart."

"You always take care of us."

"We have to help *you* now."

"You only killed Jack because he killed your son," said the corgi.

"You must have been temporarily insane," said the toy poodle.

"Yes," the Shih Tzu told Carol. "They will go easy on you for that."

"But not if you shoot these people in a premeditated way," said the Yorkie. "They will put you away forever."

"You need to give yourself up," said the miniature collie. "After all, there are extenuating circumstances."

"This is unbelievable," I said. "How can they all be talking?"

"Geri, have you not heard the old folktale about animals being able to talk at midnight on Christmas Eve?" Pepe asked me.

"Well yes," I told him. "I do remember something about that. But it's not midnight yet."

"So?" he said. "What is the *problemo*? If you can believe that animals talk at midnight on Christmas Eve, why not at eight p.m.?"

I didn't have an answer for that.

"It's a Christmas miracle," said Sarah, her eyes wide and soft.

"Wherever the law puts you," a sheltie told Carol, "we will bring you treats."

"And always make sure you have enough food and water," added the toy poodle.

"That's nice," wailed Carol. "But I can't leave you!"

"Don't worry," said Sarah. "I'll take care of them. They can stay right here where they belong." She was keeping her eye on the pistol in Carol's hand.

So was I. Carol's grasp was loose but not so loose I could wrestle it away from her. I saw Pepe sneaking closer to the sofa, but I wasn't sure about his plan. Normally he could have told me since I was the only one who could hear him talking, but if Pepe spoke now, everyone would hear him. The Christmas miracle was a mixed bag.

"We would like that," said the poodle.

"Sarah has always been good to us," said the Yorkie.

The miniature collie ran over to Sarah and danced around her, saying, "Yes, Sarah is our friend."

"That's true, dear," said Carol, her voice wavering.

"I know you love animals. And they know it, too." Her fingers lost their grip and the pistol dropped to the floor. I took a few steps forward and grabbed it.

Pepe gave a deep sigh. "I am *muy* glad I did not have to bite her. I do not think Santa would approve of me biting someone on Christmas Eve. I did not want to risk going on the naughty list."

I held the pistol on Carol while Sarah dialed 911. But Carol was no longer a threat. She just kept fussing over her dogs, marveling over the many stories they were sharing with her about their lives before she rescued them. When the police arrived, she was beaming with excitement and kept telling them about her amazing talking dogs. Who were now silent.

"The police think Carol is *loco*," Pepe told me when they left. "Her dogs were right—they will surely go easy on her."

Sarah kept her cool. She convinced the police to let the dogs stay in the home where she could watch over them. When we left, she was calling her little sister and trying to persuade her to come over for some popcorn and hot chocolate and dog gossip. Pepe and I would have loved to hang around and talk to the dogs, but we had a more important errand to run. Returning Chiquita to Sophie.

Chapter 7

When we got back to the Black Forest Inn, we found Santa Claus knocking at the door to our room. Slung over his back was a small brown canvas bag.

"That is not the real Santa," Pepe told me. "Santa does not knock on doors. He comes down chimneys. Everybody knows that."

He looked real enough to me, I thought, until he turned around, lifted up his fake white beard, and gave me a big grin.

"Felix!" I said, running into his arms. I was amazed that my boyfriend had driven all the way to Leavenworth and was standing in front of me wearing a Santa suit. "What are you doing here?"

"I came to surprise you," he said. "I couldn't stand us being apart on our first Christmas Eve together."

I gave him a big hug. He felt good in my arms, his body lean and strong.

"I'm so glad," I said.

"Who's this?" asked Felix as we separated, noticing the small dog I held in my arms. I was carrying Chiquita, who was exhausted, emotionally and physically, from her long ordeal.

"It's a long story," I said, "but it has a happy ending. Come on in, and I'll tell you."

Once in our room, I put Chiquita on the bed. She curled up and went to sleep while I filled Felix in on all that had transpired.

Felix was impressed. "You are going to make one little girl really happy," he said.

Meanwhile, Pepe was rooting around in the canvas bag that Felix had dropped on the floor. He wrestled something out. It was a Christmas stocking, decorated with an appliqué candy cane.

"This is it?' asked Pepe, incredulous. "Where are the presents?"

"I brought one for each of us," Felix said, pulling out two more matching stockings. "I thought we could leave them out tonight and see what Santa leaves for us." He winked at me.

"That gives me an idea," said Pepe. "What if we put Chiquita in the stocking so she looks like a present? Then Felix can deliver her."

"I love that idea!" I said.

"Great!" said Felix, pulling out the stockings and draping them across the TV. I realized he had misunderstood me.

"No, I was talking about Pepe's suggestion!" I said.

"What suggestion?"

I turned to my dog. "He didn't hear you speak," I said. "How could that be? Everybody could hear you and the other dogs just a little while ago."

"Sadly, I do not know, partner," Pepe told me. "Perhaps that magical time in the old folktale has already passed."

I looked at the clock. It was just past midnight. It had taken longer than I thought to talk to the police.

"Geri," said Felix, putting an arm around me, "don't be upset. You told me that Pepe talks to you, and I believe you."

That made me feel better. I'd finally told Felix about Pepe talking while we were on our last case. And when he said he believed me, I knew he meant it.

"So," Felix continued, "why don't you tell me what Pepe said? Tell me about his idea that you like so much."

I recapped my dog's suggestion. Felix liked it, too.

"And I have another idea!" Pepe said. He was rolling around on the carpet trying to wriggle out of the pink sweater. "I want to give Chiquita this sweater!" Pepe said. "Christmas is the time to give to others!"

"It does look good on her," I agreed, after trying it on Chiquita. She was adorable in pink. We stuffed the sleepy Chihuahua into the smallest of the stockings. She fit perfectly, with her head just peeping over the top.

Pepe and I decided to go visit Tim and Sophie first. Felix would knock on the door a few minutes later, making his entrance as Santa, with Chiquita.

Snow was falling as Pepe and I went down the balcony to Tim and Sophie's room. The air was alive with dancing white crystals. Across the empty highway, the fairy-tale-like Bavarian buildings twinkled with white lights.

The festive mood did not extend to Tim and Sophie's room. Tim answered our knock, but his face fell when he saw that I only had one dog with me. Sophie was already tucked into bed, but she was wide awake, watching a TV show. Her eyes brightened when we came in but quickly filled with tears when she saw we did not have Chiquita.

"I guess you didn't find my doggie," she said. Tears spilled over, leaving tracks down her cheeks. I felt bad that we had postponed their reunion for even a minute.

"Geri," said Pepe, "do you not think this would be a good time for Santa to make his entrance?"

I was about to agree when there came a loud knock at the door. Felix's timing couldn't be better, I thought, as Tim went to get it.

And in strode Santa with the biggest "Ho-ho-ho" I'd ever heard. His cheeks were all rosy, and his beard was fluffy and white, and his big belly shook whenever he laughed.

"Santa!" screamed Sophie. She scrambled out of bed in her pink flannel pajamas. Santa knelt down as she ran to him. Snow clung to his shiny black boots.

"Have you been a good little girl?" asked Santa.

"Oh yes!" Sophie told him.

"I know you have!" said Santa. "And I have something very special for you."

"Hey," Pepe told me, "there is something odd about this Santa."

"Shhhh!" I told my dog.

"And here it is, little Sophie," said Santa. He took the Christmas stocking out of the large bag he carried. Chiquita stuck her head out of the stocking as Santa handed it to Sophie.

"Arf-arf!" said Chiquita happily.

"Chiquita!" yelled Sophie, hugging her dog close. "Oh, Chiquita, I thought you were gone forever!" she added as Chiquita licked her face.

"Thank you, Santa," said Tim, a tear in his eye as he gave the big guy a hug.

"And this is for you," Santa told him. He handed Tim a very small package, about the size of a jewelry box.

When Tim opened it, it contained a gold ring with a dark red stone.

"I can't believe it," Tim said, taking the ring out of the box. "This is my grandmother's ring. I gave it to my wife on our first anniversary. She dropped it down the drain in the kitchen sink years ago and we thought it was lost forever."

I was mystified. How did Felix come up with a present that would be so meaningful to Tim?

"Nothing is lost forever," said Santa. "Especially not the love between two people who have pledged to spend their lives together."

Tim's eyes filled with tears.

"This is heartwarming, Geri," said Pepe. "But I tell you this is not Felix. This Santa smells of sugarplums and spice and everything nice. Felix always smells like the dogs he trains."

"Merry Christmas!" said Santa, opening the door to the balcony. He stepped outside and seemed to vanish into the night air. The door blew shut with a bang.

"Wow!" Tim said, staring at the ring. He sank down into the chair beside the little table in the room and looked over at Sophie, who had scrambled back into bed and was tucking Chiquita in beside her, kissing her repeatedly on the head. "It's almost enough to make me believe Santa is real."

"Of course he's real, Daddy," said Sophie with a bit of scorn in her voice. "He found Chiquita."

Just then, there was another knock at the door.

"I'll get it," I said.

"Ho-ho-ho!" said Santa, entering the room. As he passed me, he winked and asked, "How's that for timing?"

I recognized his voice. It was Felix! "Weren't you just here?" I asked him.

He shook his head. His beard was not as fluffy as the previous Santa's. Nor was his stomach as protuberant. And his "ho-ho-ho" was not as hearty.

"Told you so," said Pepe.

Felix turned to face Tim and Sophie, then noticed that Chiquita was already in the room. He looked confused, groped around in the canvas bag he carried, and came up empty.

"Hey," said Felix. "What happened to the stocking? How did the Chihuahua get into the room?"

"Never mind," I said. "Everything is fine now. I think it's time for us to leave."

Of course, we couldn't go without multiple hugs and kisses from Sophie and Chiquita. Finally we scrambled along the balcony through the thickening snow back to our room. When I opened the door, my jaw dropped.

There was a punch bowl full of frothy eggnog sitting on the bedside table and two crystal cups beside it, already filled with the beverage. A plate of shortbread cookies sat on top of the TV. There was a bite taken out of one of them. Christmas lights were strung up over the bed. And sitting in the middle of the table was Arturo, the funny little tree I had left on my dining room table back in Seattle, but now he was all decorated with blue ornaments and white lights and the special golden star ornaments that my mother had collected and given to me and my sister in Christmases past.

I whirled around and gave Felix a big hug. "Wow!" I said. "No wonder you were delayed. This is amazing. How did you pull this off?"

Felix took off his Santa cap and scratched his head. "I didn't do any of this," he said. "Where did it come from?"

"Santa?" I asked.

"Told you so," said Pepe, looking up from where he was gnawing on a bone that had been left under the table.

"Here to make all your dreams come true," said Felix, tumbling me down onto the bed.

It *was* the best Christmas ever.